BOUND BY DREAMS

BOUND BY DREAMS

CHRISTINA SKYE

THORNDIKE PRESS

A part of Gale, Cengage Learning

GALE
CENGAGE Learning·

Detroit • New York • San Francisco • New Haven, Conn • Waterville, Maine • London

GALE
CENGAGE Learning

LP
SKY

Thorndike Press® Large Print Romance.
The text of this Large Print edition is unabridged.
Other aspects of the book may vary from the original edition.
Set in 16 pt. Plantin.
Printed on permanent paper.

LIBRARY OF CONGRESS CATALOGING-IN-PUBLICATION DATA

Skye, Christina.
    Bound by dreams / by Christina Skye.
      p. cm. — (Thorndike Press large print romance)
    ISBN-13: 978-1-4104-2296-5 (alk. paper)
    ISBN-10: 1-4104-2296-8 (alk. paper)
    1. Large type books. I. Title.
PS3569.K94B68 2010
813'.54—dc22
                                2009040071

Published in 2010 by arrangement with Harlequin Books S.A.

Printed in the United States of America
1 2 3 4 5 6 7 14 13 12 11 10

BOUND BY DREAMS

■ ■ ■ ■

PART ONE

■ ■ ■ ■

One crow for sorrow,
Two crows for joy

PROLOGUE

Sussex, England
Draycott Abbey
Summer

The night is alive, restless with dreams.

Almost two decades have passed since he walked this soft grass. Touched these worn stones of Draycott Abbey.

The name flows off his tongue, rich with history. Near his hand a mound of lavender stirs, cool with dew and perfume. The scent he remembers well, along with his hours of peace in the abbey's shadow.

Every detail of the great house is branded into his memory.

For twenty years he has not come back to these green hills. The danger is too great, carrying the threat of what he once was . . . and can become again.

The wind draws him to the moat's edge. He smells the tall grass, feels the brush of young leaves on his skin. Somewhere in the darkness a hunting bird calls sharply.

The night flows around him. Then the past rushes in with a surge of bitterness. The pain slams down.

He remembers the betrayal and lost hope. From his innocence had come death.

His muscles flex. Tendons move, blood sings. Power slides down like swift moonlight spilled across endless seas. The life he'd left behind rushes in, carrying the slap of the wind, the harsh rhythm of an old Gaelic curse.

He remembers the hammer of callused hands at his neck and then the cold taste of blood.

His own blood. From wounds that had left him dead, or close enough to call dead.

He slips off his shoes.

Thyme and mint crush beneath his feet, just like the last time he was here to visit his oldest friend.

Sweat glistens on his bare skin. The night is cool, but to him it is warmth enough when the wind calls. Better to run, to hunt. It is safe here, because darkness is his home and haven.

Roses brush his arm, scenting the air with perfume. His skin burns. The time of power floods through him.

Muscles flex, changing to match a new shape and all its strength.

His hands clench. He touches the low iron fence. One hand grips the cool rail as the power snaps. He lets down the final wall, feels the explosion of dark strength that surges through him.

He remembers another night, too many years ago to count. His first taste of power — and the death it carried. He remembers a boy's raw, bone-wrenching terror, understanding nothing. That night there had been no control, no confidence, no hope. Only death.

Old history.

Dead ashes.

He mutters an oath and snaps his bond to the past. In silent fury, his body rushes into life, driven by the energy of the hunt. Across the hill he can hear a leaf fall and feel the weight of moonlight on his bare hands.

Alive.

More than alive — with such power as no mortal man can know.

His jacket drops. His clothes fall to the soft earth.

The abbey is as much of a home as he has ever known, and Calan MacKay feels the power of its welcome as he stands in the night, face to the north. The wind from the woods brings the rich scent of prey and the taste of rain before dawn. He runs, a shadow in the trees. A shadow with keenest sight and unthinkable strength. His muscles gather and stretch. Senses burning.

Then he is gone, swallowed by the darkness.

A bird cries. Moon rising.

Strange footprints dot the mud above the abbey's moat.

He smells her across the hill.

A touch of softness. A hint of warmth.

Woman.

Her perfume holds soft ginger. Orange. A hint of cinnamon.

Without looking, he knows her location. Her scent marks every step. Hidden by a mound of lavender, he waits.

She thinks she is alone. Every step she makes is quick, wary. She is small. Fast. Careful. This is what he sees in the space of a breath. The other details come slowly. Yet they are mostly about what she is not.

Not beautiful.

Not frightened.

Not sure of where she is going.

And because he is an intruder here himself, Calan MacKay does not interfere. He marks her progress, sensing the force of emotion that drives her over the damp grass to a gray boulder above the great sweep of the abbey's west meadow. From here every detail of motion along the driveway is visible.

But at three in the morning, there is no movement. The grand house is empty. He has already checked to be sure. He is alone.

The woman in the black sweater stops suddenly. One hand to the gray rock, she closes her eyes and sinks down. Tears shimmer. Her head touches her open hands.

He smells the salt of her tears then. The scent is physical, painfully intimate, as if he had shared her body in the most primal form of sex. Her tears smell like youth. . . . and sadness.

Ginger and sunshine.

He is stunned at his sudden awareness of a stranger's body. It has been years since he has felt such sharp curiosity about a woman.

Curiosity turns to something darker.

If things were different, he would make it his goal to taste her passion and her body. He would drive her slowly, making her burn as he suddenly burns. He would hunt and then possess her until his curiosity was slaked.

Something tells him that could take a lifetime.

But he has no lifetime to give. Because Calan MacKay cannot be gentle or trusting, he crushes his desire. She has stirred up emotions he can never afford.

He curses, summoning anger instead. It will

13

be an easy thing to frighten her away. Slow, he moves through the arched rose bower, a shadow amid shadows, making no sound. Almost at her side.

She gives no sign, perched on the rock, eyes intent. Suddenly she sways and pushes to her feet. Her fingers dig furiously at one pocket.

He tenses, no longer a simple observer. She is an intruder on Draycott soil and he plans his direction of attack, the timing of his approach to overpower her.

But the choked sound of her pain is not what he expects. What she pulls from her pocket is not a weapon. Only a folded piece of paper.

Small and fragile, it covers her palm.

He can smell the age caught in its fibers. Salt is locked within faint layers of human sweat, as if the sheet has been carried for years in trembling hands.

Her jaw tightens. She does not have to read the words on the fragile sheet to know their secret. Sliding to her knees, she searches the dark earth. Her eyes are hard with anger as she grips a small stone and hurls it toward the distant house. "Damn you," she rasps. "Damn all of you."

She throws another stone, and now he sees the tears spilling down her pale cheeks. He smells the salt of her skin and his body tightens in harsh response. He wants to know her name, her breathless laugh, the heat of her thighs.

He wants to know her body and everything about her.

Reckless wishes. He will never know her.

The tall Scotsman doesn't move, though every nerve shouts for him to cross the darkness between them. Who is this stranger to hold him, tempt him?

She stands awkwardly, her shoulders tense. No more tears now. Only anger.

She lifts one hand in a fist. "Leave us alone," she orders hoarsely. "Let it end."

His curiosity is caught hard now, so he follows when she climbs the hill, hidden when she kneels beneath an ancient oak. She digs with bare fingers and a simple kitchen knife, raking the earth in long lines. He can barely hold himself back when she leans down to the wet earth.

To find what?

She twists suddenly, and her pale face is caught in the moonlight, something from his deepest dreams. Dark eyes glint with tears and fury as she tosses the knife.

It spins high — and lands at his feet.

An accident, or has she sensed his presence after all?

"Gone." Her harsh whisper drifts on the

wind. "Taken like everything else . . ." She stands, unsteady, one hand white against the ancient tree. With a sigh, she pulls her jacket closed, staring around uncertainly.

And then she turns.

Away from the house. She crosses the dark grass, her shoulders stooped with weariness. Questions storm into his mind as she passes, close enough to touch.

He holds his distance as she crosses the meadow, climbs a small stone fence. From there she winds through the copse that borders the road.

Somewhere in the darkness a car engine coughs.

He draws back. She is still walking when two men emerge from behind a tangle of weeds. They block her scream. Her hands claw and scrape in her struggles.

Anger explodes through him. With their scent like a beacon, he opens to the hunt. But not fast enough.

She fights well, but the men are stonger and they take her just the same. The car motor whines.

Silent and deadly, the Scotsman hunts.

CHAPTER ONE

They came at her without warning. One minute Kiera Morissey had been cursing Draycott Abbey and its arrogant owner, determined to make her visit short so she could be gone forever.

Now she was struggling for her life against violent men in black masks. Her mother's deathbed request had led her straight into a nightmare.

A rag blocked her mouth, making her gag. Rough hands gripped her wrists, twisting until she moaned. She was supposed to be fighting memories, not violent assailants. Who *were* these people? What did they want with her?

Security guards? Kiera would have expected the Draycott family to post a team of bad-tempered Neanderthals to guard their precious privacy. But would they condone this kind of violence?

The wind snapped through the trees.

Birds exploded over her head as she fought harder. Plastic bonds locked her wrists sharply. She couldn't see, striking out at her attackers by feel alone. She knew there were two of them, and so far they had said only a few words, all of them in a language that sounded Slavic.

This was a private unit of hired foreign thugs, meant to protect the aristocratic owner of the abbey and his family? Hard to believe, even for the arrogant Draycotts.

She didn't frighten easily, though she hadn't been prepared for an attack on a quiet country road in the English countryside.

Now she was focused, ready to fight back. Her father had taught her self-defense as soon as she was big enough to hold a *Muy Thai* stick and play at kickboxing moves. Yet in her emotion at her first glimpse of Draycott Abbey, she had violated the crucial rule: Always stay prepared.

Now her attackers were going to get a little surprise.

Kiera made the move exactly as her father had taught her. She went completely limp, toppling sideways. Before her beefy captor could adjust to her sudden falling weight in his arms, she snapped forward and kicked him solidly in the groin.

His wheeze of stunned shock told her he had expected fear and blind compliance. *No way, dog breath.*

The second his hands loosened, she dropped to her knees, rolled and then shot toward the woods. She was in good shape. She also had a five-yard lead on the second attacker. She grabbed the top of the abbey's stone fence, pulled herself up and threw one leg over.

But her pursuer lunged and managed to grab her ankle just before it cleared the fence. He jerked her backward, her face scraping against the stones. Blood gushed over her lip, but when he tried to shove her down beneath him, she clawed at his eyes, sending him reeling.

Unfortunately Attacker Two had sewer breath. He was also the size of a Mack truck. With a jerk of his callused hands, he drove her flat onto the ground. Then he stood over her, one heel pressed at her throat.

Bad sign, Kiera thought.

Any second she would have a crushed windpipe.

"What do you want?" She hated that her voice was high and spiky. The heel pressed to her throat started to grind down. "Okay, are you some kind of private police? Security guards from Draycott Abbey?" She spoke wildly, saying anything that came to mind.

His foot froze. A good sign.

"I mean, if you're hired by Viscount Draycott, I can explain."

His breath caught.

Kiera still couldn't see his face in the darkness, but she heard his clothes rustle and then the click of a cell phone opening. He muttered something in a language that definitely sounded Slavic, then waited for an answer. Hoping for a distraction, she went perfectly still on the ground, but the pressure on her throat never loosened, nor did his gaze leave her face. Clearly this gorilla had military or professional security training, and now his focus was almost palpable.

Simple tricks weren't going to work with this one.

In the distance she heard the low growl of a motor. Picking up speed. Coming closer.

Straight in her direction.

Attacker One grunted, slowly recovering, one hand to his eyes. Kiera's mind raced through escape scenarios. Her father had taught her dozens. No way was she going to be a statistic on the evening news.

When the gorilla closed his cell phone, Kiera focused. He reached down, jerking her to her feet.

She twisted and dug two fingers into his neck, precisely at the vulnerable notch of his collarbone. Muscle flexed and then cartilage tore nicely. While he was still hunched over in shock, she sank her teeth into his palm, deep enough to feel skin part. Bone ground beneath her teeth.

She spit out blood but the man's grip held firm. His growl of fury didn't quite cover the sound of the car motor nearby.

Panic squeezed hard. Damn, damn, damn. How many more men were inside the car?

Then Kiera heard leaves rustle.

Something was moving toward her from the far side of the fence. There was no mistaking the snap of twigs, the harsh breathing, the sounds made by a very large animal.

There was something strange about that rough breathing. Or maybe it was hypoxia starting to kick in. She aimed two more satisfying collarbone jabs as her attacker's fingers locked around her throat.

Dizziness tore at her vision.

Oxygen almost gone.

A dark shape exploded over the stone fence. Kiera heard the slap of a body and then the sound of bushes shaking. She could see almost nothing as she fought her furious captor. Then abruptly she was free, her attacker sinking to one knee.

Car lights cut across the road, closing in fast as Kiera shot across the pavement to the far slope, where the ground fell away abruptly at the edge of a creek. Diving over the bank, she tucked sharply and landed in a sprawl at the bottom.

The sounds were muffled here. Up on the bank she heard the squeal of brakes and harsh voices, followed by a scream of pure terror.

Something growled. The sound made Kiera's hair stand on end. She had seen predators in zoos throughout Europe, but she had never heard *that* kind of growl, a sound that held cunning and intelligence.

Whatever the animal was, she wasn't staying around for introductions. She stumbled along the muddy edge of the stream, keeping her body low so she would be invisible to any attacker looking down from the road. Following the stream would bring her to a second road. Her rental car was parked only a few hundred yards away from that point.

Safe.

Her hands shook. She forced herself to stay calm. She was alive, no one's captive.

Then a bullet hit the bushes only inches away from her hand. Kiera plunged straight

22

into the mud and stayed down, breathing hard.

Reining in her urge to flee blindly.

But that was what they'd expect. Rule Two: *Never do the expected.*

Behind her the wind carried a man's guttural shout of pain and a rapid burst of gunfire from the road.

She heard another growl, this one the short, angry sound of an animal that was cornered. Wounded maybe. Something about the pain held Kiera still. Her hands opened and closed jerkily. Climbing the slope, she crept through the woods far above the point where she had been attacked. In a beam of car lights she saw motion and dim, grappling figures. Another burst of gunfire drilled the creek she had just left. Back on the road a man shouted angry orders, again in a language that sounded Slavic.

Kiera's foot struck a boulder. When she looked down, she saw she had stumbled over a man's body. He was alive, judging by his labored breathing, and a revolver lay on the ground inches from his twitching hand. She didn't think twice, scooping up the weapon. Instead of turning toward her car, she crept back toward the road.

Going back? This had to be insanity, even with a weapon.

Then the animal, probably some kind of mastiff or mixed-breed husky, gave another sharp howl of pain.

Kiera's fists clenched. They were killing the dog.

The moon broke from behind racing clouds, giving her a glimpse of the scene on the road. One man was climbing into a waiting car. A second man swayed sharply, clutching his arm. He turned and gave harsh orders, gesturing to the far side of the road, where Kiera had crossed minutes before. He was sending his men after her, she realized.

Two figures vanished down the slope of the creek, and she saw the remaining man back up, suddenly frozen by something near the stone fence. Her breath caught.

A shadow separated from the tall grass. It was the biggest dog she had ever seen, long and sleek. Every motion carried the stamp of effortless, fierce power.

The man with the gun cursed, but the animal was faster, leaping through the darkness. Kiera heard four shots in quick succession.

She flinched, certain that no animal could survive such an attack at close range. With the pistol weighing against her palm, she reacted by instinct, flicking off the safety,

24

dropping behind the foliage of a small tree and aiming carefully.

Her first bullet drove up gravel near the car's back tire. Her second shot hit the back windshield, cracking the glass. She didn't stay to see more. One small diversion was all she could afford. As Kiera dodged back into the trees, bullets tore off a branch near her hand. Footsteps pounded over the road.

He was coming after her.

She ran through the woods, caught in darkness as the moon vanished behind the clouds. With the attacker bearing down, she caught the lowest branch of a tree and swung one leg up. She clawed her way up another ten feet, then curled into a ball, absolutely still.

Grass rustled, and then a man ran directly beneath her. His footsteps hammered on into the trees.

Long seconds passed. The car idling back on the road gave two sharp bursts on the horn. Leaves scratched Kiera's face and she felt a bug fall down the back of her jacket, but she kept resolutely still.

Twigs snapped. The man with the gun returned slowly, swinging his outstretched arm directly beneath her.

Through the leaves, Kiera saw the car lights flash to high, then flicker twice.

Some kind of a message, that was clear. She prayed it would call him back. But the man didn't move, studying the darkness intently.

Sweat trickled between her shoulders. Another bug hit her cheek. The car horn sounded sharply.

The man strode off. Seconds later the car roared away.

Silence fell. The wind brushed her face.

But Kiera didn't move. Her legs were locked, her muscles taut with the aftereffects of fear. The temperature had fallen and she began to shiver. Running through damp fields and crossing streams hadn't been in her game plan when she'd dressed that evening.

But she was *alive.* There was a sharp beauty to the night, to the chiaroscuro pattern of the leaves caught against the faint moonlight. Closing her eyes, she breathed a sigh of thanks.

Still shaking, she swung her legs over the lowest branch. With trembling hands she hung for a moment and then dropped to the ground, wincing at a sudden pain in her foot. There was no sign of pursuit. The night was silent as she crossed the road warily.

Dark tracks lined the mud. A man's jacket lay nearby, dropped and forgotten. There was no sign of the big dog that the men had been tormenting, probably a guard dog from one of the surrounding estates. Yet there had been something strange about the animal's size and its powerful movements. Even now the memory left her with an unsettling sense of savage strength held in precarious control.

And as she stood in the clearing at the edge of the road, looking at the distant line of the abbey's roof, Kiera had the strangest sense that someone was watching her.

But nothing moved; nothing barked or stirred in the foliage.

"Who's there?" she whispered.

A bird cried in the distance. Goose bumps rose along her arms. Time to leave, she told herself firmly. If someone found her here, with the marks of the attack all around her, she would have no easy way to explain. And there was always a possibility that the thugs might come back.

Fortunately, she had planned for a quick escape. Her backpack was hidden in the grass near her rental car, and her keys were under a rock nearby. Yet still she didn't move. Something called her gaze through the trees, toward the moon touching the distant hills.

In the sudden silver light she saw the

sharp outline of Draycott Abbey's parapets. Kiera fought against a strange, almost hypnotic force of calm from the sight. Despite her anger at the Draycotts there was so much beauty here. So much history.

Then she felt the weight of the gun shoved into her pocket. It would have to be disposed of safely. She remembered there was a church about a mile from her hotel. She could remove the last remaining bullets and then slip the weapon into the mail slot.

One problem solved. Kiera took a deep breath.

That left her whole future yet to tackle.

He lay in the high grass, shaking.

Shaken.

His speed was gone, his muscles jerky. Blood covered his ear and dripped into his eye. He remembered the metal blade and then the sudden slam of bullets. He hadn't reacted fast enough, never suspecting an attack at Draycott's very border.

No excuse for bad judgment. No excuse for stupidly letting down his guard. He had too much to hide to ever be stupid or careless.

He made a short, angry sound and stood slowly in the darkness, wincing at sharp pains in a dozen places.

Wind in his face. A thousand sounds from the forest around him. None of them were caused by men.

He shook off the grass and dirt and watched the moon's fierce silver curve climb above the abbey's roof.

Change, he thought.

His nails dug at the damp ground, muscles tensed. But his body refused. Every nerve fought the familiar command.

From the woods came the low cry of a bird. The night called him to run, to feel the moonlight on his bare skin. *Change,* he thought furiously. And still nothing happened.

He remembered a sharp stab at his shoulder. They had used some kind of needle during the struggle. The darkness blurred as he sank to his knees. With a fierce effort of will he clawed his way back over the stone fence, back onto abbey ground.

He had to change. All his will focused on the command, yet no muscle shifted. Weakness pulled at him. The ground swayed.

Death moved in his eyes and he smelled its bitter breath on his face.

Not yet, he swore, struggling over the grass. Instinct told him he had to keep moving, that the toxin coursing through his veins would affect a man far worse than the

29

creature he was now.

Damn them.

With a growl of pain he leaped over the cool earth, forcing stiff muscles to full stride. His vision blurred with pain, but he kept moving.

He smelled her suddenly. Loping through the woods, he came to the boulder where she had sat in the moonlight only minutes before.

Minutes that felt like a cold eternity now.

Her tears still clung to the damp grass. The scent dug under his skin, spelling the essence of female, and his body responded with almost painful awareness. Searching the rock, he found more of her scent, captured in a fallen square of cloth. His hunger grew and he realized there was danger here, danger from the blind urge to leap the fence and stalk her faint tracks until he ran her to ground.

And then he would have her.

He turned to stare back toward the road, pulled in every nerve and muscle, drawn by unexplainable need. In that heartbeat pain became his friend, forcing his focus to the cuts and welts that throbbed fiercely.

Still groggy, he burst over the hill, driven by sudden anger.

And then the world tilted. Darkness swal-

30

lowed him under its wings like the rest of its creatures of night.

CHAPTER TWO

The Scotsman opened his eyes slowly. His skin burned with the clarity of his dreams. He felt sated, still wearing the heat of a woman's naked skin on his.

For long moments Calan MacKay savored the dream memories of sleek sex, of soft laughter and passion given and fiercely taken. Then pain swallowed the pleasure, spitting him out into cold reality.

Naked and bruised under a tree in the abbey's high meadow.

He was bleeding at his shoulder and forehead, his arms streaked with mud. A harsh, metallic taste filled his mouth.

Drugged, he thought. The injection had knocked him out for the rest of the night, no simple matter given his strength and size. The attackers had been well prepared, damn them.

The sun was just clearing the treetops as he stood up, grimacing. All the night's memories flooded back with sharp clarity.

He knew that Nicholas Draycott was expected home at eight, and Calan wanted to be ready for his old friend. First he had to recheck the grounds and study the footprints near the road. With luck he could find the used syringe, too. He was headed in search of his clothes when he saw a piece of white silk caught on a lavender plant.

Hers.

The scent was clear, even to his weakened human senses, a mix of cinnamon, sunshine and lavender. Calan wondered who she was and where she'd gone. What had left her full of such anger at the abbey?

He frowned as he closed his fist around the scrap of soft silk. The pull toward her was fierce, and for a man like him this attraction was dangerous.

But he needed answers, starting with why she had been attacked. He remembered how she'd returned from the woods, boldly firing to frighten off their attackers. Calan had been half blind, struggling against the numbing effect of the drug at the time. Without her diversion, his fight might have been far more harrowing.

What kind of woman would come back to save a wild creature?

He rubbed his burning shoulder, frowning. He did not take any gift lightly, and hers demanded a grave weight of repayment. He had no choice but to track the mystery woman down. At the very least he had to be certain she was safe.

In the distance a truck motor raced, and he drew back into the shadows of the trees, following a path to the small glade where he had left his clothes and belongings the night before. He had two hours to scan the road and the attack scene. From there he would pick up her trail, which should lead him to her car. At the least he would note the direction she had traveled. Then he'd put all the details in Nicholas's hands.

One thing he knew without question. He *would* see her again. She had saved his life and he must offer her an equal service in repayment.

But Calan had a grim suspicion that he would see their attackers again, too.

This time he would be ready for them.

The dusty old Triumph arrived twenty-two minutes early. The tall English driver looked distracted as he strode across the abbey's cobblestone courtyard. Then his handsome face curved into a broad grin.

Calan was sitting on the abbey's bottom step, waiting for Nicholas Draycott's arrival.

He had washed away all traces of mud and dried blood in the stream beyond the meadow and the long welts on his arm were now hidden beneath his jacket.

As Calan's oldest and closest friend, Nicholas was aware of Calan's chaotic boyhood and strange talents though Calan had never revealed all the details. Nicholas had respected that reserve, never prying further.

"Just look what the tide has washed in. Are you flotsam or jetsam?"

"According to maritime law, am I goods floating after a wreck versus goods intentionally thrown overboard? I don't recall jumping from any nearby ships, so that must make me flotsam. Floating debris — probably from the wreckage of my life." Calan smiled with a trace of bitterness. "As for you, rules of salvage are in effect. You must return me in the event of any official claim from contending parties."

Nicholas shook his head. "You're not going *anywhere*. It's far too hard to track you down. You never leave contact numbers or an e-mail address. It's as if you vanish from the face of the earth between visits."

"Call me a throwback that way. When I'm gone, I'm gone. Since I usually end up in remote places, neither type of message would do much good anyway." Calan stretched, eyeing the viscount. "For a bureaucrat and landowner you look remarkably fit."

"I've been outside a good deal in the last month." Something passed over Nicholas Draycott's face, though he tried to cover it with a laugh and a handshake. "All that can wait. I'm afraid Marston is in London, but I can round up scones and some lapsang souchong tea for you."

"You remember all my dark vices, I see."

"Only the ones fit for mixed company." Nicholas opened the front door and moved to punch in an alarm code. Then he turned, shooting his friend a knowing look. "There are other vices, as I recall. And given that lean, tanned look, I see that you've been keeping yourself extremely active in those exotic places you favor. Where was it this month? Tanzania? Kashmir?"

"Sri Lanka and Morocco, if you must know." Calan looked at the sunny entrance and giant spiral staircase. The abbey was as beautiful as he remembered, rich with the smell of freshly cut flowers. Every inch of wood and marble gleamed with polish and care. "So Kacey isn't with you?"

"No, the family is in London at the moment." Once again, tension crossed Nicholas's face. "Let's go up to the library. I've

36

got some new wiring plans I'd like you to look at, if you wouldn't mind. While you do that, I'll track down that food and tea."

"Sounds like a fair trade to me. Marston's scones were always worth a king's ransom." Calan kept his tone casual, but he was considering how best to bring up the attack of the prior night and the woman whose rich, seductive scent kept drifting through his thoughts.

"Something wrong?"

Calan realized that Nicholas had turned to stare at him. "Why do you ask?"

"Because I know you damned well by now, MacKay. Nothing troubles you or frightens you. Yet right now you're distracted — and you don't want me to know it."

"I forget you were our government's best field agent, with a reputation for missing no detail."

"Don't change the subject. What's wrong? Not your . . . health, I hope?"

"I'm in excellent shape. As shapes come and go," the Scotsman said drily. "As for the rest, I think I'll have that tea first."

"So are you ever going to stop?" Nicholas frowned at his friend over the silver tea set.

Even with Nicholas, Calan's habitual distance was firmly in place. That reserve

37

never left him, even around his few friends.

Calan sank into a thick leather chair beside the open French doors. "By that, you mean I should stop dropping in on you with no notice? I apologize for the inconvenience," he said stiffly.

"Rubbish. I'm delighted to see you, notice or not." Nicholas turned to fill their teacups. "I'm talking about this damnable travel obsession you have. I've barely seen you in the last four years." Nicholas Draycott put down his scone, untouched. His eyes narrowed. "You never stay here in England. You're constantly on the move."

Exactly. And he would stay that way, Calan thought. Right up to the day he died. Ancient clan prophecies could not be changed, though Nicholas knew nothing of that.

Calan gave a casual shrug. "I enjoy new languages and new people. I wasn't aware that travel was a crime." He inhaled the smoky scent of the dark tea and smiled. "I'd forgotten how much I miss England. I'd also forgotten how beautiful this old abbey of yours can be."

Especially by moonlight, with the clouds drifting like silver froth and rose petals carried on the wind. Such a night could make a man forget every promise, every duty.

But Nicholas didn't know about his earlier visit or the attack that followed, and Calan wasn't giving him the details yet. First he wanted to know why someone would be staking out the road at the abbey's edge.

And who the woman was.

"Don't change the subject, Calan. It's time you turned in your frequent flyer cards. Settle down. Open another six software design studios, or whatever it is you do to make such obscene amounts of money."

"Satellite mapping technology," Calan said. "And I would hardly call my fees obscene."

"More than anyone needs. I know you give away a large part of it to charities. I also know about your dangerous sideline."

"Windsurfing?" Calan tried to keep his tone cool and just a little flippant. He hadn't expected his old friend to turn their first conversation in months into an interrogation of this sort.

"Hardly. I am referring to your land mine and ordnance disposal work." Nicholas drummed his fingers on a gleaming Georgian side table. "I found out last week from a Red Cross colleague in Switzerland. He filled me in about your work in developing countries without the equipment or expertise to clear their old fields. In all these years you never mentioned it to me."

He sounded especially irritated, Calan thought, as if this secrecy had betrayed their friendship. "It didn't seem relevant."

"You nearly get yourself *killed* every six months and it's not relevant? I saw the file about your last job in Azerbaijan. The government had several small remote detection vehicles, but they couldn't get across the rocky terrain, so *you* went instead. You managed to save four children who had wandered into the minefield, I heard."

Calan tensed. He kept this part of life as quiet as possible, and secrecy was always a stipulation of his help. The last thing he needed was a horde of journalists badgering him for human-interest stories or inquiries about his unusual skill at detection. "Who told you, Nicholas? My ordnance work is meant to be private."

"The man who told me is high enough for access to all personnel records. And in case you've forgotten, I'm your *friend.* I know that you need your privacy. I accept your choice to have no contact or involvement with your family. But I'm hardy a stranger raking up details for a tabloid story."

Calan didn't answer.

"Fine, I'll go back further. I'm the friend

who dug you out of the mud when you were eight after the upper-form boys buried you up to your waist at summer camp in Scotland. *I'm* the one who bandaged you up afterward. I recall giving you your first cigarette as a consolation."

"It was a Gauloise. The thing tasted like straw and old pavement, absolutely awful. So was that whole summer in the Hebrides." Calan stared at his teacup. "I haven't forgotten a single detail, you see? You made certain that my scrawny Scottish backside was not further harassed that summer."

"They called you an orphan and you didn't deny it. Why didn't you tell them the truth?"

"Because I prefer to keep my family private." Calan smiled grimly. "And for the record, I do appreciate all the help you have given me over the years. My . . . adjustments haven't always come easily, so I'm grateful for a place of safety and your sound advice."

"I don't want your *gratitude.* I want you to come home and stay home, damn it. Be normal. Be *happy.*" Nicholas cut off a sound of irritation. "Why can't you just settle down and find a smart woman who loves you? Start a family before you forget what the concept means."

"I think not." Calan's eyes hardened.

"Wife, children and holidays in St. Tropez are not in my future."

"You want to die in a wretched little shack at the mouth of the Amazon or crossing a minefield in Africa? What kind of end is that?"

Last night's rain had washed the air clean. Calan watched a bird circle slowly above the moat. Looking for food, no doubt. Nicholas made it a point to keep the abbey's waters well stocked with trout.

Predators and prey, always circling. This was the natural order of life. One day you were a predator, and the next you were the prey. "Since I won't be around to notice if I'm dead, how it happens hardly matters."

"I'm serious, Calan."

"So am I." Calan stood up, carrying his teacup to the window. In the clear sunlight the abbey's slopes were startlingly green. Roses framed the path with a riot of color. In the distance the moat gleamed like a freshly polished mirror, three swans caught on the bright surface. "It's . . . an old kind of restlessness. You could call it a curse of my blood. I can never manage to stay anywhere for more than a few weeks."

He had no real home. Definitely no family.

Restlessness was a friend when you trusted

no one — not even yourself.

In every sense his family was dead to him, their memory no more than ashes tossed on barren soil. His past was closed, his future bound by ancient laws that Nicholas Draycott would neither understand nor condone.

Some things were best kept secret.

"You make it sound like a medieval legend, Calan, but I don't believe in fate or curses. You have a beautiful house in Norfolk. You have work that can be done wherever you like and enough money so that you need never work again. Yet you keep pushing, always restless. What are you running away from?"

Calan didn't turn around, but his back stiffened.

"It's none of my business, of course. But I count you as my friend, so I refuse to let you throw your life away, forever rootless among strangers. So come home. *Stay* home this time."

"Impossible."

"Why?"

"I don't think I care to discuss that." Calan's voice was polite, but there was an edge of warning in his words.

"And that means back off and keep my mouth shut?"

"I'd have put it more graciously. But . . .

43

yes." Calan put his teacup down on the table, wishing for something stronger.

Don't look back.

Don't think about how the sea feels, clawing at your feet in a northwest gale. Don't think about the voices in the night, come to administer clan law to a boy too young to understand.

"What's wrong? You look like you've seen a ghost."

Calan laughed shortly. "Simply the aftereffects of some tainted water in Azerbaijan."

"You don't look sick to me." Nicholas leaned back and crossed his arms. "But since you're determined to change the subject, so be it. You've come at an excellent time, as a matter of fact. It's Kacey's birthday in two weeks and I've just bought her a painting that may turn out to be a missing Whistler *Nocturne.*"

"You hardly need my help deciphering art, Nicholas. And why did you ask for my advice on your new wiring? Have you had any problems here?"

It was Nicholas's turn to look uncomfortable. "The possibility always exists. Crime is everywhere. Civilization is going to hell all around us, in case you hadn't noticed."

"I've noticed." Calan looked down at the scars on his hands, reminders of one grisly

44

ordnance job in Serbia. It was hard to ignore the world's problems when you walked through minefields on a regular basis. It was also hard to forget man's capacity for villainy when you saw it up close, written in the faces of the victims.

"My wife believes that people are innately good. I wish I could feel the same. But the things I've seen make it hard to believe in goodness and innate human kindness." Nicholas lifted a small photo in a silver frame. A grave woman with intense eyes and streaks of paint on her hands, Kacey Draycott was a recognized expert in nineteenth-century painting. Nicholas's photo had caught her at her easel, holding a jeweler's loupe to examine brush stroke and pigment layers of a suspect Whistler portrait. In a nearby photo, she stood holding a gardening spade, laughing with Prince Charles.

"She moves in good circles," Calan murmured.

"I could barely tear her away that morning. The two of them were deep in a discussion about rose grafting and compost."

"Your wife has an extraordinary ability to put anyone at ease."

Nicholas carefully straightened the row of photos of his wife and their laughing daughter. His next words were spoken softly,

45

almost to himself. "You try your best. You plan and you pray and you maneuver. But you never can keep them separate, can you?" He took a harsh breath. "On one side you have your work — your duty to your country. On the other you've got your family, and both of them deserve the very best you can give." He traced his wife's photograph, his eyes restless and worried. "But one will always affect the other. Whatever ties you to your family weakens you and makes you vulnerable to attack or influence. I, of all people, should know that." His hand closed to a fist. "Now I've let myself be caught, trapped between duty and family. But I won't have my family put at risk. I'll walk away first."

"Walk away from what?"

"A promise I made to someone in the government."

"And this problem involves danger?"

"Yes. I'm already regretting my promise. No good deed remains unpunished," he said coldly. "Then last week I thought someone was following me. When I ran the plates with a friend, he said the car had been reported stolen."

"I'd call that a bad sign. Anything else?"

"A few weeks ago a man was in town asking questions about the abbey and my family. He claimed to be an old friend trying to locate me. At first I put him down as a tabloid journalist cruising for a story. Now I'm thinking he was about a darker game. So I'm going to beef up all our security. I've already hired protection for my family. As of tonight, I'll be traveling with a body-guard."

"You're doing the right thing to be care-ful. So you're talking about a complete overhaul, gatehouse to rose garden?"

"Exactly. I haven't told Kacey any details yet, just that she needs to be especially care-ful now. She's been in London every week-end due to this new Whistler painting that has surfaced. Then it's our daughter's birthday at the end of the month. They're staying at a friend's town house in London now, and I'll see they remain there until I'm certain of their safety."

Calan didn't like anything about this news. Kidnapping was an ugly business. The attack last night appeared to be planned by men who hoped to snare a member of Nicholas's family. "You're right to take any suspicion of a threat seriously. Of course I'll do whatever I can to help. I've been toying with a new program that automatically monitors circuit stability. It will provide alerts when your response is impeded anywhere in your system."

"English would be good." Nicholas raised an eyebrow. "Not all of us are electronics geniuses, I'm afraid."

Calan shrugged. "It's still in the beta stage, but it would signal you if anyone tampers with your system. When do you want me to start?"

"What about right now? If you're free for a few days."

Free as the wind. Free as an ocean swell headed for a rocky beach.

"I'm at your disposal, Nicky. I'll need a day to find a few things in my workroom in Norfolk —"

"Give me a list. I'll fetch them myself." The viscount frowned. "There's something else you should know about that promise I regret making." Vibrations shook the old mullioned windows. Nicholas turned, gesturing as a powerful motor thundered up the abbey's long driveway. "Good Lord, not now. Does the man *never* rest?"

Calan glanced over the viscount's shoulder at the black SUV pulling toward them. "Do you know the driver, Nicky? Because I need to tell you about last night —"

The SUV fishtailed abruptly to a halt and a tall man jumped down. Ramrod straight, he studied the front grounds of the abbey and then set a small metal box on the gravel. He pulled out a cell phone and began to talk loudly.

"A friend of yours?"

"Brigadier Martingale, head of the Prime Minister's security detail. Believe me, the man is no friend. He promised me another week, blast it." The viscount ran a hand across his forehead. "Look, Calan, I've got to talk to him. If you don't mind, I'd rather keep your involvement here our secret. The man trusts no one and will want to know every detail about you. I prefer that he remain entirely out of the loop on what we're doing."

"What exactly are we doing? I'm simply here visiting you as a friend, catching up on business trends and family gossip. No harm in that." Calan's face was guileless.

"I'll stick to that story, too. But better to avoid the discussion entirely. I've only three weeks left anyway."

"Now you've lost me, Nicky. Three weeks for what?"

Nicolas watched the big man in the dark uniform circle the front of the house, take a small camera from his pocket and photograph the ground-level doors and windows.

"To set up enhanced security here at the abbey. In three weeks a meeting will take

49

place here and everything around it may become a war zone," the viscount said grimly. "I can't say more now, but I can use all your help, Calan. Look around. Dig in all the abbey's dark corners. See that nothing has been left here without my knowledge and no one has put any surveillance devices in place. You might want to start at our main power source, down at the stables. While you do that, I'll go deal with the pain-in-the-ass brigadier."

CHAPTER THREE

He didn't like any part of it. There had been no time to discuss the night's attack. His friend could be in much deeper trouble than he realized.

Calan stood in the shadows near the kitchen while the brigadier's cool, clipped voice rapped out curt questions. Officious and manipulative came to mind, along with arrogant and intrusive. Calan wished he knew more about the meeting that required the security deadline of three weeks. It had to be important if the Prime Minister's security team was involved, something that pitted duty against family in a very unpleasant way. How did you stand seeing the people you loved put at risk, even for the goal of a higher good?

He shook his head, glad that he would never feel that particular pain. *He* was never going to have a family to worry about.

Standing near the open window, he let the

morning scents of roses and cool earth play through his senses. His muscles tightened with an urge to step through the window and drop into the green shadows.

To leave human tears and regrets behind.

To hunt.

The hunger to change made his blood surge. He felt the hair stir, prickling along his neck and shoulders.

The wild thing inside him called, open to the thousand smells that a human nose could never perceive and subtle movements far beyond the range of human sight. But Calan fought the dark call. He could not risk being seen, especially with the brigadier nearby. For the Other, the wild creature he became, daylight was no friend. Exposure was a constant risk in a world where he would always be an outsider.

Suddenly a new sensation nudged his awareness. Calan felt a faint pressure at his back, as if he was being touched. But gently. So gently.

Yet the corridor was empty. Nicholas and his unwelcome visitor had moved to the far side of the front steps, caught in an argument that seemed as if it would go on for quite a while.

Slowly he relaxed his control, slipping to the very edge of the Change. With fierce force of will, he drew both parts of his mind into balance. Each part fought the other, each one claiming the right to emerge, and the struggle made Calan's muscles strain with effort.

As the itchy sensation moved up to his shoulder blades, he was certain that another presence was very close.

Offering a silent warning.

At the very edge of the Change, he opened his animal senses, yet he could see nothing more.

"Where are you?" he whispered.

A faint noise touched his ears, like the distant chime of very small bells shaken in a rough wind. The sound made his muscles tighten. The sense of a presence grew.

Low, even dreamlike, the bells seemed part of the abbey's mysterious past, which Nicholas spoke of only rarely. Calan had heard stories about an arrogant eighteenth-century ancestor with a tragic history. He recalled a legend about thirteen bells that tolled by moonlight and a great gray cat who walked the abbey's roof.

Nicholas always clammed up when the subject was raised, but the Draycott butler had savored the details, only too happy to fuel a young boy's imagination.

But Calan was no longer a boy. Ghostly

legends had no value for the man he'd become. Yet the sense of a presence persisted. Grew dense and strongly physical.

What do you want? Calan thought angrily. *Make yourself clear.*

The curtains stirred.

A bee landed on the windowsill, turning in a slow circle. Something glimmered, moving against the warm sunlight.

Calan looked up sharply, unsure of what he expected to see. A ghostly figure? Hideous, half-formed heads?

The shadows drew together, then faded. The corridor was empty.

Calan's blood hammered. The wild places called to him, very close now.

Mark your choices well, Scotsman. Beware your Changes.

The words seemed to float on the sunlight.

Darkness waits at both hands, waits with hungry breath to claim its own. Do you go or do you stay?

Do you hope or do you die?

Calan felt the fur move, felt the Other stretch, trying to claw free and leap into the vast wildness that called to him.

Who are you? He shuddered, fighting to hold his human form when the Other summoned so deeply.

There was no answer.

Wind brushed his face, bringing a sudden memory of summer and sunlight in the days before his mother and father had died. Before his innocence had been lost.

The memories slowly gathered form and force. Despite the sunlight warm across his shoulders, the past returned in an icy storm.

They had come for him at dawn.

He had expected it, feared it, but never thought it would happen so soon. All through the summer he had hidden the growing changes and the restless sleep. For weeks he had awakened at dawn to find himself muddy and bare, shivering on sand or rugged cliffs, his hands and feet bruised and bleeding. At first he had no memories of what had brought him there.

He had denied the new things he could do, hidden them even from himself. He was only nine years old, so he'd had no reference for the strangeness and strength.

Especially not the . . . hunger.

As a boy he had seen odd things on his rugged, isolated island in the Hebrides. At night he heard the cry of animals, saw icy footprints caught in winter mud near the beach. He sensed their meaning, yet he did not allow himself to truly know. A child was permitted his innocence, after all.

But not this child of Clan MacKay.

Then one moonless night Calan woke in the throes of Change, his muscles screaming, his skin on fire, and denial was no longer possible. He saw exactly what he was becoming. That night his innocence was lost forever.

He could still remember that first race of energy, the snap of tendons, the inexplicable feel of fur against his shoulders. And over that, a seduction of scents beyond the skill of any human to know.

He had made a crossing that night, bound by a dark world with new rules and new enemies.

Now they were coming for him.

Boots hammered on cold rock. Sharp voices cut through the silence. Though the boy in him wanted to flee, the braver heart bade him stay and face what lay before him. So he stood tall and proud when the door opened and a light fell on his bruised body.

His uncle first, always scowling, missing nothing as he raised his light higher. The others muttered as the beam touched Calan's shoulders, gashed and bloody.

"I've come for you, Calan Duthac MacKay of Na h-Eileanan Flannach, son of the Grey Isle. Get yourself dressed and be fast about it. You sail with us tonight."

Calan dug in his heels and did not move.

"Sail where, Uncle?"

Mutters raced through the men behind Calan's uncle. The boy dared to speak? What ill-born creature stood before them?

His uncle glowered at him. "You question me, when all on this island are sworn to my bidding?"

As if in response, the wind howled outside Calan's window and the boy heard the snarl of the sea below the hill. He wanted to protest, but the locked faces of those who should have been friend and family cut off all words. He took his sweater, looked at the spartan little room where he had spent nine years, and followed his uncle outside.

Down to the beach, the wind in his face, the spray of salt mingling with the tears he fought to contain. The water was gunmetal, all light swallowed in the hours before dawn.

They pushed him into a boat, and his uncle tossed sand over the bow, murmuring words in the oldest tongue. Only one man protested when his uncle dropped fresh sand on Calan's shoulders, in a meaning the boy did not understand.

"This is wrong." It was Kinnon, the older brother of Calan's best friend. "He's just a boy. The ordeal was never meant for one his age, Magnus. He'll ne'er swim so far. We must wait —"

57

"We?" Calan's uncle cursed the man, slapping him hard. "There is no we. The choice is made, and he will go."

There was nothing more to say. All was the True Book and the old laws. Silently the dozen men rowed straight out into the worst of the storm. After that, all Calan remembered was the sea. Almost alive now, rocking and sucking and snarling, pulling at anything on the surface to drag it down beneath its swells. They had taken him out into the worst of it, and all the while his iron-faced uncle told him why, grimly explaining the secrets of the clan and how those secrets were kept hidden at the pain of death.

Closed against all insiders, closed against all change or questioning, the True Book of the clan was clear: since Calan had begun the process of transformation every clan male experienced, he must now be tested as an adult.

They threw him overboard into the biggest swell, and the blast of icy water stole his breath. As the cold seeped in, his vision blurred. Saltwater scoured away his tears.

"You'll survive," his uncle had growled from the prow. "If you have the true skill, you'll survive. Now by all the laws of Clan MacKay, the Old Way of Testing is begun." Then his uncle turned, washing his hands of the boy who had Turned too young, an anomaly who had to be destroyed before he brought discord to the isolated island.

Calan had lashed out wildly, fighting the waves, but the big boat dipped and turned, vanishing into the storm the way it had come.

Leaving him absolutely alone, fighting to survive.

Somehow he had forced his mind to alertness, and with a brutal logic he realized that only his other, wilder form could save him. He forced the Change, felt the flood of raw strength and the snap of muscles. Driven by a blind urge for survival, he fought on toward the thread of light to the east where the sun had begun to rise.

His strength had given out just before sunset. The rest Calan knew only from those who had found his body. Exhausted and unconscious, he must have changed back on the brink of death.

By a miracle, his pale and frozen form had been discovered by a Swedish supply ship headed south for a delivery.

He had buried his family and his dark past that day. All that remained was the rough urge to survive. No longer a MacKay of the Grey Isle, he had made a new life, never returning to those who had betrayed him so bitterly.

He cursed them all.

■ ■ ■ ■

Calan's hands locked at his sides. He remembered the suck of icy water. The weight of his shoes pulling him down, down to the hungry death that was already closing in. With the memories came the old fury.

Only the most wretched of species tossed out their young to die in a rite of passage. Most animals had far too much sense and decency.

But the past was done.

Standing in the sunlight of an English morning, the tall Scotsman forced his body to relax, forced the knot of pain at his shoulders to recede. He was angry that the past could still hurt him, despite all these years.

But he willed the past away as he had done so often since he was a boy of nine. His anger, too, was pushed deep, buried so it could not impede him. He was no longer bound by the rules of the Grey Isle.

He was free, and his power would always be used in the service of those too weak or too young to protect themselves. This promise he had made to himself.

And now his oldest friend needed him.

If the abbey did become a war zone, as

Nicholas feared, they would face that danger together and defeat it.

At the door, Calan turned back, glancing down the hall.

The curtains moved gently, casting restless shadows. Time seemed to freeze.

Beware your Changes, Scotsman.

"My terms were made quite clear, Brigadier. Your team was to start work here in a week, not before," Nicholas Draycott snapped. "Why this change of schedule?"

Brigadier Allan Martingale shrugged muscular shoulders. "The timetable has been pushed up, Lord Draycott. We've had some *pings* on the radar from half a dozen Baltic extremist groups active in our neck of the woods. The Prime Minister wants everything here at the abbey swept clear before the summit, and my people need security images ASAP."

"I'll provide whatever documents you require. But my wife and daughter will be arriving soon." A lie, Nicholas thought. But with luck it would spur the man's departure. "I cannot permit any security teams in residence until next week. As we planned," Draycott added with clipped emphasis.

Irritation flared in the security officer's eyes. "I need access before that. When my attaché was here last, there were all kinds of security questions. Your backup generator looked out-of-date, too. We've got to drag this place into the twenty-first century, even if I have to take down some walls to do it."

Nicholas had a curt suggestion about where the brigadier could drag himself and what he could do to himself there. But he kept his face expressionless. Diplomacy was supposed to be his strong suit, after all. "Draycott Abbey has withstood civil war, plague and bombardment. I am certain it will be ready for the Balkan economic summit here next month."

"Your confidence is remarkable, Lord Draycott. But then your type always is *confident*." The officer made the word sound dirty. "And then it falls to me and my people to see that nothing goes awry. Rest assured, I will do exactly that, even if it becomes invasive. Wires will go everywhere they need to go." *A warning.*

"I appreciate your enthusiasm, Brigadier. Your efforts should stand us all in good stead when the Croatian, Serbian and Albanian delegates arrive here. But procedure is still procedure. I'm sure you understand that."

The security officer made a flat sound, then swung around, studying the abbey's manicured lawns and lush heirloom roses. "I'm surprised you consented to host this summit, Lord Draycott. Your home is a rare piece of English history. William the Conqueror passed over that hill. Some of the greatest artists of our country have worked here under your family's patronage."

"That history is always with me, Brigadier. But so is my family's sense of duty. The delegate from Serbia went to Oxford and we became friends there. Using the abbey was the only way to secure his participation in this summit. He seems to feel this is safe ground."

"Anyone would enjoy the abbey's luxuries." The brigadier turned, watching a small bird soar over the distant moat. "Do you know as a boy, I came here for picnics and hikes up to Lyon's Leap. After forty years, I still remember those walks. And the legends." He glanced narrowly at Nicholas. "Your family has had a singular history and not all of it pleasant. Is the house still haunted?"

"I don't believe in ghosts, Brigadier. Only in things that I can pinpoint in my government assessments or track in a range finder."

"My old nanny told me the abbey ghost is said to walk the parapets on moonless nights. And there was a story about thirteen bells, but the details elude me."

The viscount's brow rose. "Right now I'm only interested in recent history," Nicholas said flatly. "Things that might affect our preparations for the summit."

The brigadier didn't turn. "But your family history may become very relevant, Lord Draycott. You may have forgotten enemies from your work and arrest in Asia. I believe you were held captive in a place called Bhan Lai for several years."

Nicholas nodded coldly. This was *not* a subject he would discuss casually with the brigadier or any other person. And Nicholas didn't believe his long-finished work in Asia would affect the summit in any way.

"I believe that your younger sister, Elena, died in the Philippines during your captivity. She was a lovely woman. I met her once at a ball held at Chatsworth. Her death was a terrible loss," the brigadier said slowly.

Nicholas fought back shock and fury. Who was this man to dredge up Elena's death? His sister was in no way relevant to the security of the upcoming Balkan event. "Your point, Brigadier?"

"That the past has a way of coming back to haunt us, usually at the most inconvenient times, Lord Draycott. From people you least suspect."

"I'll keep that in mind. If we're done here, I have a good deal of work to finish."

"I am finished for now." The brigadier flashed a last glance across the grass, where sunlight touched the dense forest. "A beautiful estate, to be sure. I only hope that none of us has reason to regret the summit being held here at the abbey. Good day, Viscount Draycott."

Nicholas breathed a sigh of relief as the brigadier's big SUV thundered off. "Drag the abbey into the twenty-first century indeed," he muttered. There would be no drilled walls. No ghastly Day-Glo modern alarm fixtures or camera kiosks installed during his lifetime. Everything could be updated while preserving the historical appearance of the house and grounds, and Nicholas was counting on his old friend for guidance in that task.

But there was no sign of Calan. He wasn't at the stables or near the power equipment.

The viscount turned, circling past the beautiful roses and green lawns he loved so well. There was still no sign of his friend as he climbed past the moat to the edge of the high woods. Calan had been about to tell him something when the brigadier arrived.

Now Calan was gone, off stalking the

grounds for information. The viscount wondered what form he was in at the moment. He didn't relish the idea of facing down a snarling beast with wintry blue eyes.

Even now Nicholas knew only part of Calan's real story. His Changes, as he called them, were linked to his bloodline by an ancient curse that came into play when a boy reached manhood. The whole idea seemed borderline — until you stared into the creature's keen eyes and realized the intelligence that blazed there.

No animal could focus with such clear intensity. Yet Nicolas had seen the beast twice, and he still had goose bumps at the memory. He gathered that something about the usual pattern had gone wrong in Calan's case. The Change had begun too early and too hard, and the boy had nearly died in the process.

Calan would tell him nothing more. Now, as an adult, he had settled into a rootlessness that saddened Nicholas.

So where are you now?

At the top of the hill the forest began, dense with oaks that dated back generations. From here the grounds fell away, offering views of two counties and the glimmer of the English Channel to the south.

As Nicholas stood beneath a great oak, he

was struck with the odd feeling that he was no longer alone.

Then he saw the outline of a leather shoe, half-hidden beneath a giant rhododendron bush. A second shoe was pushed into the foliage nearby. Human footprints dotted the damp earth beyond.

And then vanished abruptly.

Marking the very moment of change, foot to paw, body caught midleap.

Nicholas stood motionless. He felt the hand of nature brush him along with the call of something dark and unexplainable. The woods around him fell silent, as if in hushed awareness of a predator stalking nearby.

Nicholas knew exactly who — and what — that predator was. He didn't like the idea of a savage creature prowling the abbey grounds, but for now his home would be safer for its presence.

So he hoped.

CHAPTER FOUR

Wet ferns covered the ground. Broken stems from hard rain left a green smell that marked the passage of a man only hours before.

He followed the track, every sense fully alive. The prints held gravel bits from the coast, car oil, the rancid hint of grease.

More prints dotted the ground beneath the abbey's stone fence. Here he stopped, gathering the smells like small stones, holding each until its meaning was locked into his mind.

The sun brushed his shoulders and the stirring from the woods called to him, but he waited, gaining a clear impression of the men who had crossed the fence in the night.

Their footprints had the stink of beer about them even now. Spices clung to their shoes. Chemicals. Harsh cigarettes and the smell of seawater.

The mix burned through his blood. All of

this he would remember.

Then he caught the softer trace of *her* — the woman who had come back to save him. His skin tightened in sharp response to the memory. He moved closer, testing the smells. Her footprints carried the clays of high mountains and the pine forests of France. Nothing of the sea marked her smell.

She had no scent connection with the men from the car.

Was there relief in the knowledge?

Either way, his search here was done. The sun had already passed to the far side of the valley.

He turned in a tight circle, hungry to know who the woman was, and what had formed her scent of regret and bitterness, mixed with her tears. She called to him and he had to know *why*.

There was only one way to find out.

Twilight was gathering as something jumped the stone fence near the road, following the woman's trail down into the streambed.

Kiera winced as she closed her laptop.

Her last e-mail to her sister was done. If Kiera didn't keep in frequent contact, her sister had vowed to come after her, for

69

backup and moral support. Standing up, she stretched carefully. There were cuts on her arms and legs and her face was scraped in three places. She knew she had come close to serious harm at the hands of her attackers. The responsible thing to do?

Simple.

Call the local police and report everything, including the fact that she had been trespassing at the time.

Right. And how she would explain that? Next would come the questions about her own background and what had drawn her onto Draycott grounds at night.

She shoved a hand through her short, curly hair. The color of a good crème-brûlée topping, her mother always said. Kiera was the only child with hair that wasn't jet-black, and her father had teased her once with the possibility that she was a changeling.

Hard to believe that she had cried for a week, even after all of her family tried desperately to explain it had been a joke.

But now her mother was gone. Her father, always so hale, had lost his spirit after her mother's death. Now he lived with full-time care, and a short walk left him at the edge of exhaustion. After two heart attacks, his doctors had warned the children to prepare for the worst.

Kiera couldn't imagine losing him, not so close on the heels of her mother. But life had taught her that change came whether you liked it or not. She had begun to prepare, hoarding her years of rich memories like a shield.

When she saw that her e-mail had been sent, Kiera shut down her laptop. Maddy was probably curled up by the nearest window, reading some scholarly research text on the properties of sound. The subject put Kiera to sleep, but her sister was an expert on acoustics. The two had always been very close and, despite her mother's request, Maddy had not wanted Kiera to come on this errand.

But a deathbed promise could not be ignored.

Kiera was to collect an old letter and a box from the abbey's conservatory. Both had been precious to her mother, left behind during her midnight flight from her home. Her mother had desperately wanted to be assured that they would be restored to her family at her death, and Kiera was determined to honor that wish.

Restless at memories of home, Kiera paced the room, then pulled back the bright chintz curtains. Her hotel was small, only fifteen rooms, but it was the closest place she could find to the abbey. She had already spent three days walking the local streets and driving the quiet lanes while she planned her best point to climb the abbey fence.

For all the good her plans had done.

And now a return trip to Draycott Abbey was the last thing Kiera wanted to do. She hated the memories and emotions being stirred up. On top of that, three men were walking free tonight, though they should have been behind bars for assault and attempted kidnapping. One call would send the police out after them. It was the responsible thing to do.

Kiera stalked to the phone. Picking up the receiver, she dialed the operator.

And then she'd say *what?*

She happened to be driving by and was attacked?

Too many questions.

Frowning, she held the phone. Maybe she could make an anonymous call. But those were traced, too.

With a sigh, she put down the phone. She would make a call from a pay phone in the next county, choosing a crowded spot where no one was likely to remember her face. At least the crime would be reported. But not until after she was finished and ready to leave.

One decision made.

That left the question of her return visit — and how she would get back out undiscovered.

She spun around at the chime of the cell phone resting on her bed. A quick look at the number had her smiling. "Maddy? I just e-mailed you."

"I'm not at my computer, and I wanted to be sure you were all right."

"I'm fine. I should be packing up and heading out tomorrow."

Kiera's sister took a quick breath. "You found the things?"

"Not yet. But I've been on the grounds, and I know my way now."

"No problems?"

Trust Maddy to keep probing. "No," Kiera lied. "Just —"

"Just what? Kee, are you okay? You sound upset."

"I'm a little restless, that's all. It's complicated." Kiera wouldn't say more. Her sister would worry too much.

"What's complicated?"

"Visiting here. The abbey is like every postcard of a perfect English estate. And the roses." Kiera paced the room. "Everything's so beautiful that you forget what lies beneath the surface. The secrets and the pain."

"Then finish and get out of there. That's an order," Maddy said sharply. "If you aren't done by tomorrow, I'm coming to your hotel."

"Stop worrying. I'm the practical one, remember? You can count on me to get this done without a hitch. But I'd better go, Maddy."

"Just keep me updated."

"Aye, aye, sir."

Kiera was smiling when she hung up.

Outside her window, the moon was huge, and cool light covered the garden that bordered this side of the hotel. Kiera opened the door to her patio and was instantly engulfed in the lavender fragrance that would always spell England to her. The rich, sweet scent made her a little dizzy.

Though she would have given a fortune to be on her way home to her family in the rugged stone house in the Pyrenees, something about the moonlight tugged on her senses. As if there were hopes and dreams that waited this night, if only she dared to accept them.

But Kiera had never had time for dreams. Life was too full of adventure to sit still and let empty images slip through your head. She was always on the move, always exploring the next village and valley, putting together adventure tours for one of Europe's best known travel companies.

She was determined to have her own company by the time she was thirty. If she kept building her client list, she might succeed sooner. And building a company didn't come through idle imagination.

As she stood at the window, she saw a movement in the trees beyond the garden. Something blended into the restless shadows beneath the oaks at the far end of the village. Kiera's breath checked as she saw the movement come again.

And then the shape — whatever it was — folded back into the shadows.

Probably just a fox. She'd seen two since her arrival. Or maybe it was no more than her imagination. She'd been jumpy from the first moment she'd set foot on English soil, jumpier still when she'd walked along the road and climbed the fence onto Draycott land.

Odd, she'd half imagined there had been a man in the woods. The sense of being watched had grown as she'd crossed the meadow above the moat.

She glared out at the darkness. There was

no one in the trees beyond the garden now. No reason for the little hairs to stand up along her arms.

Yet the feeling that she was not alone grew stronger. The darkness seemed to reach out to her.

Kiera reined in her errant thoughts. She had escaped. She was safe now. No one in this hotel or in this country knew her connection to the Draycotts and she meant to keep it that way. She would make her plans well. There would be no mistakes the following night.

And after that she would be done with the Draycott family forever.

It had taken Calan less than an hour to find her.

Her prints had led him straight to a small dirt road and the tire tracks of a parked car. It had been easy enough to follow the car's unique scent, crossing two small hamlets until the car stopped in a village with an isolated hotel at the far end.

Her room was on the north side, facing a garden full of lavender.

He saw her light and the blurred movements inside. Then her patio door opened, and he caught her scent. Cinnamon and pine trees. Mountain hills after rain. There was strength to her body as she leaned against the door, staring up at the moon.

Lost in thought.

Stubborn. Angry. Confused.

All those emotions clung, carried in her scent, clear for him to read. She was alone in the room, too.

The thought pleased him.

He stepped closer, silent in the shadows, his head raised. Every time she took a step her fragrance drifted toward him like a gentle touch. She was restless. He could almost feel the nervous energy slide from her as he stood, silent and watchful behind a row of topiary plants.

She turned slowly in the moonlight. Her arms crossed over her chest. "Is . . . someone out there?"

He didn't move. Wind stirred his fur. Her eyes were trained on the spot where he waited, motionless.

"Hello?"

She blew out a breath and leaned her forehead against the door frame. Exhaustion seemed to grip her. He saw her shoulders slump.

What weight did she carry? he wondered. What fueled this kind of anger and regret?

He wanted to turn away. He needed to make one more effort to trace the attackers' car, which he'd lost near a major highway exchange on the far side of the valley.

He had to put her out of his mind before this strange attraction pulled him any closer.

Yet he didn't move.

Moonlight brushed the patio outside room fifteen. He felt the sharp twist of muscles, tensed to hunt. One leap would bring him closer.

One more leap and she would be sprawled on the floor beneath him.

Dazed. Submissive.

Open to whatever he chose.

A low growl began at the bottom of his chest as hunger drove sharp nails through every nerve end. He wanted in a way he had never wanted before.

But submissive was not how he pictured her or needed her.

He looked up at the sound of a latch closing. The glass door was shut now, the curtains drawn. Her smell remained, drifting out in a subtle torment to his senses.

And then he saw her silhouette as she tugged off her robe. Slowly her body was revealed in shadows that burned into his memory . . .

Hunger blocked all logic, all control.

He fought the urge to hunt and possess. Muscles twisted, claws dragging through the soft earth.

Slowly control returned. Hunger was shoved deep. Loyalty to a friend made him turn, slip through the lavender. Then he vanished into the night.

Chapter Five

In the middle of the quiet hotel patio, Kiera leaned forward and tried vainly to read the paper. No luck. Her eyes kept blurring.

Too much coffee the day before.

Too little sleep on top of the excess coffee.

She smiled absently as a housekeeper passed, bringing her copies of the London and Paris papers. But her smile immediately faded afterward. Memories of her attackers had kept her tossing until dawn; worries about the gun she needed to dispose of made her glance nervously over her shoulder now. Except no one else knew about the gun. Her secret was safe.

Just as the secret of her identity and her purpose for coming to England were safe, no matter how jumpy she was. It was time to stop worrying.

The little restaurant in the hotel's courtyard was deserted at this early hour. Kiera finished her scone with clotted cream, stretched and reached for the big wool bag that held her knitting. When she was restless, knitting was her drug of choice. Right now her fingers itched for wool slipping in soft rows and smooth loops settling into place.

But even with patterned cables racing off her needles, she still couldn't relax. Something told her it would take more than fine threads to put the attack out of her mind. Maybe she needed to concentrate harder . . .

A shadow fell over her table.

"That's lovely tweed yarn you have there."

A living, breathing man who knew quality yarn? *Be still my beating heart.*

Kiera craned her head back, looking up. And her heart dove straight down to her unmanicured toes.

The man was at least six foot four. He wore his rough Harris tweed jacket as if it had been hand cut to fit his lean body. Which it probably had been.

Who had the money for that in these trying times?

He was handsome as sin, to boot. Rich azure eyes blazed from a tanned face that made her think of priests, poets and ancient highland warriors. So did his rough voice with its gentle lilt of Scotland.

"Sorry to intrude, but I couldn't help noticing your yarn."

"Excuse me?"

"Knitting's something of a tradition in my neck of the woods. My aunts used to win prizes for their sweaters every year."

His voice was deep, smoky like good, aged whiskey. It settled onto Kiera's senses with the same volatile kick. Smoke and heat. Depth and complexity. For some reason the man made her think of all those things.

Not that it mattered.

She cleared her throat. "You're from Scotland, I take it?"

"That's right. From a little slip of land on a quiet ocean inlet that time forgot. A lovely place, as long as you want to leave the modern world behind."

Kiera wondered vaguely if you could fall in love with a voice. If so, this man had the perfect requirements.

She frowned.

Love?

Not on her flight plan. Not for another five years at least. She had treks to plan and valleys to cross, assessing cost and safety for her tour groups. Men, with their theatrics and emotional demands, took far too much time away from everything that mattered. The idea comforted her, reassured her that her calm, orderly world was exactly as it should be.

So this heat she felt was the simple nudge of hormones, which she had managed to ignore nicely for months.

But something told Kiera the hormone-free zone had just been left behind in a blaze of glory. All because of blue eyes and a smoky voice.

She realized he was waiting for a reply. She'd been too distracted by her tangled thoughts to notice the question. But there was something remarkably distracting about the man, and not just his voice or his damnable good looks. Not even the calm power of his presence. Suddenly it became very important to understand why *this* man was different from the others who had slid past, never catching her attention.

His eyes were the oddest shade. Almost gray one minute, they shifted to azure and icy aqua. Probably a trick of the light, caused by clouds racing overhead. And right now his eyes were focused completely on her. As if she . . . mattered. When was the last time a man had looked at her that way?

Never.

And this utter focus was why he seemed different.

"What?"

"I asked if I could sit down. Is that a problem?"

"Sit here with me, you mean?" Kiera took a short, irritated breath. What was *wrong* with her? "It's just — clearly every other table is available. So why sit here? I don't even know you."

He leaned over and refilled her teacup calmly. "I'll take a chance if you will."

Way too smooth, Kiera thought. She should wave him off and be done with it.

But she didn't. Couldn't.

"You may have noticed that this place is empty."

He just kept waiting, polite but firm.

She still didn't ask him to sit down. Kiera was pretty sure that if he sat down, it would be dangerous to her peace of mind.

"All I seem to notice is you. And for the record, that isn't a line. I've been watching you from the doorway ever since you took out your wool and needles. I like how you work. You're slow and thoughtful, but there's sensuality in your hands."

Boom. This went way off the pickup-meter. He had watched her knit and called it sensual?

"Nice try."

"Beg your pardon?"

"Something tells me you've scored with

84

lines like that before. Some women might even be fascinated. Not *me.*"

"I simply told you what I saw."

She'd give him points for delivery, Kiera decided. But that didn't mean he was going to sit down. A man like this could turn a woman inside out if she let him.

"I'm sorry, but I'm waiting for someone."

"Then I'll keep you company until he comes."

He.

Kiera didn't bother to correct him. "You don't seem to take no for an answer, do you, Mr. — ?"

"MacKay." His brow rose. "You're right. I don't like wasting time. If I want something, which isn't very often, I go after it."

Heat swirled through her, working slowly up her chest. "Is that a warning?"

"Not at all. I'm just explaining what could appear to be rudeness. But it's the practical thing to do. You're alone. I'm alone. Why not share this beautiful morning, even if we both just read the paper? The waiter will have less work, and we'll have companionable silence."

Kiera shook her head. "I know one thing. This is way too good to be true. All of it."

"I don't understand you."

"Sure you don't." Frowning, Kiera stood

85

up and began to gather her notebook and papers. "I'm not in the market for conversation or companionable silence or anything else. Goodbye, Mr. MacKay."

When she turned toward the lobby, Kiera was surprised to see him move in front of her. A crease ran down his forehead. "Don't go." His hand rose, then fell back.

Almost as if he was afraid to touch her. As if he was searching for a way to put something difficult into simple words.

"Give me one good reason to stay."

"I can't explain it but it feels important that we get to know each other."

"And talking with a stranger over breakfast is important? Why should you possibly care about sitting here with me, someone you've never met?"

Something swirled through his eyes. "I'm still trying to figure that out myself. I'm hoping by the time breakfast is over I'll have an answer. Maybe both of us will."

More of that smoky Scottish accent. Each sound teased at Kiera's prickly defenses. She didn't have to believe him. She didn't have to pay attention at all. She could simply listen to him talk.

"You're a frightening man, Mr. MacKay."

"Calan." He didn't move. His air of controlled concentration seemed to deepen.

"And why would you think that?"

"Because you make everything you say sound sincere. You make a woman believe . . ." She ran a hand through her hair, shoving the short curls back off her face. "Never mind."

"No, go on. Believe what?"

His low question seemed to play over every inch of her skin.

"It doesn't matter." Kiera lifted her bag, her decision made. "Enjoy your breakfast. I'm leaving now." As she turned, two balls of her favorite red tweed yarn spilled free, rolling over the table.

He twisted and caught them both, long, powerful fingers curved around the wool. Gentle but expert.

Just a way a lover would touch. Madness, Kiera told herself.

"Nice ply. Not Scottish, though. I'd say this wool was made somewhere else."

She closed her eyes, feeling her cool decision fade fast. "Don't start talking yarn ply to me. That's really hitting beneath the belt."

After a moment he laughed. The sound started low, almost a rumble, then grew, spilling free from his chest and filling the whole patio. The sound made him seem younger, less controlled. "So I have a secret weapon now."

"I mean it. That is truly low. Men don't discuss yarn. It's a sacred law. It makes the world a safer place."

"I think you'd have liked my aunts." He looked up, watching a bird soar along the horizon. Emotion threaded his voice. "Many a winter night I spent before the fire, helping them wind their handspun wool. Each knitted cable and rib had a meaning. I used to think that the whole world lived within the space of those waves and cables."

Something dark crossed his eyes. Then his smile faded. Kiera was stunned at how fast the transformation came.

"You miss them."

"Every minute of every day. And looking at that yarn of yours . . ." He seemed to shrug off bad memories.

Kiera felt her last bit of resolution fade. You couldn't turn away a man who knew yarn.

She dropped her bag back on the table. "I give up. Have a seat."

He moved behind her with the casual grace of a man who used his strength and reflexes for a living. Tennis star? Golf pro?

No, she guessed it was something more exotic.

He refilled her teacup. "The keemum

smells excellent. I'll track down more hot water."

He turned the silver pot, using that same spare grace that made every movement fascinating. She couldn't help watching him cross the patio and then vanish inside. When he returned he had a new pot and steam played around the spout.

Fast, she decided. Competent at whatever he did. But there was more at work here than politeness or competence. She just couldn't figure out what.

"So what do you do? Butler? Purveyor of hand knits?"

He smiled a little and shook his head. "Afraid not." Kiera could have sworn his eyes changed color again, azure flashing into rich gray.

Curious, she slid into her favorite game, studying the strong, broad hands and the small scars on his fingers. No rings. No jewelry. Not even a watch. "How do you know what time it is?"

He followed the angle of her eyes and pointed east. "Right over there."

"The sun?" She drummed her fingers on the table. "Are you an anthropologist? Wildlife photographer?"

He shook his head.

"You're not a mountain climber because

you don't have the right build." Kiera pursed her lips. "They're smaller as a rule. Broad shoulders, with all their weight focused in their arms and chest. You're too tall. Your legs are probably even stronger than your arms." She cleared her throat. "Just a theory, of course." Suddenly self-conscious, she pushed the plate of scones toward him. "Feel free. I couldn't eat another bite."

"The tea will be enough for me."

"You don't wear a watch. You don't eat. Now I'm really curious."

"Don't bother. You'd find me very boring. But I see that you're interested in Draycott Abbey."

She tensed. "Why would you think that?"

Gently, he moved a paper out from beneath her knitting project. Kiera realized he had found her map of the surrounding county, part of a color hand-out from the local bookstore.

Unfortunately, she had folded the page so that the abbey lay right in the center. She might as well have burned her intentions on her forehead.

"Oh. You mean, this? The gardens looked somewhat interesting," she said casually. "And I've always been a sucker for a good ghost story."

"Ah, yes." He studied the sheet filled with tourist information. "Did they mention the thirteen bells? And the eighth viscount, who is said to walk the abbey parapet on moonless nights?"

"Not that I remember." Kiera pushed the folded paper away. "After a while all these grand houses begin to sound alike. Ghosts and traitors and spies." She began to knit, determined to avoid the force of those gray eyes. "Do you know the place?"

"I more than know it," he said quietly. Now Kiera was certain he was watching for her reaction.

Her heart missed a beat. "Don't tell me that you . . . own it?"

"Me? No. I'm only working there."

"What kind of work?"

"Outdoor work. Checking lines. Straightening out problems."

"You're no landscaper."

"No, I'm not." He leaned back, half of his face shadowed by a towering oak. "Would you like to see the grounds?" he asked abruptly.

She almost dropped her knitting needles. "No thanks. I've been on enough house tours." She wanted to stand up, to run away. How had she been so careless as to leave that folded tour guide out on the table?

Because she'd only slept two hours the night before. Because she hadn't expected to share her table for breakfast, Kiera thought crossly. She forced herself to stay right where she was and smile back at him. "No, I'm in the mood for bright lights. I'm headed for London tomorrow. Clubbing," she lied.

Something told her he wasn't the clubbing type.

When his lips tightened, Kiera saw that she had guessed right.

"Tomorrow? Then you have today. I'll be an excellent guide. I'll show you all the secret places, even where the treasure is hidden."

"I'm not interested in treasure — or in secrets," she said sharply.

But a voice whispered that this would be the answer to her prayers. One chance for a covert assessment, a check for major security obstacles to avoid later that night. She'd be a fool to refuse him.

"No," she said huskily. "Thank you, but it's really not on my list."

"You would be making a mistake, Ms. . . ." He paused, his eyes unreadable.

"Morissey. Kiera. And why would it be a mistake?"

"Because the abbey is glorious this time

of year. The centifolia roses are just coming into bloom, and the air is full of their perfume. It's impossible to describe. You need to experience it directly. Besides, aren't you even a little curious?"

Kiera had the sharp sense that they were playing cat and mouse now. That he had picked up the details of her secret plan.

And that was completely impossible. "The roses sound lovely, but I'm going to take it easy today. I'll sit here in the sun and knit."

"Oh, my aunts definitely would have liked you," he murmured.

"Calan?"

Kiera turned at the sound of footsteps. Silk rustled and ruthlessly high heels tapped across the tiled courtyard. A striking woman in a skintight suit that screamed *Versace* lasered toward the table.

"Calan, *darling!* What amazing luck to find you here."

CHAPTER SIX

"Whenever did you get back?" The woman raced on breathlessly, not waiting for an answer. "And you didn't even call me, you great vile creature." With every word she pouted more, making her full scarlet lips look even bigger.

Silicone. The thought made Kiera a little smug. Also a little jealous. The feeling grew when the Scotsman stood in that way of graceful power and hugged the new arrival, who seemed to vibrate with pure animal satisfaction at their contact.

"Bad boy. You've lost weight. Lovely muscles, from what I can feel, however." She ran long red nails along his tweed lapels. "How long has it been since Paris? Or was it Portofino?"

Kiera shifted restlessly, feeling far out of her element.

"Three years, Magritte. And it was Venice. You wore gold. I wore black." His lips curved slightly. "It rained for a solid week."

"I didn't mind a second, darling. We had far too much to do inside to be bored." Her voice fell, a husky caress. "You *should* have called me, you know."

"Sorry. Work has kept me on the move."

A little frown worked down the woman's perfectly Botox-smoothed forehead when Calan stepped back, polite but resolute as he moved out of reach. She turned slowly and studied Kiera. "But you haven't introduced me to your friend, Calan."

He didn't answer. Kiera sat up straighter.

She put down her knitting and held out a hand. "Kiera Morissey. How nice to meet you. Magritte, wasn't it?"

"Magritte Campbell. But you are American." She sounded surprised, slanting a look at Calan. "You *hate* Americans. You told me so yourself, during the dinner when that basketball team from Dallas got drunk and —"

Calan cut her off. "Don't remind me of my rudeness, Magritte. Are you staying here at the hotel?"

"*Here,* in this threadbare outpost? Hardly. I was on my way to Norfolk when we had a puncture. Henry's having it looked at now."

Was Henry the husband, the lover or the chauffeur? Kiera wondered. Something brushed her leg and she looked down at a white Maltese dragging a rhinestone-encrusted gold leash. He sniffed at Kiera's feet, then trotted to his owner, who scooped him up against her amply enhanced chest. "Rupert, there you are. You mustn't go away like that, darling. I've told you a thousand times."

But the dog didn't seem to hear. He was staring alertly at Calan. The dog sniffed the air and its fuzzy white ears went back. It growled, low and anxiously, small teeth bared.

"Rupert, do stop that. It's just Calan, you silly sod. He's not going to hurt you."

But the dog seemed to flatten, shivering in Magritte Campbell's arms.

As if it saw something that left it very frightened. Kiera found the thought unsettling.

"Ms. Campbell, would you like some tea and a scone while you wait? I have plenty here, all of it delicious."

"What a divine offer. I can see why you like her, Calan. But no, I'm sure that Henry will be by shortly. I don't mean to interrupt your knitting . . ." Her eyes slanted measuringly at Calan. "Or to interrupt anything *else* you two were planning."

"Put your antennae down, Magritte."

Calan smiled coolly. "Ms. Morissey and I had just met. We were discussing a visit to see Draycott Abbey."

"Good heavens, it's been years since I've visited the abbey. How are Nicholas and Kacey these days?"

"Very well. I'll give him your regards when I see him tomorrow."

Kiera felt her heart pound. A buzzing filled her ears and she curled her fingers over the table's edge. Suddenly Draycott Abbey felt too close, weighing ominously over her like a chill shadow. It was one thing to slip over the fence at night — and another to find herself face-to-face with the hated Draycotts.

"My dear, is something wrong? You're very pale all of a sudden."

Kiera leaned down quickly, glad to hide her face as she searched for her fallen needle. The table seemed to spin in a rush of dizziness. Dimly she heard the woman's surprised voice, followed by Calan's deeper pitch. His hand touched her wrist, skin to skin, and the whole patio seemed to lurch.

"Kiera — what's wrong?"

She didn't have a clue, but it was getting worse. "Sorry — don't feel well all of a sudden."

"Too many late nights, perhaps. Calan,

let's go outside for a walk and let her rest. We have so much catching up to do, after all."

Kiera heard the breathy, seductive voice as if from a great distance. She gripped her yarn and needles, keeping her eyes on her hands to fight the sense of vicious spinning.

". . . all right here?" The rough Scottish voice came and went. ". . . back before long."

"F-fine. Go. Don't need to stay," she rasped.

She felt his hand touch her shoulder and then the two moved away, Magritte's brittle inquiries filling the air as soon as they left the patio. She was inviting Calan to join her in Norfolk. Some kind of weekend theatrical party at her estate.

Kiera closed her eyes, taking deep breaths. Slowly the spinning began to fade. With the sun warming her face, she forced her hands to relax.

When she looked up, Calan was standing in the doorway watching her.

Just watching her. There was an intensity to him that should have made her uncomfortable.

For some reason it didn't. It left her . . . awed.

Kiera saved that little anomaly to ponder later.

"Magritte?"

"Gone. She said to give you her regards. But let's forget about Magritte, shall we?"

"She wouldn't like being forgotten, I think."

"Three minutes and you know her perfectly. Smart of you." He leaned down, frowning. "How do you feel?"

"Better. I think."

"You're still too pale. What happened?"

"I don't have a clue. Something in the food, maybe." She took a slow breath, rubbing her neck. "Dogs don't seem to like you very much. But I suppose Magritte made up for it with her enthusiasm."

"She can be very . . . enthusiastic," he said drily.

Kiera looked away. She refused to ask about any details of the time he had spent in Venice — or what happened afterward. It was absolutely *none* of her business.

"She's a good soul, really, even if she hides it well under that painfully glossy exterior."

Kiera decided to reserve her opinions on the woman who had clearly been Calan's lover and seemed eager to be his lover again.

"Have some tea. It will settle your stomach." A teacup pressed against her hands.

"If you like, I can fetch the local doctor."

"No need. I'm feeling better now." She slanted him a glance, frowning. "You're being very nice to me, Mr. MacKay."

"Calan."

"Calan then. And I never trust strangers who are too nice. My father taught us well."

"Us? How many siblings are there?"

"Three. I'm the oldest. And we are *not* talking about me." She pushed away her tea as the nausea struck again. Without warning the courtyard spun violently. Her fingers opened, clenched on the table.

"Look, you should be in bed, resting. I'll help you to your room."

For once, Kiera agreed with him. She stood stiffly, only to stagger at another wave of dizziness.

Calan cursed softly. The next thing Kiera knew, she was pressed against his chest, his arms tight around her. "I'm getting a doctor," he said flatly. "You've gone completely chalky. Kiera, can you hear me?"

Just barely, half swallowed by the hammer of her blood. "S-sick. I am never sick," she said through gritted teeth. His touch seemed to make her dizziness worse. She shoved at his hands, trying to stand up. "Put me down. I refused to be carried around like — like a child."

"Then don't act like a child. Was there ever a woman so prickly?" He caught her fist and settled it against her chest. "Relax. I'll have you at your room in a minute."

Kiera stiffened. "How do you know which room is *mine?* I never told you that."

His eyes darkened. "I asked the desk attendant. I wanted to see if you were traveling with a husband — or a lover. I don't poach."

Poach.

As in trap someone else's property. "That's downright medieval. I'm not anyone's property. Put me *down.*" She clenched her teeth, fighting more nausea.

He sighed. "Fine. Since you appear to have the temper of an Asian water buffalo. In heat."

Her feet touched the ground. Kiera felt her body slide slowly across his, thigh to thigh. If she hadn't been fighting dizziness the experience would have been distinctly intriguing. Even erotic.

But dizziness claimed all her attention as she stepped away from him. She could do this. All it required was focus and willpower. Her sisters always claimed that she had too much of both.

She took a careful step, then another. "See. I'm fine. Thank you for your help and concern, but I'm going now."

"You're sure?" He sounded far from convinced, Kiera thought.

"Absolutely." She stopped abruptly and grabbed a chair as another round of dizziness struck.

She heard him mutter. To his credit, he didn't harangue or say I told you so. All he did was pick her up in one powerful movement and stride along the cobbled walk to her room. He stopped at the threshold. "Give me your room key."

His voice was clipped, distinctly impersonal now. Reassured by this distance, Kiera searched her bag and held out the key. He shifted her in his arms, opened the door with his foot and strode inside. He settled her on the room's small bed, pulled off her shoes and spread a quilt over her. "I've put a full glass of water here by the nightstand. If you need me, call. I'll be nearby."

Her eyes slitted open. "Outside? But why — ?"

"Stop arguing with me," he said. "And I warn you, if you aren't better in an hour, I'm going for the doctor. Whether you like it or *not*."

Damned officious man.

Kiera realized she must have said the words aloud because she heard him chuckle as he closed the door.

Restless, Calan paced the deserted parking area beside the hotel. The irritating woman had twelve more minutes. If she wasn't better by then, he was calling in a doctor. She'd been sheet-white and shaking when he'd put her on the bed, and her pulse had been racing. He'd given her all the time she was getting.

But first he had a phone call to make. Nicholas Draycott would be impatient for news and updates. After scanning the nearby area, he fingered his cell phone, and called Nicholas's private line.

The viscount answered on the second ring. "About time. I was preparing to call out the cavalry."

"Anyone I know?"

"I doubt it. I like to have a few cards up my sleeve. Where are you?"

"Here and there." Calan frowned. "Do you have the name of a local doctor?"

"Are you hurt? Blast it, you should have —"

"Not for me. Someone else. I'll explain next time we talk." Calan wrote down the contact information, then shoved the paper into his jacket pocket. "I've made some headway on that car. They've been back and

103

forth near a large port, somewhere that handles a great deal of seafood — shrimp largely. I can give you a tire size and type, as well as the direction they were headed when I lost their tracks. The syringe used in the attack we discussed is in a plastic bag on your desk, ready for analysis."

"I'll send a courier. Tracing the injection will be helpful. How are you feeling now?"

"Disgustingly healthy." Calan frowned at the memory of his initial disorientation and the powerful effects of the drug. "But someone *else* might not have been so lucky. I'm convinced you or your family were the targets. You've got them under a twenty-four-hour security net?"

"All arranged. I've brought in a private contact. He's working as we speak."

"I hope that he's good enough. These people seem tough and committed, Nicholas."

"He's as good as I've ever met. He watched my back in Asia and he took a beating for it. But nothing cracked him, not ever."

Calan felt some of his anxiety recede. "I'm glad to hear you've taken precautions. Next point — I'd like all the information you can find about a leased Mini Cooper, 2007 model." Calan rattled off the plate number.

"Driver's name?"

"Kiera Morissey. That could be an alias, but I don't think so. See when she entered the country and where she's been. Full work and medical background would be helpful. Friends and family, too."

"Is there anything I should know about this woman, Calan? Since I'll be digging deep, I'd like to know why and how many favors I should call in."

Calan stared at the door of room fifteen. Something about her continued to bother him.

Her face. The way she talked.

But now the angle of the sun above the country hotel told him that Kiera's time was up. "Not yet, Nicholas. Let me decide how the pieces fit together first. I'll check back within the hour, but in the meantime it would be best if you sent anything you have directly to my computer."

"So I'm finally to be given an actual e-mail address?" Nicholas said wryly.

"It will work this month. I'll be in touch, Nicky. Now I'd better go." He waited a moment. "Keep your head down."

"Same goes for you."

Calan stalked up the narrow path to Kiera's room, prepared for anger, distrust and outright rebellion.

Instead, Kiera answered the door looking calm, rested — and beautiful. Not that her beauty matched that of a fashion model. Her brows were too thick and her cheeks were too angular. But her face pulsed with color, and strength radiated in her eyes. She was arresting and her full mouth was enough to drive even a sane man to his knees.

"You're feeling better?" He cleared his throat.

"Wonderful. I took a nap, never slept better. Strange how much good some sleep can do. A protein bar and a cup of tea — now I'm ready to move." She hiked a backpack over one shoulder, slid a knitting needle behind one ear and dropped a notebook into her pocket. After surveying her room — neat as a pin, Calan noted — she brushed past him and opened the door.

Then she waited impatiently one hand on her hip. "Well?"

No resemblance to the woman crippled by nausea. No resemblance to the stranger in the night, racked by anger and grief in the shadows of the abbey.

Who was she? Calan refused to believe that she was connected with any dangerous plot threatening the abbey. No, whatever drove Kiera Morissey was a personal torment. And Calan was determined to find out the nature of those demons.

He, of all people, could give her extensive advice on living with shadows and bitterness.

"Well, are we going?"

"I'm a little surprised, that's all."

"I've recovered. Hardly a surprise. But the day is half gone already and I have quite a lot to see before dark. I'm taking you up on your offer."

"Which offer in particular? I made several."

"Your offer of a guided tour of Draycott Abbey." She stared at him, sunlight touching her face and glinting off her hair. "You're an interesting man, and I've decided that I'm going to find out everything I can about you. No rules, no holds barred." Her lips curved. "And I warn you, when I set my mind to something, I don't give up until I succeed. Right now, *you're* next on my list." She handed him one of the two water bottles from her end table and raised an eyebrow. "Unless maybe you want to back out?"

Something dark stirred in him, drawn up from the hunter who never rested, never relaxed. He watched her with an intense focus, measuring the way heat flared in her face as their shoulders brushed for a moment.

She was offering a challenge, open in her warning. He *should* have been irritated at her clear intention.

Instead he pulled the door shut, broke off a piece of lavender from the path and slid it gently behind her ear. "I never turn back once my mind is made up."

His voice was low, rough with sudden emotion. For a moment neither of them moved, caught in shimmering awareness of how close they stood. Of the way their shoulders bumped. Of how easy it would be to move closer, skin to skin.

"Never?" she whispered.

Wind tousled her hair. It required a major force of will for Calan to keep his fingers out of those dancing, sunny strands. Suddenly touching her seemed a thing of deep and serious worth in a world that held far too much artifice and pain.

"You'll have to find that out for yourself, Kiera Morissey. Unless you're afraid of what you might find out before you're done."

CHAPTER SEVEN

Afraid?

Oh, the man was the king of smooth. The absolute model of all dangerous attraction that mothers warned their daughters against.

And girlfriends secretly lusted for.

She was going to have to watch her step, keep her impulses strictly under control and, above all, remember her agenda.

Because right now Kiera was a major fraud, a walking, talking lie. She wasn't feeling her normal self and she definitely didn't feel calm around Calan MacKay. Nor did she understand what had triggered her strange bout of dizziness. Despite her question, she had awakened with the awareness that this was an opportunity she couldn't afford to miss. She could study the abbey and have informed answers from someone who knew it well, all under the guise of a little sightseeing. So she had to go. Even if she encountered one of the hated Draycott family.

Her skin prickled at the thought.

Nearly as bad, she couldn't seem to keep her thoughts calm and controlled around her rugged guide. The man unsettled her more every minute they spent together. Sometimes he seemed generous, attentive and completely sincere. Then the vast distance settled into his face and hardened his eyes and they might have been enemies facing off on opposite sites of a trench.

Oh, yes, some kind of war was in progress. Silent and subtle, it carried her forward as ammunition was prepared and embankments were placed. But she didn't yet know his real goals and how loyal he was to the owners of the abbey. So she would test him and read every response, using the information to complete her mission at the abbey.

And then be gone forever.

Yet something warned her that if this man wanted to track her down, he would succeed.

Another shiver.

This one crossed her neck and raced lower, but not from fear. Instead it was an infuriatingly complex feeling of uneasiness, anger, expectation and, yes, desire. More desire than she could ever remember. A woman couldn't be close to a six-foot-four-inch specimen of rugged Celtic fantasy and not feel her blood stir and her body come alive. One glance from those glorious azure eyes had her shifting in the seat, torn between jumping from the moving car and gripping his jacket and hauling him against her for a slow and unbearably intimate tongues-only kiss.

"Something wrong, Kiera? Not feeling sick again, are you?"

Oh, she was feeling sick. At herself. She wasn't used to having sexual fantasies about men she barely knew. "Nothing like before. Just a few twinges. Is it far? I can't wait to see the roses. The brochures say they are spectacular." She stopped abruptly, aware that she was chattering breathlessly.

"The abbey roses are all that and more." Calan was looking at her intently. "This is a great deal of enthusiasm for someone who had no interest in the abbey less than two hours ago. Did I miss something?"

She managed a little shrug. "Do I really need to explain it? You were an utter stranger and I had no intention of telling you anything about me or my plans. That is the first rule of travel safety."

"I see. And the clubbing in London? Was that a lie, too?" Calan said gently. "Along with the man you were to meet?"

Kiera studied her neat, unmanicured nails and frowned. "I don't think I'll answer that. Not until I know you much better. And *I'm* the one who is supposed to be prying out answers here, remember? Let's talk about you." She turned slightly in her seat, watching those long, competent fingers grip the wheel. "You've got quite a lot of scars on your hands. Are you in some kind of building trade?"

He shook his head. The window was down and wind ruffled his dark hair.

"No, I didn't think so. How about resort or ship design?" He had the focused intelligence for either.

"Wrong again."

Now she was baffled. She had tried all the obvious answers — unless he had lied to her, and somehow she didn't think he had.

I never lie about the important things.

They rounded a curve, and ahead of them a row of neat cottages gleamed in the sunlight, hugging the narrow road. A picture-postcard version of the English countryside, Kiera thought.

Perfect lawns. Perfect houses. Perfect lives.

How much pain and anger was hidden behind those neat stone facades? How many secrets were buried in this quiet lane?

"What's wrong?"

Calan slowed, staring out the open window, his eyes watchful.

Suddenly a dark shape shook the nearby bushes and shot over the road. Calan muttered a curse, stabbed the brake in short bursts and cut the wheel hard to the left.

Kiera flinched, instinctively throwing her hand up to cover her face as the big animal raced straight for the car. But at the last moment, Calan fishtailed onto the grass, then backed up slightly, staring at the bushes.

Two more deer shot through. Hooves struck gravel as they hammered off to join their companion.

When a car rounded the corner, coming from the other direction, he flipped on his lights, warning them to slow down.

And then, almost as if he had suspected it, two tiny deer darted from the greenery, followed by a large female. Calan watched them race past and vanish with the others.

Then he pulled back onto the road.

"Why did you wait? How did you know . . ." Kiera's heart was still pounding as she stared at Calan.

"They often travel together as families. This time of year that means four or five. I was fairly sure there would be more."

It was logical enough. Except Kiera remembered how he had slowed the car even before the first deer appeared. How could he have known what was about to happen?

She took a long breath, drumming her fingers on the armrest.

"No need to be impatient. It isn't much farther."

She let him go right on thinking she was impatient rather than suspicious and distinctly unsettled.

He was taking a different road now, one too small to be on Kiera's maps. She filed the location away in case she needed an alternate route later.

The deer forgotten, she studied the turns, memorizing landmarks and approximate distances.

Suddenly she was aware of Calan, turning to look at her, his gaze almost a weight in its intensity. The car came to the crest of a hill and Kiera's breath caught in a gasp.

It rose above the quiet valley like a dream of summer, golden light cast on old windows, bees droning in a meadow full of wildflowers. To one side swans cut perfect ripples in a burnished moat where twisted chimneys and rugged parapets swam in restless reflections.

Draycott Abbey by night was imposing.

Draycott Abbey by sunlight was heart stopping.

Kiera wanted to be untouched, unaffected, but the beauty of the ancient walls seemed to reach out, holding dreams and hiding promises she couldn't even name.

And this all might have been part of her life, a place she could call home. Kiera felt her nails dig into her palms and understood that the real test was about to begin. Everything else had been simple.

She wanted to run. She wanted to tell him to turn the car around. But a promise made could not be broken.

She forced her muscles to relax and kept her expression casual. "Is that Draycott Abbey? I don't see any roses yet."

"The road curves. One more turn and we'll be awash in them."

In a haze of golden light, he turned past a row of dense oaks and suddenly the abbey was there, all silver water and tall granite towers, the weathered facade covered by a riot of roses. In half a dozen colors, they climbed past doors and windows, tossed in the steady wind.

"So many," she whispered, moved beyond any other words.

"You won't forget your first sight. I never have," he said roughly.

Kiera fought through a wave of emotion and tried to focus on what he'd just told her.

Him, not her. She was after all the information she could shake free from and about *him,* while she kept her own feelings firmly out of reach.

After all she was the practical Morissey sister. The one with her feet fixed on the ground in every situation, so her mother always said.

But Kiera didn't feel practical now. With sunlight pouring over old mullioned windows and the heady smell of roses filling the air, she felt rudderless, insubstantial.

Caught by magic.

And she didn't believe in magic.

Calan stopped the car and punched in a security code on a remote unit. As the big iron gates swung open, Kiera sat stiffly. More trees, a pair of ancient statues. The shimmer of the moat down the hill. So much beauty.

Pulled by emotions she couldn't name, Kiera sat up straighter. "Stop," she said breathlessly. "Right here, beside the rhododendrons. I'm getting out."

Calan's eyebrow rose, but he stopped in the sunlight, studying the peaceful scene below them.

Kiera didn't wait, shoving open her door and striding over the cool grass, pulled toward the crushed gravel path that rounded the moat and then turned toward the tall glass-paneled structure set in a grove of old oaks.

The conservatory is what I remember most, after everything else. I thought and imagined and grew up there. I shed my bitter tears there, but became stronger as a result.

Her mother's words returned, clear as a struck bell, making Kiera shiver. The old conservatory was exactly as Elena Morissey had described it, tall and imposing, but with traces of pure whimsy in its ornate ironwork doors and roof. Coiled metal shapes of dragons and unicorns decorated its window. Above it all the Draycott crest guarded the big iron door, a reminder that this place and this family held great power, and their whimsy should never be confused for naïveté.

Here was the place where her quest would end.

She made her plans with every step, sure in her goal now, her head clear. Even with roses scenting the air with magic, she told herself that she was immune to the abbey's beauty. Draycott Abbey meant nothing to her beyond a promise made to a frightened, dying woman.

Kiera heard the soft rustle of footsteps nearby as Calan drew up beside her.

"Sorry if I was abrupt. I was feeling a little queasy," she lied. "I'd like to see the roses. And after that the conservatory. If you don't mind."

"Not the inside of the house? Most tourists are mad for the old paintings."

"Not me. After a while all old houses start to look alike, great art or not. I'm more interested in the grounds and these amazing flowers. Is there a gardener here?"

"Not currently."

They were almost at the end of the moat. Kiera turned. "Then you'll have to fill in. How much do you know about the history of the gardens and what roses are grown here?"

He seemed to be absorbed by her face, considering her questions carefully. "I think I can answer most of your questions."

Kiera put a hand on her hip. "You know, you still haven't told me what exactly you *do* here."

He walked past her, smiling faintly. "I don't know what you do, either. That makes us equal."

She frowned. Sometimes you had to give up information to get information. "I'm a tour operator. Trekking and adventure routes, along with active vacations in truly rustic areas tourists seldom see." She couldn't keep a note of pride from her voice. "Nothing cookie-cutter, either. I design each itinerary to suit my clients."

"You lead the tours yourself? That would mean hiking, climbing? Bicycling with a group?"

She nodded. "All of the above. I've done a few horseback trips through Mongolia and Kazakhstan, too. I only had trouble with bandits once."

"You're kidding, aren't you?"

"No, I'm not. The man wanted our bicycles, and he was well armed. It was a little prickly until we reached a compromise."

"Which was what?"

"He got three bicycles and an iPod fully loaded."

"What did you get?"

"Escorts over the mountains through a spring snowstorm. It was astonishingly beautiful. I've never had more fun in my life," she said happily.

Calan pushed open the main door of the conservatory. "I may have to look into one of those tours. Something tells me I'd enjoy seeing you in action."

Kiera didn't answer him. She was too busy staring in awe at the high glass panels covered with light condensation. The big room was full of roses, orchids, lilies and fruit trees, all spilling their fragrance through the warm air.

"It feels as if I just stepped ashore in Tahiti. There must be two hundred plants here." She touched the velvet petals of an icy purple orchid and a spotted lily. "If you wanted to impress me, you succeeded."

She wandered down an aisle crowded with air plants in a dozen shapes. Next were small pots with white strawberries and tiny herbs. "The cook must adore having these to work with. I've only seen white strawberries once."

"Then let's not pass up the opportunity. Have one." Bending smoothly, Calan picked off a ripe berry and held it up to Kiera's lips.

Feeding her, carefully, his fingers against her mouth.

Kiera simply stared at him, stunned by the feel of his rough fingers and the fruit against her mouth. All she could see was a bead of fruit sliding down his forefinger and all she could think of was how much she wanted to pull him close and then lick all that sweet juice away with her tongue and watch his eyes darken while she did it.

Because his eyes *would* darken.

Somehow Kiera already knew that. And she wanted to know more. She itched to feel his chest under her warm palm and the sound of his breath rough with the force of his desire.

She watched her hand rise. Oddly detached, she saw it move down his chest as if it wasn't her fingers, but a stranger's that opened the top button of his shirt and traced warm skin underneath.

He felt strong but immensely controlled. His focus was absolute, blazing in his eyes, and Kiera had the strangest sense that he was measuring her, tracking her mentally, both of them caught in a contest that had begun without her awareness.

Instead of being frightened or angered, she was pulled in deeper, hypnotized by the rough power of his eyes and the gentleness of his touch. The combination was arresting.

She took a jerky breath and closed her eyes.

"This is a mistake." She took an awkward step back. "I don't know what I'm doing," she whispered.

Something dark and hungry moved over his face. Kiera had the sense of a tightly coiled spring as he watched her fingers close, her hand falling away from his chest.

"I'm willing to take a chance on what I'm feeling."

"Why?"

"Because something damned rare is happening. I want to know more."

Too smooth, she thought helplessly. He sounded absolutely sincere. Her protests were already half forgotten, lost beneath the husky rasp of desire in his voice.

She stood rigid, summoning all her strength and distance. "You could be an ax murderer or a con man for all I know."

"You really believe that?" He was absolutely serious, his gaze brutally direct. "What do your instincts tell you about me right now?"

That if I let you walk away without tasting more, I'll regret it always. But she didn't say that. Bed hopping wasn't her thing; nor was a night of sweaty sex with a near stranger.

But her thoughts wouldn't stop twisting into knots. Suddenly her old life seemed painfully incomplete.

"I'm not very good at instincts." Her voice was breathless. "Not when it comes to men — or sex."

His hand slid gently along her cheek and he pushed a strand of hair behind her ear. "There must have been others, Kiera. Other lovers have made your breath tremble and your heart sing. Did you plan those times or did you simply let them happen?"

Heat swirled into her face. She didn't know how to have a calm discussion like this. Sex wasn't a game for her. There had only been two other times, in fact. Neither one had made her as giddy as she was now, fully clothed and not even kissed. That fact alone was enough to set off alarm bells. "Does that matter?"

"Strangely, I can think of little else. You keep surprising me, when I thought life held no more surprises. Maybe that's why I need to know everything about you."

She took her heart in her hands and stared right into his eyes. "Are you asking me to have sex with you?"

His brow creased. "I'm looking for more than an hour in your bed. There's magic in trusting yourself — and trusting someone else just as much. I can prove that to you, but not in an hour."

She leaned her forehead against the cool glass, trembling. She didn't like being uncertain. "I'm not looking for magic, Calan. I'm not sure it even exists. I have my work and my family. That's always been enough. I don't make decisions by raw instinct. I'm the calm and practical one."

"Then change. Surprise yourself." Plants rustled. He was right beside her now, his shoulder at her back.

He even smells good, Kiera thought, a mix of leather and cinnamon and outdoors that left her wanting to move in much closer.

Every thought led straight back to his naked body. Every thought led straight back *here,* to the thought of hot, reckless sex.

But Kiera closed him away.

Probing deep, she found her resolve. She had come here for one reason only, to satisfy the request of a dying mother who had suffered in silence for too many years. Kiera had taken on the responsibility to close the gap and bring home the things her mother had left behind before her flight years before.

Her mother had hoped to go home to Draycott Abbey one day. But her letters had not been answered, her phone calls ignored. She had never returned.

And that haunting sadness was the thing that had brought Kiera to this room, to the old tiled floor under her feet. She looked down at the broad, misshapen square her mother had described so carefully between final, racking breaths.

Third tile from the left.

A small red flower set into the center. This was what she had come to find.

But it was impossible to concentrate with Calan's hand sliding into her hair so perfectly. He traced the curve of her ear slowly as if they had been lovers for years and he knew every inch of her body.

As if she could trust him.

Stupid.

Because he was part of Draycott Abbey, and that world held only bitterness and broken promises.

She bent slightly, touched the heavy crimson leaves of a double-stemmed orchid near the glass wall. Leaning lower as if to sniff the leaves, she reached below the table and traced the big water pipe. One quick tug was all she needed.

But she hesitated, aware of Calan's hand at her back, his thigh just behind her hip.

Pointless to wish things were different.

Almost desperately, she tipped a heavy pot onto the floor. At the same time she twisted the small handle beneath the table, silently opening the pipe. Water hissed, then burst out of the open line, raining over everything within five feet. Kiera shivered as she was drenched.

Calan muttered an oath and pulled her out of the spraying water. Then he tossed his sodden coat on the fountain. Able to see again, he leaned down, following the angle of the water until he found the source.

He twisted the handle, ending the flood. "The pot must have hit it," he muttered. "I'll have to go find a wrench to check this pipe for damage, because some of these plants are priceless. Meanwhile, you're soaked. You're going to need something dry to put on."

When Kiera shivered, it wasn't an act. Even in the heated conservatory she felt chilled.

"Stay here. I'll be as quick as I can."

He walked away without a second glance.

She shivered, pulling her soaked sweater tighter, rubbing her arms. As soon as Calan was out of sight, she knelt on the wet floor and ran her fingers over the misshapen tile until she found the small nail near the upper corner.

She should have been jubilant. Her plan was a success. All she had to do was free the tile before Calan came back. In a few minutes, her promise to her mother would be complete.

A box. A letter. The past closed forever.

Strangely, all Kiera could think about was what they had both lost.

Chapter Eight

Cold began to seep in.

Ignoring her wet clothes, Kiera listened for the sound of the big door opening and the soft scrape of footsteps over gravel. She remembered how quietly Calan moved and knew she might not have much warning.

Taking a small craft knife from her bag, she probed the edges of the tile until it was free.

She worked with silent haste, lifting out the heavy glazed square and brushing at the damp earth below. Her fingers touched leather. She bent closer. As Kiera took a small red box from the damp ground, she thought of an angry, frightened girl of seventeen kneeling in this same corner, preparing a midnight escape from the only home and family she had known. A world that was no longer safe.

Her mother had not revealed all the bitter details, only the terse description of a respected family advisor, entrusted with estate affairs in the absence of her elder brother. But the advisor had tried to coerce Kiera's mother into sexual intimacy and Elena Draycott had nearly succumbed to the man's pressure. Since he controlled her accounts and all her legal affairs, he made her life hell after her refusals. So she had run away.

But there was no time for the past. Kiera had one more task to finish before Calan came back. The leather box held an old letter written by Kiera's grandmother to Elena, personal and precious. With the leather box hidden inside her shoulder bag, she stood up and paced eight careful steps toward the door. From that spot she turned left. Facing the wall of misted glass, she ran one hand over the wooden sill beneath the main window.

Nothing.

Gravel hissed outside.

He was coming back already. She had fooled him once, but Kiera doubted she would have a second chance. Gritting her teeth, she drove her palm along the rough beam, ignoring the stab of splinters as she searched for the recess her mother had described in fine detail.

Nothing.

Despite the cold, sweat dotted her brow. Calan was in sight now, a bag in his hands as he rounded the gravel path from the garden.

Kiera focused on the wood, pushing at every corner in search of the small metal latch. Splinters dug at her fingers, making her curse. Then she heard a tiny metal click.

Something moved inside the wood. Her fingers dropped as a small wooden door slid away underneath the sill.

It was there, just as her mother had promised, a box of camphorwood almost five hundred years old. Inside was an intricate lace glove, a gift of Elizabeth I, given to her most favored lady-in-waiting.

Kiera's Draycott ancestor had been very close to the queen and a powerful woman in her own right. The glove was a priceless memory of her legacy and a heritage that could not be forgotten. Now the promise to her mother was complete.

It was time to go.

Calan gripped the paper bag that held two towels and a wool coat. His normal restlessness was slipping into anger. Did she think that she had fooled him with her sudden interest in the abbey flowers?

Then she'd reached down and the water

had gushed out. She must have opened one of the water lines. But Calan had decided to let her play out her performance. The conservatory, like the rest of the house, now had fully functioning video surveillance and he could review the tapes at leisure to see every move she was making while he was gone.

He frowned at the figure in the conservatory.

He felt no guilt about the surveillance. He needed to determine whether she was involved with the men from the attack. If so, Calan would take her into custody until he could summon Nicholas Draycott.

But first he needed to know the truth — and how much more she was capable of.

The problem was that his curiosity had already changed to fascination. He sensed that Kiera was fighting a lonely battle, and her struggles set off chords of memory from his own past. Staying detached was becoming more and more difficult. Calan had spent most of his life avoiding emotional attachments, but something about Kiera called to the dark places inside him, and he refused to let her go until that calling made sense.

When he opened the conservatory door, she was at the far wall, looking outside.

"Here's a coat. Towels, too."

She didn't answer. He noticed dirt and bits of wood shavings on her hands. She had been searching for something here.

Something turned cold inside Calan as one of his questions was answered. She was a thief. She had come here for a reason. As he'd suspected, her ruse with the water pipe had been designed to send him away during her search.

He glanced at the tables and the floor nearby. One of the tiles was askew. A line of fine dirt feathered out around her feet. After noting the tile's location, Calan pulled out the wool coat and draped it around her rigid shoulders. "How's that?"

"Better. Thank you." She didn't turn, staring through the window.

"Kiera, what's wrong?"

Her finger traced a line in the condensation. "Are you ever afraid? Really afraid?"

Calan felt the force of her emotion. "Not often. But I've had some bad moments now and then."

"Bad moments." As she shoved her hands into the pockets of her coat, Calan saw that they were trembling. One of her fingers was cut.

She was still turned away, her back stiff under the wool coat. "Forget I asked."

"I don't want to forget it."

She shrugged, then drew another line down the window. "What good are questions or promises or explanations anyway? People always lie. That never changes." She shoved a hand through her hair. "Besides, it's not your problem."

"Make it my problem. I'm listening."

Her breath caught in a soft sound. Calan gripped her shoulders, turning her to see her face.

If she had found something so quickly, she had to know where to look. That meant someone was giving her private information about the abbey, and that was a crucial security leak.

He should look at her as a criminal, but for some reason he couldn't.

She was pale and determined, glaring at the sharp outline of the abbey down the hill. "I can handle my own problems," she said fiercely. "Also, I don't trust you. I'm sure that you don't trust me, either, despite that smooth act."

Calan saw her frown at the floor, then shoot a glance at her shoulder bag beneath a white orchid.

Whatever she had found was there, safely out of sight in her bag, but she couldn't hide an occasional anxious glance.

Calan prowled the room, feeling her tension. He could confront her now, with no more delays, and pressure her into revealing the names of her colleagues.

But it still didn't feel right to him. He had the sense that she was here for her own reasons, and they had nothing to do with politics or terrorism. Maybe she'd been pulled in by a lover, persuaded that she was working for a noble cause.

Or maybe it was simply greed at work. Either way, she was trouble. Calan couldn't take risks with the safety of his friend's house or family.

So he would play out the rope and let her incriminate herself. With unguarded statements caught on surveillance video, it would be a sewn up case.

She was still staring out the window, looking pale and edgy in Kacey Draycott's tailored gray coat. Even with no hint of makeup or glamorous clothes, Kiera Morissey had a way of catching attention.

Not beautiful, he thought. But her strength and calm intelligence were arresting. Right now he couldn't pull his eyes away from her face.

Her face.

Something about her wide eyes and full mouth kept nagging at his memory. Then it hit him.

For long seconds he didn't move, struggling to take in the realization. If it was true . . .

He swept up her bag and pulled her toward the door. "Come on."

"Why? What's —"

"There's something you need to see, Kiera."

"I told you, the gardens are all I'm interested in."

He felt her resistance as he opened the door. "Not in the garden. This is inside the house, and it's important that you see it. Now," he added harshly.

"I — There's not enough time. I really need to get back to my hotel. Tomorrow I have to —"

Tomorrow you'll be in jail, Calan thought. *Either that or you'll be in a serious interrogation.*

Nicholas . . .

Calan took a sharp breath. His friend had to be told immediately. "It will take only a minute or two," he said calmly. "After that I'll drive you back to your hotel. You'll have all afternoon to finish whatever you're working on."

She frowned but stopped fighting him. Though she was clearly reluctant, she let

135

him guide her along the path that led down toward the moat.

He could feel her pulse slam at her wrist. He could see the sheen of sweat on her skin, fueled by nerves.

She took a jerky breath, quickening her pace to match his long strides. "Is the owner home?" she said breathlessly.

He heard the raw edge of emotion in her voice as he unlocked the front door of the abbey and stood back. Her eyes darkened as she stared up the broad staircase. "I wouldn't want to . . . intrude."

"The Draycotts are away on vacation so we won't be disturbed. Even the family butler has the day off."

"That's . . . good. But where —"

Calan pulled her behind him up the broad staircase. "Just down at the end of this hall." He pushed open the door to the library. Four centuries of priceless books filled floor-to-ceiling shelves.

And on the back wall, just above the fireplace, a woman with clear gray eyes and a wide, generous smile kept vigil over the abbey's priceless treasures.

Once Calan had made the connection, the resemblance between Kiera and the woman in the portrait was impossible to ignore. Her name was Elena Draycott.

Nicholas's dead sister.

"Do you want to explain?"

She didn't answer, her gaze locked on the painting.

"In that case, why don't I toss out my theory?" Calan circled the room, his voice hardening. "What do you say, Ms. Morissey? Or maybe I should say Ms. Draycott?"

She hadn't spoken since he'd stopped by the fire, releasing her hand and pointing up over the mantel.

Her lips mouthed a silent word. Then her face closed down, all emotion shoved deep. "I — don't know her. Who is she?"

"Elena Draycott, of course. She's the viscount's younger sister. A remarkable likeness, wouldn't you say?"

"A little, perhaps." She shrugged and tried to turn away, but Calan gripped her shoulders, holding her where she was.

"Mother or aunt? Which is she?"

Kiera shoved at his chest. "I have no idea what you're talking about."

"Where is she now? She broke Nicholas's heart when she left. But I guess that doesn't bother her — or you," Calan said savagely.

She shouldered him aside and turned toward the door. "I am no relation to that woman or anyone in this family. Now that

137

you've shared this charming hallucination, I'd like to go back to my hotel."

"Why don't we ask the police what they know about Elena's disappearance? Better yet, why don't we ask Nicholas what he remembers?" Blocking the doorway, Calan pulled his cell phone from his pocket and dialed quickly. "Hello, Nicholas? Yes, it's Calan. No, everything is quiet. But I've got something you should know about. How soon can you be here? Twenty minutes? Excellent."

Calan heard her little gasp of shock and pain. She was staring at the painting with her hands locked. Then she spun around, hammering wildly at his neck and chest. "I won't see him. I won't see *any* of them. They can rot in hell for all I care. Damn them and damn this house, too," she said, fighting back a sob.

"Hold on, Nicholas. Let me call you back." Calan cut off the imaginary call and shoved the phone back in his pocket. "Rot in hell? What did they do to make you hate them so much? Your mother would have inherited millions, but she threw it away."

Kiera's fingers froze, fisted against his chest. Spots of angry color flared in her cheeks. "Not that it's any of your business, but it was rape that sent her away. Cold-hearted, calculated rape. Now get *out* of my way and let me go home or I'll knock you out of my way!"

It took Calan several seconds to process the words.

Several seconds more to hear the terrible pain hidden behind the fury in Kiera's voice. None of it made sense. "Explain it."

"Explain what? The late-night visits and the groping in dark corridors? Or maybe you want to know the threats about what would happen if she didn't meet him in the little caretaker's cottage near Lyon's Leap."

"She told you this? Your mother, Elena?" he said quietly.

"My mother. But she was *not* Elena. She never used that name again. This house — this family — all of that world was closed forever and locked away. It was the only way she could survive after Nicholas returned her letters unopened and told her not to bother him with further contact."

"Nicholas?" It was so preposterous that Calan could only shake his head.

"I have his letter. My mother saved it all these years. Every cold, brutal word is there."

"Impossible." Or was it? Calan knew that Nicholas could sometimes be proud and ar-

139

rogant. If his younger sister had angered him, he might have threatened to cut her off.

But . . . rape? How could that be part of Elena's past? "Who threatened her, Kiera? Because this doesn't make sense. Let me call Nicholas and you two can —"

Kiera cut him off. "Out of the question," she said in a rush. "Now I'd like to leave, unless you plan to add kidnapping to the list of criminal things that happen in this house. You're just like the *rest* of them. You get what you want at *any* price, no matter who gets hurt."

CHAPTER NINE

Just like the rest of them.

Calan hid a bitter smile. In that, at least, she was absolutely wrong. He was like no one that Kiera had ever met.

Of course he would never share that secret with her. But now at least her pain and anger made sense. Families could be the cruelest of enemies, striking at vulnerable layers of hope and innocence. Calan still carried his own turbulent memories — and the scars — to prove that dirty truth.

"I said I want to leave. Move out of my way." She gripped his arm and tried to shoulder him aside.

"Not yet. There are things you need to explain."

"Have you heard *anything* I've said? I'm leaving. I won't explain anything to you or your arrogant employers."

"Just tell me one thing. If you hate the Draycott family so much, why did you come back here?"

Anger simmered and snapped in her face. "I don't have to answer that."

"No, you don't. But it's a fair question. Assuming your story is true —"

"It is," she snapped. "Every word."

"If it is true," Calan went on calmly, "coming to the abbey would have been the last thing you would choose. Except if you were hoping for revenge. Theft for a start." Calan had to goad her. It was the fastest way to lay the truth bare. He had to know how far her hatred would push her.

As she tried to force her way past him, he turned smoothly, pinning her against the wall. Carefully he took her hand in his and opened the palm. "You've cut yourself. If you'd stop fighting me, I'd take care of it for you."

"If you're waiting for me to moan and fall apart, you're flat out of luck. My whining skills have never been very good."

"Are you always this difficult?" he said calmly.

"I don't need to be taken care of. I don't *need* anything from you." She tried to pull away, but Calan's fingers entwined with hers.

He felt her hand tremble. For some reason he couldn't name, he brought her palm up to his mouth.

And kissed the skin gently.

Her breath caught. "What . . . are you doing?"

"Something very stupid, I imagine. Odd that I can't seem to help myself." Even the sound of her husky voice did strange things to his pulse. The slightest movement of her hand made his skin feel heavy and heated, need rising viciously.

But he had learned something crucial.

She was no professional. Professionals never made the mistake of getting involved in family matters. All in all, Calan was starting to believe that her behavior had nothing to do with criminal elements. "If you leave now, if you run away with so many unanswered questions, it will always haunt you. You'll never put this behind you."

"How would you know?"

"As I said, I've had my share of bad moments. Running doesn't work, believe me." His voice hardened. "It's a waste of time to carry around more baggage than you need."

She studied him for a moment, then sidestepped without a word.

Calan moved right along with her, her fingers against his.

"Why are you doing this? The family must pay you very well to be their watchdog."

"I count the viscount as my friend. I would guard his interests for that reason alone. I would neither expect nor accept payment for that."

"Very noble." She sniffed. "But you choose your friends badly in that case." She glared at him, her eyes suddenly narrowing. "You were there at my hotel. It wasn't a simple coincidence, was it? Have you been following me?"

Calan couldn't explain how he'd found her. She would never understand the special skills that had allowed him to track her car from the abbey, down twisting lanes and over quiet country streams.

By scent alone he had found her.

No, she would never believe that.

"If you want answers, you'll have to sit down and let me take care of your hand first."

She blew out an angry breath. "Why do you care about my hand?"

"I'm not exactly sure myself."

"Then give me one reason to stay."

"Because if you choose to stay, you'll be well treated."

Calan swore that he would calm and soothe her. But then he would do everything he could to make her talk of her own will. He couldn't let her walk away. Not because

144

he thought she was a threat. He understood now that she was something far more important.

She was the key to a tragedy that Nicholas Draycott had never been able to understand or forget. Calan was going to see that his friend had that resolution. Somehow he would make Kiera stay, without restraint or coercion.

"What do you say?"

"Up to now your word hasn't stood for much. You told me you don't lie, but you do. You also said you'd take me back to my hotel, and you haven't done it."

"I said I'd take you back before I realized who you were. You belong here, Kiera, not in that impersonal hotel. Here in the house where your mother was born. Where she was deeply loved." Calan glanced at the picture over the fireplace. "I knew her. Not very well or for very long, but I remember her clearly. She loved the books in this room. She was always in here or out in the garden, trying some new scheme to grow a new color of rose."

Kiera's eyes widened. She took a long breath. "You knew her?"

Calan felt her resistance fade. When he released her hand, she sank down on the leather wing chair near the window.

"I met her at a difficult time in my life. She never asked questions. Being pointed wasn't her way. She simply gathered you in and made you feel at home. I know that she made me feel safe here. I owe you the same."

When Kiera looked up, he saw the glint of tears in her eyes. "You must have been just a boy."

Old enough to understand things a child shouldn't have to understand, Calan thought grimly. "I was eight. It was summer, and I was visiting my great-aunt in Norfolk. Elena was here, studying French with her tutor. She was leaving for a year abroad and she was desperate not to sound ridiculous in Paris. She always garbled her tenses."

Kiera seemed to sway slightly. Her hand flattened on the wall, almost as if she needed its support. "She always hated tenses. Usually she ignored them. I remember once when we —" Kiera stopped abruptly. She stared at the walls filled with precious books. "She loved history. You'd never find her without a book nearby. Strange, I've always wondered what she was like back then, before . . . things turned bad. She kept so much hidden from us, right up to the end," Kiera whispered, almost to herself.

"You have siblings?"

After a moment Kiera nodded.

Calan burned with questions, starting with why Elena had never come back to the abbey. But he saw just how shaken Kiera looked and knew he had to give her time.

He poured her a glass of sherry and waited while she sipped it. When the color began to return to her face, he found the medical kit in Nicholas's desk.

Then he took her hand and gently began cleaning the ragged welts.

No questions.

No speculation or idle talk.

He calmed her with his touch. And Calan accepted that he would do that again one day, thigh to thigh.

Soon or not, the time didn't matter. He could be a very patient man when something important was involved. And Kiera was very important to him, on levels he was only starting to realize.

Emotions shimmered. The old abbey at its magic again, offering secret challenges and stirring up memories.

He could almost see the pale, wistful boy standing at the back of the library. He could almost hear the tall, confident woman who laughed as she pulled down books for him without being asked. She had put him at ease when few people could, and Calan owed her for that measure of comfort.

He'd sent her two letters. She'd sent him two postcards from Bordeaux.

Then, a few years later, he had heard she was dead.

He turned away, frowning. The past felt painfully close as he carefully placed a bandage over Kiera's torn skin.

Then, because he wanted to touch her full, generous mouth, he stood up and walked to the far bookshelf. "I have something else that you might like to see. I only hope that Nicholas hasn't moved it."

She watched him intently, perched on the edge of the chair.

"Here it is." Calan pulled out a set of photographs in a worn leather album and carried it across the room. "That's Elena on the right. She was very beautiful, with a dozen young men always coming and going. Nicholas teased her about it unmercifully."

Kiera took the album cautiously, as if it might burn her. Her face softened as she stared at the figures sitting on the wall beside the moat, sunlight brushing their faces.

"The boy in the back. That's you?"

Calan nodded.

"But you're . . . so thin. You look very unhappy."

So much for his studied performance. Calan wondered if everyone else had seen through the act as easily as Kiera had.

"Only to be expected. The good old days were never really very good, were they?"

"Now who's the cynical one?"

"Guilty as charged." Calan glanced over her shoulder, looking at a picture of Nicholas trying to catch one of the swans. "He loved Elena. He feels guilty still. He tried to find her and his investigators always came up empty-handed."

But Kiera flinched. "He ignored her when she needed his help." Her expression hardened. She stood up, the album plunging to the floor. "We're done here. But first, here's what I think. I think that you've been following me. I don't know why or how you found me, but that doesn't really matter. If you or your arrogant employer comes anywhere near me, now or at anytime in the future, I'll see that you regret it."

Her hands were shaking.

Calan realized that she was strung as tight as a wire, and he hated the pain in her eyes. "Kiera, you're wrong about this."

"No. There's nothing more I want to hear from you. No more wistful photos, no more sad stories. No more sweet Draycott family lies." She pulled the borrowed coat from her shoulders and tossed it down onto the chair. "Now will you drive me back to the hotel, or do I have to walk?"

Her eyes snapped. Her hair was a wild tangle around her angry face. And dear Lord, he wanted her, wanted her sighing beneath his hands, wanted her reckless and hot. He knew it was madness, but from that first moment he saw her on Draycott soil, it had seemed as if his every sense was attuned to hers.

He took an angry breath, working to recover the control that never deserted him.

Until now.

"It's almost six miles."

"I've walked twice that." She smiled icily. "In a snowstorm."

The wonder of it was, he believed her. "Finish your sherry. Then pick up the bloody coat and put it on so you don't catch pneumonia. After that, I'll take you back," Calan snapped. "Sorry to destroy your imagined melodrama, but I don't intend to hold you here. Apparently you're not as important as you think," he said coolly.

Her hands opened and closed. Then she picked up the coat and tossed it over her shoulder. Still watching him, she gripped the glass of sherry and gulped it down.

Then she tried to smother a cough.

Calan picked up the fallen photo album and placed it on the desk. "I only wonder that I didn't see the connection immediately," he said quietly. "The color of your eyes. The curve of your mouth."

She flinched, swayed as surely as if he had struck her openhanded. The memories were clear in her face, sadness like a ringing bell, and Calan would have given anything to take back words that could cause her such pain.

"I don't want to hurt you more. But there's one other thing. Like it or not, you're going to hear it. I only knew her a short time. But she meant a great deal to a young boy who didn't know who he was, or his place in the world. I thought you should know."

He was already turning toward the door when he heard the sound of cloth on leather. She crossed the room slowly, the coat gripped to her chest. All the angry defiance had slipped away. Now there was curiosity and almost a sense of relief in her face. "You did miss her, didn't you? I can hear it in your voice. Not that it changes anything . . . but thank you for that."

Then Kiera rose slowly on her toes and kissed him.

CHAPTER TEN

He had surprised her. Irritated her. Intrigued her.

Then he'd charmed her right to the tips of her unadorned toes. Kiera was determined to fight the feeling. She had never been pulled to a man this way, never carried off balance by passion.

But she was off balance now. And this man was so far out of Kiera's league that her head spun with it. Everything felt wrong.

She had been ready to storm off, burning with fury — and then a simple story about a small, unhappy boy had stopped her short. The respect in his voice had held her.

Then the photograph of her mother in happier days had torn out her heart.

Thanks to Calan's story, her mother's past had become far clearer. Now Kiera had concrete images to fill the shadows and haunting gaps in her mother's life.

When she had responded with a simple

gesture of thanks, it was given as recognition of their truce. A simple brush of lips, it was meant to be nothing weighty or complicated.

But in an instant all that had changed. She hadn't expected to notice the heat of his body or the hard planes of his cheeks beneath her hand. She hadn't expected to savor every detail of their contact until her blood sang with it.

Calan made no sound as her hand slid into his thick hair. Motionless, distant, he watched her.

No invitation. No smile. No sign that he was touched.

So that was that. Crystal clear, she decided.

Her hands dropped. "Thank you."

"For what?"

"For that story about my mother. I had so little." She looked down, frowning.

He caught her shoulders in one swift movement that had her gasping. She was hauled blindly against his chest. His hands opened, rough against her shoulders. He took a raw breath. And then he held her. Tightly. As if he never meant to let her go.

As if, for now, holding her was enough.

And for some reason Kiera felt completely safe against his chest, with the harsh sound of his breathing in her ears, a counterpoint to the slam of his heart. Her fingers opened, combing through his dark hair. He muttered a low curse.

Intrigued, Kiera moved closer.

His eyes darkened.

His low hiss of pleasure was very loud in the quiet room. Kiera felt desire shiver to life, measured in the pounding of her own heart. In a matter of seconds her gesture of simple gratitude had become anything but simple.

And nothing close to gratitude.

Now she wanted something that felt dark and hungry. Edgy and dangerous.

He moved closer until their thighs met. She felt his hands open, kneading her back and sliding lower to cover her hips. Their lips touched, and she felt the hot brush of his tongue.

Brutal and swift, desire blotted out all her careful plans and determined logic. She caught his shirt and pulled him closer, determined to savor that hard mouth. But there was no time to savor when she felt so urgent, driven to take, and take furiously.

Her head tilted, opening to his mouth. Her nails dug into his tweed jacket. She sighed at the restless heat of his tongue against hers. The room, the house, and

England itself tilted and spun. She felt a sharp wave of dizziness. Her only stability was here, against his body. All she needed was the feel of his skin and the rough tweed of his jacket as need swallowed logic.

He braced her against the wall. She felt his arousal as he lifted her, anchored her against his thighs. His hands locked on hers.

Kiera stared at his tense face, caught by the shock of exploring this new terrain of desire. As shock gave way to curiosity, her fingers dug at his jacket. "Please."

He answered her with fire, his strong hands opening, shifting her hips to pull their bodies into maddening, intimate contact. Thigh to thigh, heat built between them.

It still wasn't enough. Kiera pressed closer, lifting her body against him. "Let me touch you," she ordered, breathless. "I *need* to touch you." He shifted and his jacket fell. Then she tugged blindly at his shirt.

Two buttons hit the floor.

With a low curse, he gripped her hips, driving their bodies together. Through a haze of need, she felt his tongue brush hers, slipping into a hot entry that carried promises of pleasure as old as time.

She wanted that pleasure now.

She wanted him naked and hungry, driving inside her. She shivered with the force of the image, and instantly, his arms tight-ened around her. "Kiera?"

She barely heard, tugging furiously at his shirt.

A third button hit the floor.

"Take it off," she ordered breathlessly. "Now, damn it. I want to see you. I want —"

Everything.

Images overwhelmed her. She wanted his skin on hers.

His lips hungry and hot, everywhere.

And she wanted it right now.

She felt him mutter, the words sounding like Gaelic. Reckless, she pressed closer, then winced at the sudden scrape of his buckle. As her breath caught in a hiss, Calan cursed. His hand slid between them. His belt slid free.

Her panties followed.

Kiera shivered at the sudden feel of air on her naked thighs. Pleasure swept, sharp and edgy. His fingers grazed damp skin; she pressed closer, driven to be closer, to claim him fully as his hands were claiming her.

Hunger snapped. Need took on a hot violence that seemed to fill every inch of the room.

"There are about a thousand reasons why I shouldn't be here, why you shouldn't be

touching me. So why don't they matter?
Why —"

He cut her off, his hands tightening. "You want to have all the answers, but you can't. You want this to be simple, but it's not. God help both of us for that," he said hoarsely.

He was right. Nothing about this was calm or predictable. What she felt was primitive and infinitely dangerous.

Calan bit the curve of her ear lightly. Kiera felt his hands shake as he freed her blouse, lifting the weight of her breast into his hand. Her nipple tightened in instant arousal, hard against his fingers, and he lifted her higher.

Her back shifted against the wall, her legs sliding around his waist. Fabric rustled. His fingers teased, slipping against her.

Shuddering, she arched her back, welcoming his slow strokes. She shuddered when he muttered her name roughly, whispering in Gaelic.

He goaded, and she wanted more.

She gripped his shoulders, feeling warm muscles lock beneath her touch. With her back to the wall, she was anchored, caught against him. And just like that she was there, caught on the edge of pleasure. His fingers slid deep, and she was dragged out of herself with a violence she'd never felt before.

At her sharp, breathy gasp, Calan moved his palm against her, making hot circles that snapped her back into pleasure again. Blindly, she moved against him, her nails raking his chest.

Shock bloomed, dragging her up into delirious and consuming pleasure.

She gave a soft cry and shattered while his arms gripped her and he murmured hoarse Gaelic against her hair.

As he gathered her against his chest, Kiera had the crazy idea that she answered in the same tongue.

"Kiera." His voice sounded hoarse now.

She blinked.

Someone said her name again. She realized he was motionless.

Frowning.

His shirt was pulled free, his hair disheveled and the marks of her nails lay in faint streaks on his neck.

She had done that. And she wanted to do more.

She closed her eyes on a raw, choked breath and rested her forehead against his chest. Sanity was tenuous, but she clung to its thread. "What am I doing? You're practically a stranger and . . . and you infuriate me. I've never let myself be ruled by my body. I've never even been tempted to."

159

"Liking may not be part of the equation," he said. "Not when something this deep is at work. But don't tell me this is wrong. It can't be wrong when it's pulling us both inside out this way."

"Both?" She had to be sure he was pulled as deep as she was.

"Bloody right. And I don't do things like this, either, not with a near stranger."

"So why is it happening now?"

"I don't know. But I have to find out why you make me feel this way, damn it."

Kiera wanted to know the same thing. But if he kept touching her, she was in danger of forgetting why she had come to the abbey and all the reasons she had to leave.

She took a deep breath, feeling his thighs flex against hers. "Just so you know, we are *not* going to have sex."

His lips nuzzled her ear. "Like hell we aren't." His hands rose, combing through her hair, tilting her head back until she met his unblinking gaze. "Not right now. Not until we figure this out. But it's just a matter of time, Kiera. Like tides and Christmas. You know it. I know it."

"I don't trust you," she whispered. "Maybe I don't trust myself. What's happening to us?"

"You can trust me. I am in this just as

160

deeply as you are."

He held her.

Touching her like this could be a drug, Calan thought. She was unforgettable, and that made what had just happened very dangerous.

Because Kiera Morissey was strong and stunning in her passion. Twice she'd shattered in his arms. Twice, with no more than the stroke of his fingers and the brush of his mouth. And that was far less than the ways he hungered to take her.

Her rare passion called to his own need, crying through his blood. Her heat seemed to summon dark images that felt like memories.

His muscles flexed as he drew in Kiera's scent, felt the powerful drum of her pulse, still fired by her passion.

Inside him the Other woke.

Calan took a harsh breath. Out of the corner of his eye he saw Elena Draycott's portrait. Her face made him remember the innocent boy he had been, rather than the man of darkness he had become.

The boy had believed. The man trusted in nothing but himself.

Calan's skin tightened. He felt the draw of power and the wild places beyond the

161

world of men. He wanted the power, tasted it building inside him.

Then he saw it.

Two small beads of blood on her pale shoulder.

Blood from the sharp nails that were barely visible, pricking her skin as his hand began to change.

No.

But once roused, the wild thing growled in hunger, prowling restlessly beneath Calan's skin. Now two beings wanted Kiera's passion and naked heat.

Two creatures. Only one of them was capable of any control or empathy.

Never had he felt both parts of himself brought so close, struggling for control. While their methods would differ, their goal was the same.

Kiera's breathless cries. Her hot response beneath his pounding body.

In silent rage, he fought back the Change. It pounded over him, inches from completion while the images of her climax called to the creature inside him.

Damn it, there was no reason he could not have her, here against the wall, while she bit and fought him.

No.

Biting down a curse, he carried her

roughly to the nearest chair and released her.

Then he walked away. But it wasn't enough. He could still feel her heat. He cursed the Other. He cursed the way his hands were shaking. He saw the faint outline of dark hair, shifting beneath his skin.

Dear heaven, never had he stood so close to the edge, torn between the worlds of man and Other, fighting to hold the two worlds apart while his body became the battlefield of his control.

He couldn't, wouldn't, lose. The cost was unthinkable.

He focused on Elena Draycott's portrait. Rigid, he remembered the boy who had hoped and believed, rather than the man who trusted in nothing but himself.

The image held. His skin settled, smooth again. His muscles relaxed.

The Other growled inside him, twisted in anger and then slowly retreated.

Dimly he felt Kiera's hand on his shoulder. "Calan, what is it?"

He didn't answer. As he searched for words to explain what couldn't be explained, she looked away. Buttoning her blouse, she avoided his eyes and she stood up, her body rigid. "I'd better go. Right now.

Because this . . ." She took a jerky breath. "*This* was a huge mistake."

CHAPTER ELEVEN

"Like hell it was."

He wouldn't leave her regretting what had just happened between them. It was too powerful. Now both of them were going to have to deal with that fact.

Whether they liked it or not.

He caught her wrists in his hands and pulled them against his chest. Anger fought with deeper emotions he wasn't ready to face yet. For now it was enough that she stay and admit the power of what they had just experienced. "You're not leaving, Kiera. We're not *close* to being done here."

"You're wrong. This — whatever you want to call it — was a fluke. A delusion. It's my fault for being stupid enough to let it happen."

The breathless hitch in her voice made him flinch.

"It's no fluke and no delusion," he said harshly. When her fingers slipped on a button, he pushed her hands away, finishing the job himself. How to explain what couldn't be explained, that women didn't usually affect him this way and that sex was as commonplace as eating or breathing. All those things *had* been true, up until he had touched Kiera for the first time.

Now he couldn't imagine having enough of touching her. So how did he describe things about himself that few would believe possible?

And how much of the truth could he tell without betraying his oldest friend, who needed his help now?

"Stop shoving at your buttons and listen to me, Kiera. We're adults and we can handle those things. You want to walk away because this has hit you out of the blue. You don't want things that aren't simple and tidy, black-and-white. But life doesn't come wrapped in neat little packages. What's happening here isn't tidy and it never will be."

"I don't need amateur analysis. I . . . I thought I needed a friend." She tried to step around him, but Calan blocked her way. Never putting a hand on her, he held her by the simple power of his voice and his absolute conviction.

"You've got a friend, whether you believe it or not. But a friend tells the truth."

Something came and went in her eyes. "Even when it hurts?"

"*Especially* when it hurts. What I'm telling you now is that this thing between us is important. If you walk away without answers, you'll always regret it."

She gave a little shrug, as if she wanted to push away everything he was saying.

"Things that matter aren't simple and usually they're not fair. They come at you when you least expect them. They hit you hard, knock you off your feet and leave your world in turmoil. That's what you've done to me," he said roughly.

"Hardly a compliment. And I don't want to be knocked off my feet." Her mouth was a tense line.

"Then you lose. Your life will always be the same and your joys will be a slim shadow of what they could be."

"I'll take simple. Calm and practical sounds just fine to me."

"The woman I just touched wouldn't say that. That woman has too much fire and hunger to want her life to be bland or simple." His hands slid into her hair. "You have to be willing to leap. Sometimes, with the right person, you have to run before you can walk." His fingers tightened.

"Stop. You're . . . too clever at this."

"I don't want to be clever. I want to be honest with you. I want to get under those layers of anger and distrust you don't want me to see. When life offers a gift like this, you take it, Kiera. Nicholas Draycott taught me that."

She made a tight, angry sound. Her hand fisted against his chest. "Him again."

"He's a good man. He's your *uncle,* like it or not."

"I don't like it, believe me."

"What happened can be explained. Trust me and trust him."

"We've done enough talking." Her hand locked against Calan's chest. She was staring at his shirt, but he had the feeling she was miles and years away, caught in memories of an unhappy past.

"Are you afraid of the truth? Will the monsters turn into empty shadows when they're finally out in the open?"

Emotion filled her eyes. He watched her try to close down, slowly pushing everything deep, where she could forget it existed. But this time it didn't work. She took a hoarse breath. "Since you want the truth, I'll tell you what I see. I see someone who's used to having things go exactly how he wants. But not this time. Yes, you made me reckless for a moment. You managed it all perfectly, I admit. But it won't happen again."

"Wrong. I'm going to feel you wrap your legs around me. I'm going to hear your voice break when I bury myself inside you. I can't get it out of my head," he said.

She flushed and turned her head away. "That's never going to happen. Now you can let me go." She raised her knee until her leg was inches away from his groin. "And unless you want me to do something very unpleasant, you'll get out of my way."

He frowned at the bitterness in her voice. He still had no clue what had caused it. "Why don't you explain what your mother told you? *Talk* to me, damn it."

"I can't," she whispered. "And talking changes nothing. Besides, we don't even —" She stopped as Calan turned suddenly, staring out at the moat.

There it was again.

His sudden sense of warning had been no mistake. There was a faint blur of movement through the trees on the far hill above the moat. A man with normal vision would have dismissed the motion as a simple play of light and shadow.

Calan knew better.

"Get your coat and your bag. We have to leave."

Kiera frowned at him. "Now? Just like that?" A faint rumble drifted from the far side of the hill. "What's that noise?" She leaned toward the window. "Who's coming?"

There was no time to explain, not if his suspicions were right. "Get your things," he repeated quickly. "You've got to get out of here. Here's the key."

"Key to *what?*"

"The Porsche you'll find parked just behind the stables. We can't take my car from the front of the house or you'll be seen."

"I'm not —"

"There's no time to explain. Not unless you want your face and your life story captured in a dozen government files by tomorrow morning. And after that, you might end up splashed over the evening news," he added grimly. "Is that what you want?"

"Of course not." She started to fire another question, then stopped. "Is there a way to avoid the front of the house?"

"There's a small service road that branches off the back driveway. Take a left at the stables. Follow the road for about half a mile and it will take you to a gate, which is locked. The tumbler code is nine-four-seven-one. Once you're outside, go left. In about two miles you'll pass a small church. Make a sharp right and that will put you on the road to your hotel. Can you remember that?"

She was already gathering her bag and coat. "I'll remember." She turned her head as the low rumble of motors grew to an angry drone.

From the sound, Calan estimated that half a dozen Range Rovers were headed their way. He had to see that Kiera got out fast. "*Go.* You don't have much time."

She took a deep breath. This time there were no protests or questions.

She hated him.

No, she only *wanted* to hate him.

He was everything she distrusted. He was gorgeous and confident and he'd pulled her in with his talk about the past, making her believe that she could trust him.

And now she was up to her neck in trouble. Who were these people racing closer?

Kiera darted past the back garden, following the path toward the low stone building that had to be the stable. She passed no one, and the car was exactly where Calan had said it would be.

Behind her the motors grew louder, and she fumbled with the ignition. Finally the engine turned over with a smooth purr. There was no sign of movement nearby as she followed the back driveway toward the service road Calan had described.

Before she reached the turn, another line of dark cars appeared, racing out of the woods. There was no way she could go farther without being seen.

Her only choice was to go back. With luck she could stay out of sight inside the house until these new arrivals left.

Quickly she backed up, parking the car where she'd found it. After a short run to the house and back through the kitchen, she took the stairs to the library. She shoved her bag out of sight, then looked carefully through a gap in the heavy velvet drapes. Calan was at the front door, arguing with a tall man in a black uniform. She heard the words *Draycott, security* and *unacceptable*. The man in the uniform shrugged and held out a cell phone.

Calan spoke briefly, then gestured toward the row of black Range Rovers. His frown grew as half a dozen men moved over the abbey lawns.

What was it, some kind of full-scale military operation? Kiera caught a little breath. Staying no longer seemed like an option. She had to find some way to get past them.

Three more uniformed men trotted toward the house. With small metal cases in their arms, they appeared to sweep the ground, turning as they moved.

Was this some kind of contamination check? But the reason didn't really matter. All that mattered was getting out without being discovered. The last thing she wanted was her connection with the Draycott family to be noted by a gung-ho security organization, even if they were the good guys.

Kiera watched Calan pace near the door. He was still speaking on the cell phone, and the team of uniformed men paid no attention to him, focused on their work.

What to do?

She looked around wildly. Down the hall she saw the bend of the broad marble staircase. An idea hit.

It was unexpected, dramatic and just a little bit dangerous.

She smiled grimly.

It also might work.

"Brigadier, this situation is unacceptable." Calan crossed the broad foyer, then turned to face the man in the black uniform. "I

173

have already notified Lord Draycott and you may be certain a complaint will be raised with appropriate authorities."

"Complain all you like. I have a job and I mean to do it. Since my electronics team happens to be free, I'll complete this part of my preparations today."

It could be true, Calan thought. But the bloody man was enjoying every second of this invasion. At least his men hadn't begun ripping up the lawn and installing surveillance equipment.

Yet.

"And one more thing. I'll be watching you, too. Lord Draycott told me about you, MacKay, but something is off about your records. I always perform a thorough search on anyone I work with and yours has gaps. Big gaps."

Calan glanced outside, hearing more trucks race toward the back of the house. He muffled a curse. Now Kiera's route out would be blocked.

Hell.

"Oh, darling. What in the world are those trucks doing? And what is taking you so long?"

Calan went absolutely still. He was almost certain the voice was Kiera's, except it was slow and sultry, like a woman who was waiting to make love.

No, that couldn't be Kiera.

He looked up the stairwell.

The brigadier looked up.

Two of the brigadier's men looked up.

A pin would have echoed in the sudden quiet as Kiera dangled one bare arm over the banister. A bracelet shimmered and her hair drifted over her face. As she moved, Calan saw the short, silky robe barely covering the top of her thighs. He felt a punch of desire.

The men below were mesmerized.

He'd been trying damned hard to keep her presence hidden, but now she left him no choice but to play along. Irritated, he managed to force a slightly amorous grin onto his face. "So sorry — darling. I'm afraid I'm going to be tied up after all. Why don't you —"

"No." Kiera pushed newly crimson lips into a dramatic pout. She leaned back, and her hair fell in a way that made it cover her face. "You *know* I've been planning to get away for weeks. I want to be alone with you. I want it now." Her voice was low and husky. "Why don't you just make them go away and then come up here, Calan? We'll have all afternoon."

Calan cleared his voice. "I'm sorry. It

won't be possible after all. *Darling.*"

Up the stairs, Kiera swung around in a huff. "Fine. Since you seem to be too busy for *me,* I'm going home. Get your car and drive me back to town," she said angrily.

She stamped down the hall, tossing the robe over the rail behind her.

Slowly, the bright silk fluttered down, landing at Calan's feet.

The brigadier slanted a glance at Calan. "Busy man, aren't you, MacKay? Apparently, we've come at a very bad time . . . for personal reasons."

His officers were grinning now. One of them picked up the thin robe and handed it to Calan with a smirk.

Calan hid his fury as he walked toward the staircase. "You could say that, yes. I'd better drive her back to town. There will be hell to pay otherwise." He glanced at his watch. "Give me twenty minutes."

"Don't let me interfere with your diversions. We'll be here, doing our jobs, digging in the dirt and checking the power lines to the roof. By all means, take your time with the young lady," the officer said acidly.

"Twenty minutes." Calan took the stairs two at a time. "And I'd appreciate it if you didn't start digging anywhere on the grounds until I got back."

He was well aware that there was no answer from the brigadier as he and his men walked outside.

"Almost there, *darling*. Be sure that you smile at the nice men." Kiera was pressed against his chest, her face angled down out of view as Calan drove the Porsche back down the driveway.

Kiera turned slightly, snuggling closer against his chest as they passed the brigadier.

"I'm smiling," Calan said grimly. "Just keep your head down."

He saw the brigadier's thoughtful look as they drove on.

Finally he let out a breath and felt Kiera relax slightly.

"You took a big chance. If they had seen your face —"

"But they didn't, did they? I made certain of that." Kiera sat up and smoothed her hair back out of her face. "That's the only reason I would parade around in a skimpy silk kimono in front of strangers."

"You did an excellent job of parading. We were all transfixed," he said drily. "It got you out safely."

She gave a quick glance over her shoulder. "Who were those men?"

"A team from London. They're doing some structural work at the abbey." He kept the explanation brief, pulling out his cell phone.

Nicholas Draycott answered on the second ring.

"Nicholas? Calan here. Yes, I left the message. The brigadier and his people are here at the house. That's right, I think you should get down here as soon as possible. I'll be back in about twenty minutes. There's something I need to take care of first." He glanced at Kiera, who was staring out the window, her body rigid. "Yes, I'll explain when I see you. Within the hour? Excellent." He hung up.

Kiera didn't look at him.

"You can't keep avoiding him, you know."

"Can't I?"

"Let me rephrase that. You can — but it would be stupid, and you're not a stupid person." Unable to help himself, Calan reached over to smooth a last few strands of hair off her cheek. "I haven't much time, but I'll drop you at your hotel and see you inside."

"You don't need to —" Her eyes narrowed. "You're worried that I won't be safe? What aren't you telling me?" She took a short, angry breath. "Who am I kidding?

There's a whole continent of things you aren't telling me." She hesitated. "Are you going to mention this to . . . Nicholas Draycott?"

"Not if you speak to him first."

He would help her, that much was true. But he would help her the way he knew would be best in order to bring this bitter misunderstanding to an end.

"You're not giving me much choice." Her hands slid up and down the handle of her shoulder bag, and she turned to face him squarely. "Clearly those people back at the abbey were military. So why did they come storming in with no warning?"

"I'm afraid I can't tell you that."

"You mean, because it's so secret. A covert government operation? Isn't that a little trite?"

They were almost at the village now, and Calan slowed to pass a delivery truck. "There's nothing more I can tell you about it."

"Well, you won't have to lie to me much longer," she said firmly. "I'm leaving first thing in the morning."

"For where?"

"Afraid I can't tell you that."

Calan's hands tightened on the wheel. He needed answers from her and he was getting tired of waiting for them. He wasn't about to allow her to leave yet. "I know things haven't gone smoothly today, so let me make it up to you. We'll have dinner at a restaurant owned by a friend of mine. Butter prawns with red chile sauce. Shanghai street dumplings that melt in your mouth. Stir-fried asparagus with wood ear mushrooms, and chocolate ginger crème brûlée for dessert. Trust me, you won't forget it. Then I'll drive you to the coast. The beach in moonlight is something worth seeing."

She made a small sound. "Don't."

"Don't invite you to a fantastic dinner?"

"Don't try to seduce me."

"You've got to eat. Why not eat with me?"

"Because this isn't going any further."

As they turned the corner, Calan saw the top of the topiary trees at the side of the inn where she was staying. But now cars blocked the road. Two television vans were parked beside the sidewalk, and there was no hope of her getting inside without being seen.

Kiera leaned toward the window. "What's got the traffic tied up in knots?"

"My guess is a society wedding. I just saw the bridal party leave the church across the street." Calan stopped the car. Ahead of him the road was clogged. If he drove farther,

180

he would be caught in the jam. His options had just dwindled.

With the complications looming, he weighed his choices carefully and came to a decision.

He backed up expertly, did a three-point turn and took a sharp right down a parallel street. Tricky, he decided. And he'd have to make arrangements with Nicholas by phone. Someone would have to go to the abbey immediately to work out the security plans with the brigadier.

Kiera swung around, her eyes full of suspicion. "Where are we going?"

"Since you can't go back to your room until the furor dies down, I'll take you to my home instead." He glanced back, watching until he was satisfied that no one was following them.

"On the phone you told him —" she forced out the words "— you told Nicholas Draycott that you would be back at the abbey shortly."

"And I will." Calan took another look in the mirror as he pulled onto the highway. "Now you may as well rest. I'll wake you when we reach Ravenswood."

CHAPTER TWELVE

Nicholas Draycott drummed his fingers on the steering wheel, staring at the traffic ahead of him. What should have been a snappy drive from London now held the threat of taking more than two hours. Added to the traffic snarl, he'd had to pull off the road twice to take and receive mobile calls.

He was still surprised by Calan's departure from the abbey. It wasn't like his friend to shirk responsibility, so there had to be a good reason. Nicholas wanted to believe it was personal, some kind of old attachment that required his presence. But as long as Nicholas had known Calan, the Scotsman had remained focused on his work, dating a variety of women but never lingering. None of his relationships moved into serious attachments. Ever.

Nicholas glared at the traffic on the hill to the south.

Not a single car was moving.

Frowning, he pulled out his mobile phone.

He knew the best person to contact. Over the years he had worked with an American security expert who was one step below a magician in his abilities with electronics. Ishmael Teague also had solid contacts and the highest government clearance. If interference had to be to run, Izzy would do it superbly.

Nicholas waited impatiently for the call to go through.

After much static a gruff voice answered. "Joe's Pizza."

Izzy's sense of humor hadn't changed.

"Nicholas Draycott here."

A pause. "Well, well. Nice to hear from the English aristocracy. Your family is all doing well, I hope."

"Excellent."

Another pause. "So this is business?"

"I'm afraid so," Nicholas said quietly.

Somewhere a car door shut. "Okay. I can talk now." Izzy's voice was calm. "Let me have the details. Luckily, I'm just wrapping up another project."

Nicholas felt slightly better as he rang off.

Given Izzy Teague's world-class security and electronics skills, he could field all questions the brigadier would throw at him. He would also make sure that the brigadier's men didn't attack the lawn or gouge out walls to lay down wires or surveillance cameras. Now, despite Calan's absence, the abbey was in the best of hands. And that was just as well, Nicholas Draycott decided irritably.

The traffic, snarled south along the M25 as far as the eye could see, was going nowhere.

And neither was he.

After he closed his cell phone, Izzy Teague pulled back onto the road. It wasn't far to Draycott Abbey, and he knew the winding country roads from memory.

The beautiful granite walls were equally clear in his memory. He respected the abbey's owner. Even more, he counted the man his friend after their work together over the years. Whatever Izzy could do to help, he would.

Only one thing bothered him. He was certain that he'd heard the name Calan MacKay before, but the details eluded him. Had it involved some kind of humanitarian mission overseas? He had the sense the man was connected with satellite software of some sort.

Since he couldn't pull up any files while he was driving, Izzy would have to go in cold. The thought left him uncomfortable. He didn't believe in working with people he hadn't researched. Experience had taught him that when you were unprepared, every little detail could backfire in your face.

With luck, this time might be different.

Except Izzy Teague didn't believe in luck.

The hedgerows flew past.

Kiera watched hills dotted with sheep run into tiny villages with small stone cottages. As they drove east, the throb of the engine, coupled with Calan's expert driving, eventually made her relax.

She yawned.

Five minutes later she slid into a strange dream where huge black cars drove in slow circles around the abbey while she stood shivering beside the moat, wearing only a silk kimono and a pair of white gloves. She waved, trying to make them stop.

The cars didn't pay any attention. They lumbered on, then veered toward the house. In a moment they were all going to crash into the abbey's front door. She tried throwing her gloves at them, but the gloves turned into owls and then into some kind of wolf.

She shuddered, lurching upright. Barely

185

awake, she felt her hand slam into Calan's shoulder. *"Stop. Have to — make them stop."*

"Kiera." He gripped her arm, smoothed her hand. "It's a dream. Nothing's wrong."

She blinked, swallowing hard. Why had it felt so real? What had happened to those strange animals? "Sorry about that."

She brushed at her eyes. They were on a narrow winding road. Below them sheep grazed in the low marshes along the ocean in a scene of timeless peace. Even the power lines blended into the woods above the road.

As Kiera sat up and stretched, she forced the dream from her mind. Calan had been right about one thing: she couldn't keep avoiding him or what had happened between them. Maybe the circling cars were a warning that something had to give.

Armchair analysis?

She gave up trying to understand the dream and tried to picture Calan's house instead. Probably full of minimalist rooms with pale furniture. Sleek windows, no curtains and lots of modern art.

Looking down, she realized his tweed jacket was draped over her shoulders. The smell of his skin blended with tantalizing hints of leather and sandalwood. All of it tangled in her senses, rich with Calan's presence. Every detail of tweed and man

186

was seductive.

Powerfully male.

Trying to ignore the intimacy of wearing his jacket, feeling every movement of the rough wool sliding against her bare arms, she sat up straighter. The last bars of golden sunlight covered the road. It wouldn't be long until twilight. "How much farther to Ravensgate?"

"Ravenswood."

"Nice name. Is it much longer?"

He didn't answer. When she glanced over, his gaze was focused on the top of the hill. His hands seemed tense on the steering wheel.

"We're there."

A house appeared in the golden light, all twisting spires and vine-covered walls. Honey-colored stone met stained-glass windows beside a small garden that spilled in irregular lines, looking even older than the house.

Enchantment.

The word leaped into her mind. The sense of place and age was unmistakable, as was the love of a careful owner.

Her breath caught as they came closer. Plane trees grew in an arch over the road. Up ahead, beyond an ornate metal gate, Kiera saw the curve of a driveway. The cobblestones were smooth with age, worn to a beautiful gray-pink, and a rugged sculpture of a wolf brooded from a rise beyond the gate.

She realized they were slowing down. Calan stopped and set the brake, then strode to the big ornate gate. After unlocking it, he pulled back the heavy ironwork, giving Kiera a clearer view of the house.

When Calan walked back to the car, he looked younger, more relaxed. There was an unmistakable pride of possession in his face.

"This is really yours?"

He nodded, his eyes never leaving the view ahead. "I've been gone too long. The trees need to be trimmed, and the roses are top-heavy."

"It all looks lovely to me. And . . . not at all what I expected."

"I suppose you pegged me for sheer glass walls and Swedish modern furniture. Abstract art in plain white rooms."

She gave a guilty laugh. "Something like that. Nothing like this. It's lovely."

"Look." He nodded in the direction of a small summerhouse beneath a huge oak tree. A family of red deer ranged around the old building, grazing calmly.

Suddenly the old stag raised his head, showing huge antlers. He stared up the hill toward Calan and the car, and the air seemed to crackle with a strange sense of awareness between the two. The big stag stood stiffly, then pawed the ground with a battle-worn hoof. It almost seemed to be a mark of respect, one old warrior to another.

Calan hadn't turned. She realized that he was still watching the woods, his hands gripping the wheel.

He seemed to be waiting for something.

"Calan, what's wrong?"

"It's . . . nothing. I thought I saw something, but I was wrong. Let's get you settled, shall we?"

It was all beyond strange.

Yet something about the quiet dell made her feel welcome. Inside, the house carried a similar sense of intimacy and welcome. Kiera's first impression was of exquisite old tartans and blue-gray walls with very fine prints. Calan moved quickly through the downstairs rooms, showed her the three upstairs bedrooms, then vanished to make a call.

When he came back, he was wearing a fleece jacket. He looked distracted. "I have to go back to the abbey. I don't like leaving you alone this way, but Aunt Aggie will be over shortly."

"Aggie?"

"My great-aunt. She's English, and this was her home until about ten years ago, when I bought it. She married my great-uncle Duncan."

"But isn't your home in Scotland?"

Something locked down in his eyes. "Not anymore. And that's a story for a different day." He leaned down, picking up a big canvas bag near the door. "Make yourself at home. Poke about if you like. Use the library freely. I have some fine old prints there."

The beautiful inlaid mahogany clock in the hall began to chime, a reminder of the duties that called him away.

Kiera walked with him toward the door. "I'll be fine. I've got my knitting and a dozen proposals to finish. I doubt I'll even notice you're gone."

That was a serious lie. She'd notice every second of his absence. She was too honest not to admit it to herself.

"I may be back late, so don't wait up. Try to get some rest." He shifted the heavy bag, frowning. He seemed to be assessing her body language and missing nothing. "You won't run off, will you?"

Kiera shook her head. "Not tonight. I make no promises about tomorrow."

"I'll accept your word on that. By the way,

say hello to Aggie for me. Tell her I'll catch up about the mail and any estate matters."

"How will I know her?"

"She'll be wearing a red sweater."

"You're sure?"

"Trust me, she will be. And now I hate goodbyes." He leaned down, skimming her cheek, his eyes very dark. "Go back inside. I've started a fire in the library for you." He said something in Gaelic. "Read my books. Drink my whiskey. Enjoy the welcome of my house and all within it," he said in a husky voice.

"You're being far too nice. It makes me uneasy."

He laughed. The quick, warm sound suited the comfort and beauty of the old house, adding another layer of welcome.

Down the lane a car motor started.

"Ah, that will be Aggie. She always did have the eyes of a hawk. That hasn't changed."

Kiera glanced in the nearby mirror and ran a hand through her hair. "I'd better do some damage control before I see anyone."

Cool air moved over her face. She felt something prick the small hairs along her neck. "Calan?"

There was no answer. When she turned around the hall was empty. Calan was gone.

191

■ ■ ■ ■

The little red Mini Cooper that pulled into the front driveway five minutes later was well used and covered with mud. A tall woman emerged. The setting sun glowed on her long silver hair, bright purple glasses and the large fabric bag caught over her arm.

Just as Calan had assured Kiera, she was wearing a red sweater. She knocked twice, then pushed the door open without waiting.

"Ms. Morissey? I'm Agatha MacKay, but please call me Aggie. Everyone does. I take it Calan has left already?" Without stopping, she crossed the foyer, put down her bag and then took Kiera's hands in a tight grip. "He asked me to make you feel at home, and so I shall. Let's start with a cup of tea and a nice splash of whiskey. I know where he keeps everything." Her bright blue eyes took on a glint of mischief. "The good silver, the best whiskey and all the family ghosts. All the dark secrets, I assure you."

She released Kiera's hands, frowning a little. "You look . . . familiar. At first I didn't notice, but here in the sunlight it's remarkable. Have we met somewhere before?"

"I'm afraid not."

"But I'm certain . . ." The old woman moved in a small circle, staring at Kiera. "It's your mouth. Or maybe the color of your eyes." After a moment, she shrugged. "I suppose it will come to me. My mind isn't always as sharp as it was." She took Kiera's arm, clicking her tongue. "Such a rascal, that boy is. I haven't seen him for two years, and then he flashes away with no more than three words on his tongue. I'll rake him over the coals for *that* when he gets back."

Kiera smiled at the thought of Calan being reprimanded by this sprightly woman. Clearly the bond of affection between the two was deep, and had been for years. "You were married to his great-uncle, he said. That was in Scotland?"

The old woman looked down. Emotion shimmered in her eyes. "The Hebrides. Such a long time ago, it was." Her fingers tightened on Kiera's arm. "It feels as if I am a different person now. Duncan's been dead these twenty years, but I still miss him like part of myself." She looked a little pale.

"Are you all right? Maybe you should sit down."

The woman shook her head, squaring her shoulders. "Nonsense. Of course I'll see to the tea, and I've brought some lovely apricot

193

scones. I made them yesterday, when Calan called. He always loved them best." She looked back down the driveway. "I wish he would stay . . ."

Kiera waited, feeling the force of the woman's hesitation. "Stay here, you mean?"

"Did I say that?" Agatha MacKay cleared her throat. "Forgive me. I must have been thinking of something else," she murmured.

He took the corners fast, just beyond the speed limit, checking his rearview mirror often. He hadn't told Kiera that they'd been followed from the village near Draycott, but he'd managed to lose the small green van en route.

He'd sent a text file of the license and driver description to Nicholas, and hoped for an ID soon. It was probably one of the brigadier's men, but Calan had to be certain.

As he rounded the curve above the beach, twilight stole over the lonely marshes. He saw the sheep moving home, white patches against the purple light, easy prey for hunters or for wolves.

He smiled slightly. Good thing there were neither nearby.

His smile faded as he came out of the curve.

The green van was back. He gunned the motor, shot past a low hedgerow, then pulled off the road in a spray of gravel. Out of sight, he cut the motor and waited.

Fifteen seconds later a dusty van raced past, its driver hunched forward, frowning.

Calan exploded back out of the twilight, picking up the van from behind, his brights in the man's rearview mirror. They wound over the barren marshes for almost a mile, barely a yard apart, and then Calan pulled onto a side road that put him out at the top of the hill.

He was waiting for the van when it appeared. As it slowed, Calan jumped out. Pistol along his leg, he strode to the car.

"Get out."

The man stared at him, his expression rigid with fury.

Calan leveled his pistol. "Why are you following me?"

The man said nothing.

"Do I need to ask you again?"

The door opened slowly. "You're making a mistake, mate. We're . . . on the same side," the driver snapped. "Just ask the brigadier to —"

"Oh, I certainly will. Give me your keys."

"You're going to regret this." Muttering, the soldier handed over his keys.

"You'd better start walking. This road over the marsh is deserted at night. Don't lose your way as sinkholes can be unpleasant. I expect you'll get to the abbey before midnight if you put some effort into it. Don't expect to find a lift."

Smiling coolly, Calan tossed the keys up into the air. They spun over and over, landing with a faint splash out in the darkness of the marsh. "Be certain you put that into your report to the brigadier."

CHAPTER THIRTEEN

The moon was rising over the trees.

Calan parked his car beside a deserted stretch of road. Silent, he slipped through the grass and climbed the high stone fence onto Draycott property. Then he stood in the darkness, listening to the night.

Warily, he turned into the wind.

Dozens of small movements around him took on form and meaning. A rabbit crouched two yards from his left foot. A mole sank low in its burrow farther away up the hill.

The smells grew more intense. He recognized a dozen kinds of roses, along with fresh lavender and crushed mint. Acrid diesel smoke from the distant A-1. He closed his eyes and let the wind bring every scent to him.

Nothing big moved through this side of the woods. No men crouched with the hint of aftershave and cordite on their clothes.

No metal gear clicked softly.

Quickly, he stepped out of his shoes. The dark force inside him jolted to life, wary and focused. Calan stretched out one arm, watching moonlight touch his wrist. So many small bones in a human hand. Such a marvel of engineering.

Now he was about to force those tendons and muscles into impossible changes . . .

Inside him the Hunter felt the call of the night and growled, aware of what was to come.

Now.

The earth was cool and damp beneath his feet as he shook off his clothes and let down the final wall. An explosion of seething life and raw strength hit his body, muscle and bone shifting.

He took a deep breath, savoring the power he could sense but never quite feel as a man.

The Change howled through him. The Other ran free. . . .

Izzy turned in at the weathered gate he knew well.

The moon was wreathed in clouds, and he caught the drifting scent of roses. There were no lights down the driveway, no signs of movement.

But some instinct held him where he was.

Turning off the car engine, he sat back and called Nicholas for an update.

"It's Teague. I'm at the gate. So far nothing's moving."

"I'm still an hour away. Bloody traffic is strung all along the M25 tonight."

"Take your time. I'm on it."

"Any sign of the brigadier's people?"

"No lights. No vehicles." Izzy pulled out a pair of night-vision glasses and scanned the far line of trees. "Of course they could be hunkered down somewhere in the woods or behind the house. I won't know until I go in. You expecting anyone tonight?"

"Only my friend Calan. He knows you're coming, so keep an eye out. He seems to turn up without any warning. Just so you know."

Izzy felt a strange sense of being watched. He looked down the slope, into a pool of dense shadows. Nothing moved.

But the prickly sense didn't go away. "I'll keep that in mind." Carefully, Izzy opened the car window completely, listening intently.

He heard nothing but the wind. Somewhere the brief cry of a bird.

"Nicholas, where is the —"

A hand moved, covering his cell phone, flipping it closed and ending the call.

When Izzy tried to move, the fingers closed hard around his arm.

Not many men were able to get the jump on Izzy Teague; this man had just done it without breaking a sweat.

Was this Nicholas's Scottish friend, the one who was supposed to be keeping an eye on the abbey?

"You're Teague?"

"Who wants to know?"

"The man with the keys."

At least he knew the code phrase Nicholas had given him.

"Okay, man with the keys. I'm Teague. Now do you mind giving me back my cell phone?"

The small silver unit slid over the car window.

The man's clothes were streaked with dirt, Izzy noticed. His voice sounded Scottish.

You're fast, Izzy thought. *Clever, too. But I need to know more than that before we start working together.* "Very smooth. Just the same, I could have been the pizza delivery guy."

Calan MacKay walked around the car and slid into the passenger seat. "Nicholas Draycott doesn't like pizza." He spoke quietly, staring into the darkness. "The brigadier has three men in place around the moat.

Directional microphones and Taser M18s. The brigadier has decided to flex his muscles and take charge, despite the arrangement with Nicholas. He'll call it a training exercise."

Izzy breathed a curse. "Where's the great man?"

"Making calls inside his Range Rover, which is parked behind the stables."

"The sooner we get him out of our hair, the sooner we can get to work on the upgrades Nicholas needs." Izzy grabbed a bag and stepped quietly out of the car. "Which is the quietest route to the stables?" he murmured.

The Scotsman loomed up beside him, silent and capable. "This one. We'll approach the brigadier's car from the south, away from the moat. Less than five minutes to get there."

"I like it." Izzy shouldered his bag and then programmed his cell phone to silent mode. "After you, MacKay."

Brigadier Martingale was on his fourth call and his second cup of tea when his car motor died.

He glared at the sudden darkness around him. "Find out what's wrong, Rollins."

"Yes, sir." His driver jumped out of the

big Range Rover and vanished around the hood.

Four minutes later the officer still hadn't returned.

Martingale cut off his call, peering through the glass. "Rollins?"

Fingers tapped on the window.

"Call off your men, Brigadier. Any information you need will be provided, but not until all your team is assembled here — with their hands in the air."

The brigadier's eyes narrowed as he recognized Calan. "You? I'm surprised you could take time away from your lady friend. After all, she seemed so enthusiastic. I hope your visit was productive," he added acidly.

"Business before pleasure, Brigadier. I'm standing in until Nicholas Draycott arrives. Anything you need, you can ask me about."

The brigadier glared into the darkness. "Who's that behind you?"

"Someone Nicholas sent to help."

"I need names for my records," came the curt answer. "Full background information, as well."

"Those will be provided."

"I don't like working with civilians," the brigadier said icily. "Where is my driver?"

"He won't be coming back for a while."

"Why *not?*"

"Because he's tied up behind that rock," Calan said. "With your distributor cap and wiring removed, you won't be going anywhere, either. So if you'd be good enough to call in the rest of your men, we can get to work. Tasers will not be required."

"How did you —" Martingale's eyes narrowed. "I don't trust you, MacKay. Something's off here. I'm going to find out what it is."

Ten minutes later, seven men ranged in a stiff line across the abbey's front driveway. Each soldier stood at attention, every face stony with anger.

They still couldn't believe someone had gotten past them unseen and unheard, Calan thought. That was their problem, not his.

He motioned to the brigadier. "Let's get started."

"This is my attaché, Staff Sergeant Wynston. He'll be keeping records on our assessment."

Calan nodded impatiently and moved toward the abbey's big front doors. "Why don't we start with the exterior installations on the roof?"

"No. First I want to finish my assessment of ground-level security. I've noted that this part of the abbey has substandard wiring. I hope Draycott has managed to move this place into the twenty-first century," he snapped.

Calan's smile was cold. "I think you'll be satisfied with Lord Draycott's enhancements. If you will stand right here . . ."

As the brigadier stepped onto a brick square next to a bank of white roses, Calan's cell phone LED screen sounded a loud klaxon. A command code flashed off and on in red.

"You just triggered a pressure-sensitive window plate. There are similar plates installed outside every window and at all access points."

Martingale tested the windowsill and newly upgraded locks, then stalked toward the big plate-glass window in the dining room. "I trust that Lord Draycott can document all tests run on windows and door security? I'll also need an updated set of plans for the abbey."

"You will have all of that directly."

Martingale made a gesture to his aide. "Make a note of that, Wynston. I want those documents before we leave here."

"Yes, sir."

The officer looked across the abbey's shadowed grounds. "Where is this man

Teague you're working with?"

"He's taking care of some things inside. Why don't we have a look at the roof next?"

The brigadier began shooting questions at Calan even before they reached the stairs. "Is there an antisniper post? What lines of sight have you considered for attack probability?"

Behind him, the efficient aide made notes in a PDA.

Calan pushed open the heavy, reinforced door to the roof. "No direction has been ruled out. There is marshland to the south and accessible coastline not far to the east. Nearest airport is Hastings. Your people will be in place monitoring all flights there, I assume."

The officer nodded curtly.

"We'll set up a post right here." Calan gestured over the wide expanse of the roof, which had an unobstructed view of the front and back lawns. "The team will have three-hundred-sixty-degree perspective and minimal obstructions from architectural features to block preemptive fire. Lord Draycott has an antisniper infrared tracking system housed in that small building to the left of the conservatory. It can detect weapon type and location instantly."

It was the best spot for countersurveillance. Calan knew that his friend had spent long weeks assessing every part of the grounds to be certain of that location.

The officer glanced at his aide, as if making sure he was getting every word of the conversation. "Impressive. But at first light, an operator would be in shadow. Second problem — the angle of that large parapet." The brigadier shone a powerful flashlight over the roof, picking out chimneys and carvings. "With the sun in his eyes and the shadow thrown by that parapet, even a trained sniper could miss a small plane, coming fast, until it was too late."

His voice was cool, certain in its arrogance.

Calan pretended to assess the view and then check the distant trees due east of the abbey, where the sun would emerge. Then he smiled calmly. "Quite so, Brigadier. Which is exactly why my surveillance report to Lord Draycott has stipulated two operatives, positioned back to back. I suppose you haven't read it yet."

The officer blinked. "I prefer field assessments to reports," he snapped.

Calan raised an eyebrow. "I prefer *both*. I've checked the coordinates carefully. Using two people working in tandem will give maximum exposure and near-zero chance of vision obstruction. Anything less would be negligent."

The brigadier crossed his arms, staring coldly at Calan. "I know your record, MacKay. I know about your electronics firm and the mapping software you've designed. But what I don't understand is why Lord Draycott insisted on calling in a civilian. Why someone with no military training? That's damned odd to me."

"You'll have to ask Lord Draycott that question. Is that your only problem, Brigadier."

The officer made a flat sound, then swung around abruptly. At the edge of the parapet, he leaned out over the weathered granite, shining his light over the abbey's manicured lawns and heirloom roses. He continued to study the grounds for several minutes. "Where is the man I had following you?" he finally asked.

"The one driving a green van? He lost his keys. He'll be walking back to the abbey."

The brigadier's mouth flattened.

"Is there anything else you need to see here, sir? I believe we've covered the key entrance points and optimum locations on the roof." Calan hid his impatience, thinking about the fiber-optic wires yet to be run at the back of the property and all along the perimeter.

"I'm finished for now." The brigadier flashed a last beam of light across the shadowed roof, casting tall shadows from the twisted spires of the abbey's chimneys. "Easy to get lost up here," he muttered. "One almost has the sense . . ." He cleared his throat. "Never mind."

Wind tossed gravel in small eddies at his feet as he motioned briskly to his aide. "The viscount will have my security assessment in two hours." He shot a glance at Calan. "I trust that my distributor cap and wiring will be back in place by the time I reach my car."

"It's feels cold all of a sudden. Or is it just me?" Agatha MacKay rested her elbows on the sink, staring out at the dark outline of the summerhouse.

"It does feel a little colder. Why don't we go back into the library?"

"I'll bring in the tea."

"You'll do nothing of the sort." Kiera lifted the big tray, smiling. "I do the heavy work while you tell me about Calan. I want to know about his family, all the details."

"It's always about family, isn't it?" Agatha brushed back a strand of white hair from her immaculate red sweater. "I knit a new red sweater every year. I've done it for almost forty years now, starting with that first summer on Skye. I met Duncan at a little pub. Five minutes later he said he loved me in red, and I . . ." Her voice caught and she leaned down, helping Kiera to tea, homemade scones and tiny sandwiches with herb mayonnaise.

Kiera didn't push her for more details that would make her uncomfortable. "It's a gorgeous sweater. But I've never seen that kind of cable before. It's not a staghorn or a traditional Celtic style."

"No, it's an old design. I'm told it was first made by Calan's great-great-grandmother. Of course, that could be a legend. There are a great many tall tales where he comes from." Her eyes took on a distant look again. "They are an unusual family."

"Unusual as in pirates, patriots and thieves?"

"Worse." Agatha handed Kiera another scone. "They can be a dark lot, broody and charming by turns. Duncan took me by storm that long-ago summer in Skye. Within a day I knew I was in love, and within a week I said yes."

"Yes to what?"

Agatha's cheeks took on a sudden flush. "To whatever the man wanted. Very fortunate for me that he was a gentleman, so what he wanted was marriage." She gave a little sigh. "It's often that way with the MacKay men. I warn you, if they set their minds on you, they'll reel you in and very soon they convince *you* to want the same things they do."

"Like some kind of . . ." Kiera cleared her throat, feeling a little ridiculous. "Not some kind of mind control?"

"Good heavens, no. It's simple chemistry, the kind that a confident and powerful man uses without any thought. But it's strong stuff just the same. And if you have half a love for Scotland, for the long summer twilights and the wild beaches of the far west, you could find yourself caught forever." She toyed with a bit of her scone. "Just the way I was."

It all sounded a little Gothic, Kiera thought, unconvinced. "You mean, you fell in love with Scotland first and the man second?"

"No." The old woman shook her head vehemently. "That's making it clear and simple, but it wasn't simple. It wasn't just the passion, though we had that, most definitely. He was handsome, but I've known men who were more attractive. It wasn't anything I can explain neatly even now. I thought I had my whole life planned, from the place I would live to the kind of man I would live there with. But one look at Duncan and I knew it was all wrong, and I would follow him anywhere." She stared at her untouched tea.

"Just like that? As easy as one look?"

"Who said anything about *easy?* Falling in love is the hardest — and the most frightening — thing in the world, my dear. We want things that come wrapped up in neat packages. We want clear explanations for what we think and feel. But life can have different plans in store."

Kiera frowned, remembering how Calan had used almost the same words to her that afternoon. That memory brought hot images of his hands as he'd brought her to stunning pleasure.

She looked away, feeling an odd pressure at her chest. "I wouldn't know anything about falling in love," she said stiffly.

"No? I see the way you look at his photo on the dresser over there. I've seen you glance down the driveway, as if you're listening for his car."

"You're wrong."

At least Kiera prayed she was. Love wasn't anywhere in her monthly planner. She didn't intend to toss away her logic, her independence or her careful plans for a man she barely knew.

She stood up, determined to shift the conversation to a safer topic.

But the old woman reached out, clasping Kiera's hands. "If you need a friend, I'll be here for advice or just to listen. If this thing between you is meant to happen, it will, though you can fight it all you like. But remember this. Once you find a good and true man who wants to share his life with you, don't let him go. Not for career. Nor for family. Not even for fear you'll lose yourself. I almost did that." Her voice fell to a whisper. "Walk on glass and don't mind the pain, not for a good and true man. Otherwise you'll always regret it, my dear."

"Did you . . . did that happen to you?"

"Almost. My family thought I'd lost my mind to run off with Duncan. And his family was completely opposed." She frowned. "There were other things in our way, too. The rituals. The Calling. The three tests."

Kiera frowned. "I beg your pardon."

"Oh, dear." Agatha sat up straighter. "I shouldn't have . . ." She reached for the teapot with fingers that shook.

"But you said —"

"Never mind what I said. I'm an old woman. Sometimes my mind wanders." Agatha stood up, straightening her sweater, touching the linked cables slowly, one by one. "They call it the binding cable. It was the first sweater a girl learned how to knit. So beautiful." Outside in the hall the old clock began to chime.

"I — I must go. I had no idea it was so late. My number is there by the phone. Please call me if you need anything."

Kiera followed her out into the bright light of the alcove. "Let me drive you back. I'll walk home. I could use the exercise."

"It's kind of you, but there's no need. I'm quite able —" Agatha's head tilted. She took a slow step, staring at Kiera under the bright light of the chandelier. Her eyes widened.

"That mouth." She put one hand to her chest. "Dear heavens, but you almost look . . ."

She made a little breathless sound, raising Kiera's chin, staring at the lines of her face beneath the chandelier.

"Who are you?"

Shadows gathered on the abbey's granite roof. A bird called shrilly from the woods.

Something moved, space taking shape.

Specks of light gathered. Lace cuffs formed, caught by elegant sleeves of black velvet. As clouds raced across the waning moon, the abbey ghost strode from the shadows.

At his feet a great gray cat ghosted over the cold stone.

"Again the danger. Again the intrusions. We are never permitted our rest, my friend. Such penances."

Adrian Draycott stared out beyond the moat, where uniformed men flashed strange electrical sensors. "If one of them dares to harm these ancient walls, I'll materialize and smite them all, by heaven."

At his feet the gray cat gave a low growl.

"Of course I know they are here to protect my abbey. Were they not, I'd have sent them bolting long ago. But their anger and distrust rub against all my senses. And the Scotsman at the center of it."

The cat's tail flicked from side to side.

"The woman? Yes, I've seen what you tell me. Her blood is Draycott." Adrian stared out at the swans on the moat. "So much sadness she carries. The memories haunt me still. I could not save Elena, though I tried. Had she stayed, maybe . . ." He shook his head. "Now the daughter and her Scotsman must find their way, tested gravely. I've planted what seeds I may, but their bonds call out. Even I may not interfere."

The cat's eyes gleamed as he stared up at

his oldest friend.

"Yes, bound they will be. Already it has begun. Their hearts call out and if they turn away, they will regret it most bitterly. All their days they will feel the loss." Adrian rested one boot on the parapet, brooding. "But the choice must be theirs." His face hardened as he watched the Scotsman talking with a tall man in a dark uniform. "And the danger draws closer. He hunts well, Gideon. But he will need all his skills as the net closes around him."

Adrian Draycott stiffened as one of the soldiers trampled on a young rosebush. "Let them touch another of my roses and I'll smite them all down. Some powers are left to me."

Gideon meowed softly, perched beside him on the roof.

Guarding as he always did, loyal to death and beyond.

Adrian saw the light gather at his hands, tingling sharply at his wrist and ankle. "Fading so soon. There is no more I can do, in truth. It is their choice, to go or stay. The Scotsman must beware the Change, for there his testing will begin." Adrian's eyes closed. He remembered his own choices, and the love he had found only after the gravest testing.

Wind played through his hair. She waited for him even now, waited for his duties to be done and one more penance completed. What would remain to fill his soul without her?

Leaves spun up at his feet. Wind gusted over the granite roof.

I'm coming, Adrian thought, casting the words out to the night.

Lace cuffs fluttered.

The moon spread out a veil of silver behind cold clouds. And then the roof was empty.

Chapter Fourteen

Calan stared at the darkness.

Something seemed to brush his shoulders. He moved to the window, suddenly restless.

Outside a tree branch tapped at the window.

Izzy looked up from the wiring diagram he was studying. "Something wrong?"

Calan didn't answer right away. He probed the night for dangers, letting his senses play out, reaching for anything out of place.

Smells teased. Sounds seemed muffled. Nothing was as clear as it should have been. The Change called to him.

His muscles tightened. In the space of a heartbeat he could read the shadows . . . with every sense sharpened by the hunt.

Too dangerous.

"MacKay?" Izzy was staring at him. "I just asked if you heard something outside?"

Calan felt the sense of danger recede. "No. It was just an . . . instinct."

"Never good to ignore an instinct." Izzy put down his papers and glanced outside. "You think the brigadier's back? Maybe some of his men?"

"It's possible. I'm going out to check."

"Want me to tag along?"

Calan shook his head. He required privacy for the search he had in mind. "No need. I'll call you if I find anything."

Izzy nodded. "Fine. It's going to take me an hour to go through these diagrams anyway." He drummed his fingers on a big sheet of paper. "Did Nicholas mention any wiring upgrades to you?"

"Only the backup generator and its feed to the house near the kitchen."

"I saw that." Izzy rubbed his neck. "But there are a few changes in the upstairs switch wiring that don't make sense. It's not like him to skip over a detail like that." After a moment he pulled out his cell phone. "I want to know why."

Anger and accusation burned in Agatha MacKay's eyes.

"Well? I think I'm entitled to an answer."

Kiera sat very still, her heart pounding. "I don't know what you mean."

The old woman's teacup rattled loudly as she set it on the side table. "In the daylight

I would have noticed immediately. You —
your face. The resemblance to Elena is
unmistakable now. Maybe you will explain
that to me."

Kiera looked down. Her hands were laced
as she searched for answers, for a way to
avoid lies that would give extra pain. But
the search was like trying to pick her way
through quicksand, with the ground sliding
away beneath her. "You . . . *knew* Elena
Draycott?"

"Of course I knew her. I knew her mother
and her father. I know Nicholas." She took
a breath. "She and my eldest daughter were
—" Her voice broke. "Why did you come
here, Ms. Morissey? Or should I call you
Ms. Draycott? You would save us both a
good deal of time and pain if you told the
truth."

How could she start? And where would it
all end, Kiera wondered. Something twisted
inside her. She was tired of lies and denials.
"Elena was . . . my mother."

It hurt to say the words. But the shadows
of her mother's past could not be avoided
any longer.

"She's dead. She died several months
ago."

"What we were told was a lie?" Agitated,
the old woman stood up and walked to the

fire. Her back was stiff. "So many years. So many questions we had. And now . . . to find out like this. Where were you born?"

Kiera looked at the old books, feeling the deep peace of Calan's house. In its quiet way the house seemed to demand her honesty. Kiera took a deep breath and told Calan's great-aunt all of her mother's story, from the night she left Draycott Abbey, to her marriage and finally to her death.

The old woman shook her head. "France. So close and yet all these years, we never knew." She turned abruptly. "Does Calan know?"

Kiera sat up straighter. "He knows who I am."

"Good. Because he knew Elena, too. Not as well as I did, of course. My daughter and she . . ." Her fingers opened and closed. "It hurts to remember, even now." She seemed to force out the words.

"You'd better sit down. Please. Right here at the fire." Kiera helped the old woman into a big wing chair, then spread a blanket over her lap. "I'm sorry to shock you with all this. I don't know much about my mother's past in England. She . . . never spoke of it."

Agatha stared into the fire. "For two years she and my Maeve were inseparable. Dance classes. Drawing lessons. Then Maeve was accepted at art school in London. It hurt Elena, I think. And a few months later, Maeve —" The old woman took a hard breath. "She was killed in a car accident as she was coming home for her first break."

"I'm so sorry."

"A lorry went out of control. The driver died, too." Agatha's voice was rough. "For a while, I was cut off from everything, everyone. I tried to call Elena, but she never phoned back. I understood that there were some difficulties, and since Nicholas was off in Thailand then, I drove to Draycott. But she wasn't there. No one knew when she would be back. There seemed to be nothing more to be done." Agatha frowned. "I wonder if she was too proud to see me. She was never one to reveal her emotions easily, Maeve said. But if I hadn't lost touch with her . . ." She lifted her hands to the fire, shivering as if struck with cold. "A few months after the accident I lost Duncan to cancer. Everything was a terrible muddle. When I was stronger, I called the abbey to ask Elena to come stay with me here. Yet again I had no answer. It was all very peculiar. Then we learned she had been in a hotel fire in the Philippines. Someone from the embassy brought her passport and a few belongings that were found." Agatha frowned. "It wasn't true."

Kiera didn't move. "No, it wasn't."

The old woman continued to study the fire. "Why did she pretend such a thing?"

"My mother wanted the past buried. When the fire left so many dead, she saw her chance. She had already met my father and she had no reason to come back to England," Kiera said flatly.

"Not even for Nicholas?"

"He didn't answer her letters. When she phoned — well, he left the message he wanted nothing to do with her."

"I don't believe it. But then Nicholas came back from Thailand so very, very changed. So many terrible memories."

Kiera felt every word slam at her heart. "Thailand?"

"Didn't you know? He was held captive there for months, beaten terribly and starved. He nearly died before the government got him out. When he came back home, he was . . . not the same."

Another explanation fell into place, though Kiera fought to deny it. Her uncle *hadn't* turned his back on his sister. He had been busy fighting his own battle to survive.

This had to be the key, somewhere in that time of shadows. How could she possibly sort out so many missed chances?

So much pain and misunderstanding.

Down the hall the old clock began to chime.

Agatha stood up. Her fingers tightened on the linked cables of her sweater. "In those terrible weeks after I lost Maeve, I made one of these sweaters for your mother, but I never saw her again to give it to her. I still have it somewhere. I must remember where." She looked sad. "Maybe it was lost. So much was lost." She shook her head, as if to free painful memories. "I must go. It is very late and I'm too tired to think clearly. I've left several packages for Calan when he returns. They're important, even if I don't like to think about it."

As the clock continued to chime, she took Kiera's hands, staring into her face. "You are beautiful, as your mother was. Maybe you are as proud, too. Pride can be a dangerous thing, especially when you are young."

Kiera felt new emotions twist and whirl until it was painful to breathe. "Let me drive you back."

"There's no need. It's only a few minutes to the cottage. I could find my way blind-folded. Besides, I need to think tonight, and I'll do that best alone." She touched Kiera's cheek. "Dear girl. Elena's daughter. Remember what I said. We all want our days measured out quietly, in neat packages. We want clear explanations for what we think and feel. But life usually has different plans in store. It did for me, and it did for your mother. I think it will be the same for you."

She squeezed Kiera's hand and then left, her face tired.

Did it all come down to this? Kiera wondered. Could the real problems her mother faced have been made far worse by her pride? Had her mother closed the doors to her past because the truth was too painful to bear — or because she was too stubborn to ask for help?

Kiera thought of the fragile lace glove, safe in its old box. She thought of her mother's letter of explanation to her brother, safe in Kiera's suitcase now. Her mission in England was done, a promise completed. Down the long row of trees, the lights of Agatha's Mini Cooper slowly faded.

In the sudden darkness, Kiera felt starkly, painfully, alone.

A branch tapped at the broad French doors of the second-story bedroom. The moon climbed higher, shrouded by rising clouds. Rain before morning.

Too restless to sleep, Kiera tried to knit, but for once she found no peace in her fiber or stitches. On the wall, an exquisite map showed the old coast and ships at sail.

Captivated by the map's exquisite details, Kiera rose to trace the coast, her fingers sliding over cool glass.

There were so many memories here. So much history and so many lives.

Nearby another map hung. This one showed a high keep and a twisting moat. The term *Draycott land* took on a new meaning as Kiera studied the yellowing paper.

Nine centuries of Draycott hands had protected the abbey's slopes and woods, spilling their sweat and blood. This image of that history touched something deep inside her.

But she didn't *want* to be touched. She wanted nothing to do with the Draycott family or its long, convoluted history.

Air stirred. Did she hear a low rustling in the hall? Maybe Calan had returned?

Kiera crossed the room and threw open the door.

Shadows gathered beneath paintings of hunting scenes and wild Scottish crags. Dim light touched beautiful old carpets. But the corridor was empty.

Of course the corridor is empty. He's not coming back until very late. And when he does come back, he won't be lurking outside your bedroom.

Angry at her own restless emotions, Kiera ran a hand through her hair and muttered crossly. She refused to give in to temptation. As soon as it was light, she was leaving. She had promised Calan she would stay for one night, but tomorrow she would put Draycott Abbey out of her mind forever.

It was her family's wish and her mother's wish.

With sleep retreating as a possibility, she decided a cup of her favorite herbal tea might work miracles. A few minutes later she stood in the silent kitchen, impatiently waiting for water to boil.

As she was pulling down a cup and saucer, Kiera saw two boxes with foreign postage, pushed to the front of the counter. A hand-written note from Agatha was taped to the larger box.

She didn't want to snoop, but even a quick glance left her frozen. Unable to look away, she stared at the sealed lid.

According to Agatha's note, the boxes held some kind of new field safety gear. She mentioned a tactical suit and new Lexan face shields. They had been delivered that week for Calan's work.

Tactical suit and face shields.

Ordnance? Some kind of military work? No, Agatha's note mentioned "your new field safety gear."

Calan did safety work that required armor and face shields?

Cold brushed her skin. Her mouth felt dry and gritty as she stared at the big box with rows of foreign stamps and special handling instructions.

She stood listening to the teakettle begin to hum. She remembered how intense he could be, how deeply focused. She remembered how careful his touch could be. Was he a dedicated idealist or was he a cool, cynical playboy far too skilled at persuasion?

The shrill whistle of the kettle finally cut through her tangled thoughts. She poured her tea and walked back through the silent house.

She couldn't stop thinking about those boxes.

Light from an iron sconce touched the beautiful room with its blue silk wallpaper and blue damask coverlet. Crisp white bed linens shone beneath antique lace, some sort of ancient Scottish crest embroidered on each pillow.

It was a very long way from her family's rural stone farmhouse in the foothills of the Pyrenees. Every inch of the room held the mark of Calan's keen mind and good taste.

Irritated, she finished undressing and climbed into bed. With her clothes still at the inn, all she had to sleep in was a soft shirt of Calan's. With every movement the fine cotton played over her skin, teasing her senses.

Heat filled her face. Who was the real Calan MacKay? He had seduced her first with that smoky, lilting voice, and then brought her to stunned pleasure.

Now he captivated her again, this time with the charm of his house. Kiera sensed this was a man who hid his talents well.

Despite her best efforts, she couldn't drive him out of her mind.

Wanting came, sharp and unmistakable. How could she possibly leave when she had so many questions clamoring for answers?

CHAPTER FIFTEEN

A small current of air brushed Izzy Teague's neck as he finished a call to Nicholas Draycott. He spun around, scanning the room, missing no detail.

No one there.

Scowling, he peered into corners and shadows, then turned back to his titanium case.

He was still irritated at how the Scotsman had caught him unprepared in the car earlier that evening. There had been an uncanny silence and speed in the man's movements.

Frowning, he hunched over a wiring diagram that just didn't make sense.

Draycott Abbey was a perfect place for ghosts. Experience had taught him that the ancient house could get under your skin and make you imagine all kinds of strange shapes and noises.

If you let it.

Over one hill and around a wooded curve.

Nicholas Draycott muttered as he shot along the deserted country lane. He'd finally escaped the murderous traffic from London. Now the abbey was only a few kilometers away.

As always, the sense of home called to him, restoring his sanity after a day of chaos and uncertainty. Out of the corner of his eye, he saw a deer plunge from the trees. Biting back an oath, he slammed on the brakes.

The deer bolted back into the darkness.

Minutes later the abbey's great iron gates rose up before him, ornate in the car lights. Although he preferred his habit of opening them by hand, he'd been persuaded to add a remote unit as a security precaution, so he sat in the car, watching the heavy iron panels creak open.

The sound was warm and familiar, part of the abbey's welcome. This always was and would be home, he thought. The place that had been his lodestone, his first and best haven. His wife understood his love for the old abbey. Nicholas suspected that she loved the place almost as much as he did.

The thought of Kacey sent a smile curving over his lips. When the Balkan summit was done, he was going to take her and their daughter away to a quiet island in the Caribbean for a long holiday.

No cars. No cell phones. No faxes. No death threats or extremist groups.

But before that there were a thousand problems to negotiate and dangers that could not be ignored. His mind continued to race as the gate halted, and he scanned the trees for unusual movements. Reassured that all was well, he drove inside, cueing the big iron panels to close behind him. If anything broke the infrared beam behind his car, it would trigger the new security alarm inside the house. The upgrades were a step in the right direction, but Nicholas knew there was much more to be done before the summit.

He should have called in Izzy sooner. He should have —

Regret was a waste of time. His safest option right now was to back out entirely and have the government switch to another venue. Yet Nicholas knew the reality of volatile Balkan politics. The meeting was too important to jeopardize. If there was a return of hostilities and more dead, he didn't want it on his conscience.

Behind him the gates clanged shut.

He was halfway down the hill when the moon broke through the clouds and he had his first glimpse of the abbey. Wind ruffled the silver face of the moat as a bird called somewhere in the high woods. Moonlight clung to the twisted chimneys on the roof. Then a movement. Something seemed to drift in shadow near the north face.

A figure or a dream from memories?

The skin tightened between Nicholas's shoulder blades. He heard the distant sound of church bells on the wind, rising and fading, half real and half phantom.

More old legends that would not die.

As a boy he had been raised on stories of a brooding ancestor who walked the grounds on windswept nights, accompanied by his faithful gray cat with keen amber eyes. Old family servants and relatives had insisted there was truth to the stories. Nicholas had seen too much over the years to scoff at any of the odd tales that he had grown up with.

Tonight the faint bells sounded like a warning.

There was danger in what he had offered, danger to his house and to his family. But he had taken all possible precautions to protect Kacey and his daughter. That left the abbey to consider, along with the difficult process of dealing with the brigadier's security team.

He needed an update from Calan. They would go over the details of the summit preparation, while Calan and Izzy targeted any weak spots in the planned installations. After those additions were complete, the abbey would be in safe hands.

Nicholas frowned at the ghostlike movement on the roof.

Safe?

Life had taught him that you were never as safe as you hoped. His months in Thailand had brought him bitterness and betrayal. He had nearly died during his brutal captivity, and when he'd come back, he was a changed man, withdrawn, emaciated and unable to trust anyone. He had lost his sister during that grim time, and the loss still clawed at his memory.

Elena had been headstrong, beautiful and proud. Half his friends had been in love with her when they were growing up. Even young Calan had been touched by her kindness. Damaged and frightened, the young Scottish boy had needed all the friends he could find that first summer Nicholas had met him.

Now he was the strongest person Nicholas knew.

If only he would stop all this rootless wandering. If only . . .

Leaves swirled up against the windshield, carried by a gust of wind.

Nicholas pushed the past out of his mind. The future was his focus now, and how to prevent anything that would shatter the safety of this place he loved so well. Tomorrow his new safe would hold detailed munitions records to be discussed during the summit, to pressure all the delegates into negotiation. Not even his wife and his closest friends could be told about this sensitive information, by the prime minister's directive. It was too late to turn back, Nicholas thought grimly.

Moonlight dappled the high roof. Wind tossed flying white petals over weather-grayed stone.

Fragrance drifted. Space seemed to gather, shimmering and restless.

Out of the night Adrian Draycott walked, carrying a patch of moonlight on white lace cuffs. He studied the distant woods and then leaned out over the parapet, his eyes dark.

Danger, he thought.

Clearly, it comes now.

There was never peace or rest for the

guardian that he was and had been for nine centuries and more. The weight of the abbey's protection fell on his broad shoulders. Always the duty and the danger.

Always one more task to complete.

Gravel raked the air, swirling over the deep shadows.

And then a rustle at his boots. Gray fur and keen amber eyes caught in a pool of moonlight.

"Ah, Gideon. Well met, my oldest friend. Just at the moment when I feared to sink into ill thoughts." The guardian ghost of Draycott Abbey set one boot on the edge of the high parapets, perched above empty space. "Do you feel this new thing carried on the air, pulling me from rest?"

The cat padded to the edge of the roof and sat on the ancient stones near his friend and master. His tail flicked sharply.

"Yes, Nicholas has come back. Almost at the moat, and his thoughts are weary. Danger follows him like trailing smoke. I wonder that he cannot feel it clearly."

The cat meowed.

"Humans. Limited in so much, and fierce when they are thwarted. Contentious and lacking in humor." Adrian ran strong fingers over the cat's thick fur. "Yes, I remember that they can hold strength and certainty. I remember what it meant to laugh and dream in human form. And well I remember the pride, which has set its hand on all of Draycott blood. Sometimes I think pride is our curse."

The cat brushed against his boot, amber eyes unblinking.

"Useful? If tamed, possibly. If used to a good end, certainly. But which of us has the strength to control his pride?"

Silence stretched out, as restless as the shadows that drifted at the edge of the roof. Cold grew, nearly visible in its density.

Then car lights appeared at the top of the long driveway.

Adrian's lace cuffs fluttered in an unseen wind.

The car stopped. A door opened.

Nicholas Draycott picked up a single bag, stretched and then strode into the beautiful old house.

"He doesn't know that nobility and honor have their limits," Adrian murmured to the cat at his feet. "He will have to learn, though the learning will cost him dear."

Suddenly Gideon meowed. With one paw he struck the air and a dim spiral rose, turning slowly.

Not physical, yet glimmering with life, its energy drawn from the abbey's very heart.

"The mark," Adrian said dourly. "Now you've done it. That is woman's power turning there. Be careful where you touch or you'll be tossed full off this roof, my friend."

The cat sat in fascination, watching the silver mark spin, slowly twisting into variations of its intertwining curves.

Fragile, restless and powerful, the image grew.

Silver swirled into new patterns. "Very old is that mark, even older than this roof. Older than the Virgin Queen who used it for her own ends. I remember the first time Good Bess made that sign, marking a secret message to the King of France. A Draycott lady among her waiting women carried the letter at great risk."

The cat's fur rose on his back.

"Difficult? Aye, so was she. Difficult and far more. But also brilliant. A woman capable of great charm, when politics or situation required. The mark became a sign of special favor to the women who served her. And one Draycott woman served her more than any others."

Adrian studied the twisting shape. "Past and forgotten, it is. Yet it is here, strong as ever. The Draycott women carry the energy about them always, even if they know it not."

The gray cat meowed.

Adrian frowned. "You saw *this* shape? But where . . ." Adrian turned slowly. "On a lace glove, hidden in a box on the floor? And you saw it also on the Scotsman?"

His eyes turned to the far woods, where a swift form moved from shadow to shadow. Only a ghost such as Adrian would have noticed the movement.

"He hunts with rare skill tonight. And the mark is truly there?"

Gideon's tail flicked sharply.

The silver image swirled again.

"On *his* arm?" Adrian rubbed his neck. "The library will hold the truth of it. Unfortunately, we have no time to be at our books. The grounds must be walked. The walls must be checked. These men brought by Nicholas are to be trusted, their skills drawn and made greater by ours, though they know it not."

Adrian raised his hand. His words drifted through the air.

"Above and below. Protection in hand and word. In all places and times." Light shimmered and grew, haloing the roof and touching the roses. The figure in lace and black velvet moved from corner to corner. "Above and below," he repeated intently.

Finally the whole house was wrapped in a

faint veil of silver.

The abbey's guardian prayed it would be enough for what was to come.

The woods were silent.

A racing shape passed the moat.

The small creatures nearby were still, frozen in burrow and nest. The terror of the Hunt touched the air.

As the moon vanished in clouds, tracks crisscrossed the muddy slope beyond the stables. A bird shot from the trees as the long grass parted and shook.

He found more footprints, the acrid ash from a dropped cigarette, the exotic mix of tobaccos burned into his memory for later reference. Up the trail, other footprints merged, drawn from separate vantage points in the woods.

These men had been waiting. The moment the abbey's alarms had been triggered by the government troops from London, these men had crossed the carefully hidden sensors, undetected in the chaos. The Hunter's muscles clenched in anger at the realization. Ten feet away he found the metallic scent of chemicals, caught in the upraised leaves of clover along a small creek.

He savored the scent, dragged it over his tongue so that it swirled through his nose.

The molecules were bitter, complex, a particular mixture of opioids that eluded him now.

No matter. Now was not for logic or science or thought.

Now was for the Hunt.

The wind sighed in the high woods.

The thing in the grass moved. Shuddered. Bones slipped. Muscles clenched, twisting in the Change.

The grass rustled and parted in a sudden wind.

Then a man walked from the shadows, his body scratched and bruised, his bare feet streaked with mud. Slowly, he took the pile of clothes from beneath a bush, stretching with confident grace.

When he was dressed, Calan MacKay studied the darkness. His muscles ached. His legs and feet were cut. Bruises ringed his right wrist. He had pushed himself to the very edge of exhaustion.

But his search was done.

The Scotsman had found exactly what he needed to find.

CHAPTER SIXTEEN

"He's taking too long, blast it."

Nicholas Draycott paced the library, glancing out into the darkness. "How long did you say he'd been gone?"

"Over an hour." Izzy Teague leaned back from the cluttered table and stretched. "I wouldn't worry. Your friend strikes me as a man who can handle himself just fine. He got the jump on me without much effort," Izzy grumbled.

"I told you to expect that." Nicholas took a last glance out the window, saw nothing unusual, and went to pour them both more tea. "I suppose I'm a little jumpy. I don't like putting my house — not to mention my family — at potential risk."

"Understandable. It's a good thing you're doing. Of course, good things don't always feel good at the time," Izzy added. "You're still travelling with a bodyguard?"

"Yes. And it's damned uncomfortable."

A shadow fell across the doorway. "What is uncomfortable?"

The men in the library turned sharply. Calan strode in, dropped two plastic bags on the worktable and went to pour himself a cup of tea.

"Having a bodyguard. It's good to see you, Calan. You look like you've been through the wringer. There's a nasty cut on your neck."

"I'll survive," Calan said drily. "I've got good genes."

Nicholas reached for the smaller bag and held it up to the light. "What have we here?"

"Mud samples. I found them on the far side of the road, just past the sharp curve at the north side of the estate. From the tracks, I make out one car. Wheelbase is 2.8 meters. Two men left the car, climbing the stone fence three hundred meters apart. One dropped a cigarette butt. You'll find it in the second bag. At a quick guess, I'd say it's a clove-flavored type imported from Indonesia. Highly addictive."

"They're called kretek," Izzy said quietly. "You picked up all that from a single butt?"

"It's still just a guess." Calan swirled the tea in his cup, then glanced at the wiring diagrams spread over the table. "They didn't go very far. One stayed near the

242

fence, possibly standing guard. The other left a low-profile digital surveillance camera at an excellent vantage point for the house." Calan rolled his shoulders, frowning. "The camera's there, but the data card is in that plastic bag."

Nicholas frowned.

"It's tough and durable, but not many bells and whistles. If I made a guess, I'd say it could be ex-Soviet block. Probably a few years old."

Nicholas breathed out a harsh breath.

"Well, well." Izzy reached out for the bag that Nicholas had put back on the table. "I'll get right on it. This could give us something to work with. I might even be able to backtrack it to the vendor, especially if it's military."

Nicholas nodded to him. "Let's make that the top priority." He turned to Calan and his voice fell. "Are you certain you're all right? Your hand is bruised. What happened?"

"I missed my footing beyond Lyon's Leap and took a tumble in the dark." Calan gritted his teeth as he rubbed his wrist. "It's a little stiff, nothing more."

"It looks as if you've got some kind of rash." Nicholas glanced at the heavy welts crisscrossing Calan's wrist. "I'll have a doctor look at it tomorrow."

"There's no need, Nicholas. It will be fine." The edge in Calan's voice indicated that the subject was closed.

"Anything else you managed to pick up?" Izzy took out tweezers and gently removed the small data card from the bag. "Any detail at all could help narrow the search."

"Not a great deal. They were careful. However, I did find traces of carfentanil on one of the prints. The mud sample was taken from the print."

Izzy put down his tweezers. "You carry forensics gear with you as a routine?"

Calan shrugged. "My company is working on some technology for field chemical assessments."

"I'll take some of that now," Izzy muttered, looking bemused. "Assessments of that order of subtlety, handled with a portable field kit? Yeah, I'd be all over that. Any idea when your company will be offering the technology for sale?"

"I'll let you know," Calan said. "As I was saying, I believe the chemical was the same as that used last night. You can verify that, Mr. Teague."

"Izzy. And give me twenty minutes for an answer."

Calan rubbed his neck. "Given the moisture remaining in the footprints, I estimate they left less than two hours ago."

"Soon after the brigadier's people arrived," Nicholas murmured. "So you're saying Draycott has been compromised by intruders who knew precisely when the alarms went off?"

"That's my assessment. They left in a hurry, judging by the force of the tire tracks, and then headed south." Calan poured himself more tea. "I followed them to the I44, where I lost them."

Izzy hadn't moved. "You followed their tire prints? How did you manage that, with all the other road traffic?"

Calan sipped his tea, rubbing his wrist. "It's another piece of new technology I'm working on. Still proprietary, so you'll understand if I don't go into details."

Izzy crossed his arms. "I see."

His voice said that he didn't see at all.

"So they have surveillance equipment to install." Nicholas continued to study the soil sample in the bag. "They also have carfentanil at hand, ready to use. That's powerful animal tranquilizer. Sounds to me as if they were hoping to take a captive." His voice was grim. "*Are* hoping," he corrected quietly.

"I'd say that was likely." Calan finished

his tea. "And they're taking chances, getting edgy. That makes them very dangerous. You're going to need extra security precautions, Nicky. Raise the level of protection on your family," he said flatly. "*Now.* Then we have to talk."

"Understood." Nicholas pulled out his cell phone. "Give me five minutes."

Kent, England
Sweat covered the driver's face.

Though he wanted to race madly through the quiet streets, he drove slowly, mindful of speed limits and merging lanes. The man beside him was just as jumpy. There was no room for failure, not after so many months of preparation.

His fingers tightened on the wheel. They needed a hostage. They *must* have one to succeed in controlling the summit.

He ran a hand over his forehead, forcing his mind to cold detachment. His cell phone vibrated and he answered immediately. "What is it?" The question was in flat, accented English.

His contact spoke in breathless excitement. "I have information. You must come back here now."

Zarof frowned at the darkness. This man was new, but well trained, from the same military unit in the war. "What kind of information?"

"Not over the phone, you told us. It involves the family you are interested in. I have found one, and she is alone. Unguarded."

Zarof gripped the wheel. "You're certain of this?"

"I had it from my sister's first cousin. She works in the housekeeping department, remember? And she had this news from the hotel manager's own mouth. It is someone in the family, he swears it. The resemblance does not lie."

Zarof reached down, taking a well-oiled military revolver from the car's glove compartment. A muscle clenched at his jaw.

The long weeks of planning and watching were done.

Now the true mission could begin. Blood would be spilled, just as they had promised. A pity that his own government had cut off all connection with his group. The new regime lacked daring and vision, always compromising. They had accepted handouts from their enemies.

Zarof was tired of handouts. For years, he had received extensive interrogation training, learned at the hands of a dozen international teachers. Now his skills at inflicting pain would once again be useful. His small group would point the way for the cowardly politicians.

He left the highway, eyes on the nearby traffic. When he was certain that no one had followed him, he took the first turn, heading south to the coast.

Kiera jolted awake.

Something was wrong.

She heard a movement nearby in the darkness. Her fingers clenched. Still half asleep, she told herself the sound was only in her imagination, shaped of restless dreams. But logic didn't shake her feeling of restlessness and danger.

She sat up, frowning. She had no more time. Her family needed her to help pay for her father's expensive medical care, and the sooner she got back to work, the better.

Kiera stood up, searching for her clothes. She never should have agreed to come here with Calan. Whatever pull or attraction she'd felt was temporary, an illusion created by the stress of her visit. It was time to be responsible and practical again.

It was time to leave, now before Calan came back to muddle her focus. She picked up her sweater — and froze.

Something rustled outside her window.

Was she being watched?

Had Calan come back at last?

She sat, frozen, her eyes fixed on the darkness just beyond the heavy curtains. But now there was only silence.

She closed her eyes, willing her body to relax. Too much had happened since her arrival in England, and nothing had turned out as she'd expected. The abbey was dangerously beautiful, and it was a struggle to keep her emotions detached from the old house, its history and its owner.

And when it came to being detached about Calan . . .

Kiera blew out an angry breath. There was no place for Calan in her well-planned future. She was going back to her town, her small office, her work and her family. She had lost herself to passion in his arms, but it wouldn't happen again.

Something else continued to bother her. What was it that his great-aunt had blurted out? Something about a test and a ritual?

Tested by whom? Was some kind of secret group involved or was the attack at the abbey something completely unrelated?

Only a fool would ignore the signs of danger at Draycott Abbey, and Kiera was no fool. Men didn't make violent kidnapping attempts for no reason. If she hadn't been so twisted up by emotion, caught up in resolute plans for her visit, she would have called in a police report to alert the owners of the abbey about the danger.

But she owed the Draycott family nothing. They could pay people to guard them, or use their friends like Calan to help. The sane and logical thing to do was to go home.

The calm, practical part of her mind knew it was true. Right now, she needed to dress and call a taxi. But something held her, making her heart pound.

She forced herself to sink back into the cool white sheets, every sense painfully alert. The night seemed to close in.

She couldn't leave now. She had too many questions, and those answers would affect every part of her future. She also had a responsibility to alert Calan to the attack outside the abbey. He would notify Nicholas Draycott and the proper authorities. She should have told him about the attack as soon as she realized she could trust him.

Trust?

The thought was sudden and jolting. She had known the Scotsman for mere hours. What gave her this certain sense that she could trust him? Kiera closed her eyes, searching for answers. She had grown up in a tightly knit family in a community where they had been respected but definitely outsiders. Both her parents had always been guarded about their pasts, with few close friends. As a child, Kiera had learned not to trust anyone outside her own family. As an adult, little of that sense of distance had changed.

Until now.

The reasons didn't spring from logic. Her trust for Calan welled up from a deeper place of connection between them. There was shimmering sexual chemistry between them, yes, but his cool intelligence and his quiet sense of duty attracted her even more. After seeing the note from his great-aunt about his explosive protection gear, Kiera realized there were layers to the Scotsman that she hadn't suspected, and she wanted to explore all those depths.

Because something else had changed. Kiera realized it was time to trust *herself*. It was time she stopped forcing herself to be detached and practical. All her careful planning had been no help at all lately. She had been at the mercy of chance ever since she had reached the abbey.

She might as well be open to the possibilities that she had never allowed herself to explore. Something told her that she would never meet a man like Calan again. She would be a fool to turn her back on him.

Something moved beyond her window. Kiera peered around the curtain. With her eyes attuned to the darkness, she saw the empty gravel driveway curving toward the summerhouse.

Something moved just beyond the driveway.

A big dog? Some kind of wolf?

The creature stopped, head raised, half-swallowed by shadow.

Her heart began to hammer. Something gave her the eerie sense that she was being seen, assessed. A dim instinct whispered that the animal on the far side of the grass knew exactly where she stood behind the heavy curtains and even what she was thinking.

That was *impossible.*

Angry at her thoughts, she padded back to bed and pulled the pillow over her head. Being spontaneous didn't mean throwing out all her sanity and reasoning powers. A dog was a dog, after all. A wolf was a wolf. They were hardly her problem.

She closed her eyes, listening to the deep silence pool up around her. Finally she drove the image of the figure on the driveway out of her mind. But when she saw Calan, Kiera was *definitely* going to tell him to keep a tighter control on the animal life crisscrossing his property.

Wind brushed the grass.

The moon drifted and then vanished behind racing clouds. Night clung to the curves of the driveway and the old summerhouse.

He stood at the edge of shadows, a creature at ease in the night, shaped from Scottish soil rich with violence and myth. Yet his muscles were real. His limbs were hard and solid.

The night flowed around him, smells of the tall grass mixed with the perfume of lavender. He tasted the pain of wasted youth and lost family.

From his innocence had come violence and death.

Dangerous to forget that. Dangerous to forget that even a moment's loss of control carried risks beyond imagining. So he did not forget. Ever.

But there was no place for thought or truth when night called him to hunt, when the cool darkness wrapped around him. Over his head he could hear a leaf fall, feel the weight of moonlight on his bare skin.

Alive, he was — with such power as mortal men could never know. He caught the faint mix of cinnamon and roses. He sensed her close by, in the room beyond the stairs.

His senses flared without warning. The dark, prowling predator inside him growled and demanded to hunt.

To hunt *her.*

To capture and claim her, forced to his will.

Stormy images broke through his mind. He burned with hunger for their bodies entangled and restless, noisy and pounding in the night. The images screamed, demanding that he make them real.

Demanding that he make her submit.

Something was wrong. He struggled to hold himself still despite the images that poured through his fingers like hot sand. His control was weakened.

Dangerously weakened.

He tried to call the Change, pulling himself back from violence and instinct, from four legs and straining lungs into the human body he had known first.

He needed reason and control.

Nothing happened.

Claws dug at the damp earth. Something drove him through the grass up to the windows of her room. He panted, muscles bunched. Hunger overwhelmed every other instinct. In seconds she could be his, her skin sheathing his heat, trapped and claimed beneath him.

His.

A low sound slid from his throat. Wrong. Even the Other sensed the loss of balance.

He dropped flat, pressing his body to the earth and fighting for the energy that would slam him back to reason. The man's mind was dim, foreign in the powerful body he still wore.

A barrier held him where he was, primitive and shuddering, gripped with images of violence. There was no sound around him, no sense of intruders.

All was safe.

Except for the threat that *he* had become.

What he feared had finally come to pass. His control was the pivot for everything he was and knew; without control he was a danger to all around him. He had seen the violence of those who lost control back on his island home and the memories haunted him even now. He carried a syringe locked in his car; two more were kept inside his house to immobilize himself should the Change be blocked.

Never had it happened before.

And never would this madness be allowed to proceed. He shot to his feet, racing along the darkened driveway to the car he had left beyond the trees.

The syringe would protect her, protect them both from all that he feared to become if raw instinct and primal hunger overcame him. He had to act while his reason was still within reach.

As Calan summoned his will the Other growled in fury, snapping and twisting. Pain jolted every nerve as the struggle raged.

Finally his Change began. Never had it come so late or brought so much pain.

Shuddering, he fell forward. Muscles twisted. Sweat dotted his naked back and shoulders.

Claws receded.

The man stood.

With pounding heart, Calan rubbed his face and turned slowly. No other sounds drifted to him as he found his clothes, dressed clumsily and walked through the cool grass to his front door. Muscles burned as he climbed the stairs, stopping for a mere heartbeat outside her door.

No sound came from the room.

All was safe.

But for how long?

The question brought deeper torment. Angry, he ran water, found bandages and a needle. He barely noticed how his feet bled and welts dried on his shoulder. His muddy clothes dropped to the floor.

Exhaustion hit him.

Only in his exhaustion would the quiet footsteps have caught him by surprise. "Calan?"

He froze.

"You're . . . back."

Her voice was a whisper. He caught the breathless mix of wariness and fascination.

Desire, more than all.

His head turned. His gaze locked on the mirror where he saw Kiera's pale face. Color streaked her cheeks.

Beautiful, he thought.

And he could never hold that beauty against him because of the harm it would bring them both.

"Go away." Better to set their future straight now. Better to hurt in one stroke rather than in a thousand mangled, bleeding moments of explanation. "Please," he said hoarsely.

She didn't move.

Her shoulders tensed.

"You should have told me you were home. You should have told me that you were *hurt*." She took an angry breath and drove one trembling fist against his chest. "I didn't

want to care. I didn't want to trust you.
Dear heaven, what is happening to me?"

CHAPTER SEVENTEEN

Not now, Calan thought.

Not with her so close, shredding his logic. So close that she made him forget what he should do.

He had to leave — or make *her* leave.

"Tell me why. I need to know *why,* Calan." Her fist ground against his chest. As she leaned closer, her hair fell in a dark tangle across his shoulder and he felt the sweat of her skin mix with his.

"I don't know. I didn't expect to meet you, to want you beyond reason or control. Maybe this is what they mean by fate," he added harshly.

"I don't believe in fate," Kiera snapped.

"Neither do I."

"There's no reason I should trust you. No damned reason at all," she whispered. "But I do . . ." She took a raw breath. Then slowly her hands opened, sliding into his hair.

Calan felt her tremble. He tasted the scent

of her raw, unwilling need. It tore through his senses, mixed with his own urgent drive to mate.

She had trapped him. Claimed him. His whole being screamed for him to claim her in turn.

Before the violence of that need robbed him of reason, Calan shoved her away. He wouldn't take her blindly, not with the lust of an animal.

But she gripped his shoulders, holding him where he was. "What is it that you aren't telling me?"

"You need to leave." Calan didn't try to hide his anger or the edge of violence that simmered. *"Now."* He took a harsh breath. "Ask your questions later." He pointed to his clean, folded clothes. "I need to dress."

"Not until we get to the truth." Kiera studied his muddy feet and bruised legs. "What were you doing, running a marathon?" Frowning, she moved past him, picking up his alcohol pads from the bathroom counter. "I'll start on that cut at the back of your right knee while you tell me what's really going on."

Calan closed his eyes, caught in a strange place between fury and black humor. "What part of *leave* don't you understand?"

She didn't respond.

Alcohol bit at the jagged wound behind Calan's knee. The sharp pain was nothing compared to her touch, razoring across his raw nerves.

You could feel too much to bear, he understood then. You could be too close and yet strain to be infinitely closer.

"Forget the alcohol. I'll do it myself." He turned, keeping his back to her in some partial concession to his nakedness. "Give me the damned box."

She pushed his hand away with a sigh. The sound made him think of how she would sigh when he shoved off her shirt and pushed deep inside her.

"Just tell me the truth." Her fingers dabbed at the dried blood near his hip. "Does that hurt?"

"Damn it, Kiera —" *She* hurt him, simply by being too close. Too damned gentle.

"I'm done. Now I'll have a look at your other leg. Turn around, Calan."

"Hell."

"Turn. Around." She frowned up at him. "Why all the drama about me touching you? I've seen naked men before. Last year during a riding trip through Mongolia —"

He closed his eyes.

Breathed a rough curse.

She'd seen naked men. Of course she had.

But she didn't have a clue what she was dealing with now because he wasn't like other men, and she shredded his control as no other woman ever had. "I don't give a damn about how many naked men you've seen or where you've seen them," he growled.

"Well." She glared up at him. "There's no need to be nasty."

"Call it self-defense. Politeness doesn't seem to register with you."

Her eyes rose. She stared at his thighs — and then higher. "Well," she murmured again. Very softly this time. Color swirled over those gloriously soft cheeks. "I think I'm impressed."

The words had an instant effect, his erection surging in a full and hot response.

The darkness always waiting inside him paced and shuddered. Something crucial had begun, and it tasted like danger in his mouth. "You don't know what you're starting here, Kiera."

For a moment there was something wistful and uncertain in her face. "Maybe not. But when you touched me at the abbey . . . you brought something alive. I was all nerve, all sensation, but it wasn't just from the desire I felt. It was —" She made a shaky sound. "That's just it, I don't know *what* it was. I've never felt like that before," she whispered.

Her breathless words left Calan speechless. But they changed nothing. "You can't stay with me tonight."

Her chin rose. "Why?"

"Because . . . I don't want to hurt you, Kiera."

"Then don't."

Two easy words. But she didn't know the things he was capable of. Right now even *he* didn't know what he was capable of.

In growing irritation, Calan wrapped a towel around his waist and tossed her the sterile gauze. "I'm trying very hard not to hurt you, believe it or not. Take this and I'll meet you in your room."

She caught the box and held it clasped against her chest. Her hand moved, closing around his waist as he tried to walk around her. "Where did you get all those old scars? There must be half a dozen of them."

"Accidents." He shrugged. "The usual."

"I don't think so. Are they from the explosives work you do?"

"I don't know what you're talking about."

"Your great-aunt left boxes for you with a note. I didn't want to spy, but I saw them on the kitchen counter while I was making tea." Her eyes darkened. "There was a shipping list attached for safety gear. A tactical suit and face shields. Is that how you were hurt, Calan?"

There was respect in her eyes, and that was the most dangerous thing of all. "No. I'm just a geek. My company makes some of the ordnance location equipment, that's all." Leaning down, he removed her hand, then scooped up his clothes. "End of story."

"I don't believe you."

"Too bad." He pulled her to her feet and angled a hand at her back, pushing her toward the door. "Goodbye."

"Wait a minute. Aren't you the one who was pitching the values of honesty and open communication? Am I overlooking something here?"

Calan made his voice hard. "I changed my mind."

She turned, leaning into him. "I don't believe you. I think something else is happening," she said slowly.

At any other time he would have been fascinated. But not with her leg wedged against his thigh and her full breasts pressing against his naked chest.

He had never wanted a woman half so much.

That thought was like cold water dashed in his face. How much longer until he did something they'd both regret? How easy it would be to hurt her when his darkest instincts took control. Every second she stayed brought that danger closer.

He gripped her shoulder. "Kiera, you know nothing about me. Not about the things that matter."

"You said I could trust you. Are you taking that back?"

"Yes."

He expected her to flinch. To mutter angrily. Even to look offended.

Instead she lifted her hand to his cheek. "Liar." Emotions played through her face. "You're just . . . worried."

The way she looked at him dug deep inside him. He didn't want her respect or her concern. He didn't want to hope or believe that he could be different with her, because that hope was empty. Calan knew enough of his past to understand that he was incomplete, malformed, damned. His Change had come too soon, marking him forever a misfit among a lineage of people already cursed as outsiders. As a boy he had been cast out without training and now his instincts ran close to the surface, always ready to push him past the edge to uncontrolled violence.

He would never be complete, never be

fully controlled. He had nearly been harmed twice, driven by the Other. Anyone close to him would always be in danger.

He thought he'd accepted that fact, but it simply hadn't mattered so much before. Not until he'd met Kiera.

"Why are you worried, Calan?"

He caught her hand and lifted it away from his cheek.

She leaned closer, putting her palms on either side of him, bracketed against the wall. "I'm not afraid. I've traveled on every continent. I walked up to my waist in mud to find my way to tiny villages on no map. I wasn't afraid then, and I'm not afraid now."

"But you should be," Calan growled. "You haven't traveled where I've been. You wouldn't want to, believe me."

"Tonight I'm not going to worry. I'm going to be impractical, just for a few hours."

"You shouldn't, damn it."

She looked down at his muddy feet. "You need to understand this. I've always been the cool, practical one. I'm the keeper of the Filofax, guardian of the BlackBerry."

Calan heard the self-mockery. "Don't. There's nothing wrong with being organized or careful."

"Isn't there? I've missed too much because of it. So I'm doing this for me. I want to take a chance tonight. I *need* to take a chance, Calan."

He breathed a quiet curse. Part of him was already giving in. Part of him could already feel Kiera's hands locked, her mouth on his thigh while a raw climax tore apart their reason. Behind the stark images, the darkness inside him snapped and growled. "Tonight, I'm a bad person to take chances with, Kiera. Very bad," he said harshly.

"I don't believe that." She looked down and touched his thigh. "You're bleeding again."

"It's not important."

"It is to me." Suddenly her eyes narrowed. "Has something happened at Draycott Abbey? Was anyone . . . hurt there?"

"I can't talk about it. I can't tell you what I'm doing or who I'm doing it for. There's a whole continent full of things I can't tell you about. Now will that make you go?" he said savagely.

She drummed her fingers on the counter and shook her head. "Why can't this just be about sex? What's wrong with having an hour of mind-destroying, stupendous sex and leaving it at that?"

If he hadn't been in the grip of a battle with vicious, clawing desire, Calan probably would have laughed. As it was, it took all his strength to keep from wrapping his fingers around the cotton shirt she wore and tearing it to shreds.

He felt his muscles tense. He felt hair prick at his chest as the Change shimmered under his skin, growing ever closer.

"Women are allowed to do the asking these days. Some men even like it."

"I'm not in the mood to debate gender behavior or the new sexual politics, Kiera."

"Tough. I'm staying until you say something that makes sense. Once in Florence, a famous Italian chef told me —"

"No." Calan cut her off, his hand gripping her shoulder. "Don't tell me about the men. Not about the ones you've traveled with or been friends with. Especially not the ones you made love to."

He closed his eyes, losing himself to the inevitable. Falling under the spell of her honesty.

No way he could fight it any longer.

"I don't want to know about any of them, Kiera. None of them matter." His hands tightened. "I'm the only one who matters now." He heard himself as from a distance, unable to stop the harsh words, unable to control the violent need behind them. "Do you accept that?" he growled.

Any other woman would have stalked out.

Kiera simply watched him, sifting through the words and then nodding as if they pleased her.

The dark and wild part of Calan wanted to hammer deep and drive the soft smile from her face. Not for her pleasure.

For his alone.

He closed his eyes, tired of fighting the force of that drive. He gave up talking and scooped her up, setting her down outside the bathroom. Then he closed the door in her face. "I'm going to dress. Then . . . we'll talk." Maybe time would give him a measure of control.

He couldn't quite face himself in the mirror, afraid to see something that wasn't human in his eyes or the set of his mouth. But the Other rippled beneath his skin, furious to be set free.

"I don't get it." Her voice was muffled. "You walk through minefields. You rescue people from terrible danger. Why, Calan? And no, I didn't buy that malarkey about your company using that gear."

"Because someone has to do it. It may as well be me." He tugged on a pair of pants and splashed water on his face. Even with a closed door between them, her fragrance clouded his senses.

He opened his hand on the marble counter, watching the muscles flex as he fought back the Change. He felt the little hairs rise, felt his muscles twist, power filling his lungs.

Take her, fool. Make her submit to anything you want.

He closed his eyes, drove down fiery images of their naked, sweating bodies. His fingers stretched out, white against the cool marble as he slowly counted to twenty, feeling his muscles finally relax.

In a few more minutes he would go out and give her all the reasons why sex was off their new agenda. If talking didn't work, there were ways to frighten her away. Heaven knew, it would be easy enough for him.

For the thing he could become.

He stood up slowly, ignoring a wave of sadness. Something rustled outside the door.

"Kiera?"

Silence.

"Are you still there?"

No answer.

When Calan swung open the door, the room was empty. The hall was empty, too. He sprinted toward the sound of a door opening in her bedroom.

Empty.

Curtains billowed out at the patio. As he ran toward the patio door, mist struck his face. He couldn't let her leave. The danger to the Draycott family touched her, too, though she didn't know that. He'd hoped to keep her here by persuasion, not force.

He jumped to the grass and caught her scent, drifting on the wet air.

She was a fool if she thought —

Branches rustled and she moved out from behind a wall of climbing roses. "I'm not running away. I wanted you to follow me, and you did." Her damp hair framed her face and her cheeks were high with color. "I need this, Calan. I need *you.*"

He heard the tremor in her voice.

Too late, he thought. He couldn't turn away when her honesty was so clearly given. "You'll regret it," he whispered. "We both will."

Then he shoved her against the house and ground his mouth down over hers. There was no time for subtlety and no hope of care.

He took for his own pleasure, took out of a hunger that threatened to explode into violence at any moment. The animal inside him snapped, fighting to be let free.

And Calan couldn't make himself care,

though this was what he'd always feared. The rage and hunger were here, devouring him, and he was beyond stopping or even wanting to stop now.

He saw beads of water gather in the hollow of her throat and glisten in her hair. He smelled the heat of her pulse against the fine rain. Closing his eyes, he let the smell of her sex fill his senses.

Even then he tried to make his hands open. He tried to shove her away. But possession was a howl that blotted out everything else.

This was what he was, what he had come from. She would finally understand her grave mistake.

"You should have run. You should have locked your door," he said roughly. "I told you."

"I'm not running."

His hands slid over damp cotton, molding her full breasts. He lifted each one against his palms, watching her nipples tighten. His pulse hammered and he drove his thigh between hers, lifted her up until she rode against him.

She trembled, whispering his name.

His mouth ground over hers again, and this time Calan tasted a hint of blood. Whether hers or his, he didn't know. It didn't matter because there would be more before this was done.

God help them.

Mist swirled around them as his fingers found her. He opened her and cursed to feel that she was already wet. Ready to be taken.

So many ways he could take her. Ways she wouldn't imagine.

He lifted her, pulling her legs higher so that her soft heat cupped his erection. She wrapped her legs around his waist.

Trusting him. Wanting whatever he would give.

Dimly he felt her fingers slide into his hair.

And then she bit him. Bit him hard enough to draw blood. She closed her eyes and licked the welt on his shoulder with her tongue.

"Do it here, Calan. Hard." She shuddered. "Fast. I want to feel you now."

Torment came in the same breath as hunger. He felt her tongue brush him again, felt her taut nipples rake his chest.

Blindly, he sank his fingers inside her, lifting her at the same time. The smell of her made him wild. *Too late . . .*

The Other howled and Calan felt the claws emerge. His heart hammered as she touched him and then nipped him again, this time on his jaw.

The claws stopped. His senses cleared briefly.

She bit him again. This time the hair slid away at his chest. Her touch, he thought. Somehow it affected his Change.

Kiera reached between them, sliding her hands under his waistband and circling him. Fury possessed him and he pinned her against the wall, feeling his erection jerk in her hands.

The Other roared to be freed, demanded to shove her down into the mud and savage her over and over for his pleasure. Calan closed his eyes, fought the need that screamed in his blood. Her teeth bit at his ear, bringing a brief awareness.

His thoughts cleared.

He stared at her, holding her locked against him. "Do that again. Use your teeth, Kiera."

She was breathing hard, her eyes glazed with desire. "I don't —"

"I need you to."

She licked her lower lip and nuzzled his upper arm, watching him. "Here?"

Calan managed a grunt.

Her eyes shimmered. "Are you sure?"

"Do it."

She nuzzled him, ran her teeth slowly over

his shoulder. Then she caught the skin at the top of his biceps between her teeth. When he stiffened, she tongued the small welt, making slow circles. "Like that?"

His penis throbbed against her. She was killing him with the hot scrape of her thighs, yet Calan could have thrown back his head and shouted in triumph. Each time her touch had caught him, pulling him back from the edge. Each time the force had steadied him, focused him, empowered him. When he chose to accept pain rather than hurt her, he had somehow driven the Other down into its fathomless darkness.

"Again," he ordered. "Bite my lower lip this time."

"I don't want to hurt you," she whispered, her hand riding along his hot length. She arched a little, pushing against him.

He was mad to sink inside her, feeling the wildness rise again, a heartbeat away. "I need this from you, Kiera. I'll explain later."

She took a breath and kissed him wetly. Her tongue slid into his mouth, wrapped over his tongue in hot circles. And after long seconds she bit him.

Hard.

Calan jolted at the sharp sensation and the absolute return of control.

And then he raised his head, unable to

believe what she had shown him. Was it possible that she had freed him from his nightmares? Had she touched the capacity for violence that had haunted him since he was a boy, with powers he could neither understand nor control? Was it something about *her* that made him different now? Or was it what they became *together?*

He felt her mouth on his, gentle and warm. Her hand closed on his engorged erection. Lust slammed down viciously.

And yet he did not shove her to the ground and hammer with blind violence. His control held.

Now Calan was only a normal man fighting to control the pleasure he gave the woman he loved.

The woman he loved.

The words burned through his blood. He watched their colors, felt their weight. And he measured the deep truth of his feelings.

Love always brought pain, he thought. Rarely were the two apart. And now, with Kiera, love and touch might free him.

"Finish," she panted. "I can't — wait. It hurts to want you so much." Her body moved against him, slick with passion. She made a soft, broken sound as his fingers stroked her, eased inside her.

Calan stroked her hot, wet center while

she closed around him and her legs gripped his waist. As she arched back, sighing his name, she fumbled for his zipper and then shoved the fabric away to bring him closer.

Her head fell back. She was a vision of reckless, breathtaking desire. She was his first sliver of hope in too many years to count.

He brought her higher, opening her legs to tease her, letting her slide over the throbbing tip of his penis. He stroked, hard and controlled, but did not enter her. Instead he seduced and maddened.

She moaned, driving her body hard against him. "Don't. No more, Calan. I can't wait —"

His fingers opened, expertly stroking as he whispered hot Gaelic praise against her throat. "You're all silk, Kiera. So much heat right here against my hand."

He palmed her, pushing deeper until he felt her stiffen, her legs gripping his waist.

And then he drove her over the edge.

Panting blindly, she bit his shoulder and plunged into a shuddering climax.

CHAPTER EIGHTEEN

Wind tossed the leaves. Mist swirled up in white waves as Kiera sank against Calan's chest. Her hair fell in a chestnut tangle across his shoulder, and he felt the sweat of her skin mix with his.

He was completely entranced.

It wasn't going to be fast between them, he swore grimly. It wasn't going to be easy, either. There was too much at stake.

And Nicholas expected him back at the abbey in four hours.

So damned little time.

"Are all the men from your town as devastating as you are?"

"There are no towns on my island. Just a few roads. Crofts that face a never-ending roar of storms and cloudy sky."

She sighed. "Sounds lovely."

"Not lovely. It's a difficult life. Yet I doubt many of the tenants would consider leaving."

"Tenants?" She leaned back, squinting at him. "You're the landlord? Laird, isn't that what you call it?"

"Aye, it's been the MacKay isle for centuries."

"You have your own *island?*"

"Not just me. I'm not the next in line," he said gravely. No point in bringing up the past. No point in telling her why he could never be accepted by his own kind.

"But it's in your family. That's very impressive." She rested her head against his shoulder for a moment, shivering.

"You're cold. The wind is stirring up."

"I'm counting on you to keep me warm." Her hand slid down and rested on his waistband. "I think it's working." Her fingers slid slowly lower. "Before you didn't —" She took a husky breath. "Finish."

"It's not a race. Getting to the finish line is half the fun."

"Tell that to my last boyfriend," she muttered.

"Past boyfriend," he said flatly. "Forget him." He drew her closer, arms around her waist. He could feel the sharp slam of her heart.

She bit her lip. "Why did you want me to hurt you? Every time I did, you smiled. That's on the edge of creepy, Calan."

279

He traced the curve of her cheek. "There's a reason. A good reason. I'll explain it to you someday."

"Why not now?"

"Because we have more pleasant things to do."

Wind stirred the lavender near the house, filling the air with crisp sweetness. Kiera looked up and blinked. "It's starting to rain."

She stretched a little. Smiled up at him. "Do I care?"

The first fine drops darkened her hair, soaked slowly into the cotton shirt that was only half-buttoned now.

"You'll catch cold if we stay here much longer." The wind rose, snapping her hair across his face, but she didn't seem to notice. Her hand tightened, drawing him fully into her grasp.

She sighed, whispered his name.

Heat hit Calan, exploding in vicious waves. Rain gathered on her face as he kissed her, tasted her, burned to take her. Need became a scream.

He gripped her closer, opened the door with his elbow and carried her down the hall. They didn't make it to his bed. They didn't even reach his bedroom. Her hand fisted on his penis as she bit his ear, threatening to force him over the edge. And he wanted to be inside her, driving her to a fine madness when that happened.

But pain had become his mentor. He welcomed the control it gave him.

"Stop hurrying things."

"I want you inside me, Calan. If this is just a delicious dream, I don't want to know it."

Muttering, he pulled her hand free.

Smiling, she slid it right back. "And I've got you exactly where I want you. Within my hand."

He muttered a dark curse in Gaelic. The last embers of the dying fire turned her skin golden as he strode into the library, shoving a table out of the way with his foot. He set her down on the thick rug, then pulled a soft wool throw off a wing chair and dried her face and arms.

"Your leg is bleeding again." She frowned up at him. "You hit it on the table."

"I don't feel anything," he said in all truth. "Are you warm enough?"

"No." Her face was grave as she stood up, freeing more buttons on her shirt.

He caught her hands and pushed them away. Moving slowly, he released each button and kissed the damp skin beneath until she dug her fingers into his hair. Despite her panting, he didn't hurry, savoring the pleasure of revealing her body inch by inch.

She muttered his name.

She dug at his back.

She tried to wiggle out from beneath him, but Calan was implacable. She had given him hope for a future, and he would give her this small gift in return.

More pleasure than she could bear.

He leaned on one knee, freed the last button and pushed the cotton away. A faint gleam touched her skin, shimmering in her eyes. It would be impossible to forget her when he left, Calan thought.

Impossible not to want more. To want forever.

He forced the future from his mind, dimly aware of her hands pressed against his chest. With a low oath, he rolled, bringing her above him so she knelt, her knees on each side of his body. Slowly he followed the lush curve of her thighs, teased the warm curls until he found the heat of her. She shuddered, arching in the faint light.

Calan rose on one elbow. His mouth followed the same searching path as his hands and then closed over her. His hands locked around her shoulders, holding her steady when she would have fallen while he tongued her deeply. Each stroke drew a breathless gasp that hissed away into a husky moan.

How would he ever have enough of her?

Something penetrated the iron concentration. Calan realized it was the faint scent of salt. A single tear glinted on her cheek. Her eyes were huge and dazed as he brought her body down against his mouth, meeting her with his hot tongue.

Pleasure shattered her. She raked his back, her legs rising to wrap around his shoulders. The force of her climax left her breathless, panting, and when her eyes finally opened, color swirled through her cheeks.

She eased backward, shifted, then pushed him down and slid her body closer until he was between her thighs, his erection caught against her.

Muttering, he tried to lift her, but she worked free. She slid lower against him to force his slow penetration.

She took him deeper, urged him slowly inside her, her expression rapt as their bodies merged.

Nothing was hidden in that moment. Her honesty was fierce and complete. And every emotion that snapped through her eyes struck Calan with equal force. Their bond was deep, beyond words.

She traced the little welt on his shoulder.

Frowning, she leaned down to kiss the small bruise nearby, then touch an old scar near his neck. Calan had been a boy when that scar had been raised.

He was a man now, and the old pain was finally just a dim memory.

When she drew him completely inside her, he gripped her hips, lost to a rush of pleasure.

"I'll have you, Kiera. With a pleasure you can't even imagine. You'll never forget this joining."

His shoulders tightened. Tiny hairs rose along his back.

Kiera touched his cheek, distracting the beast.

Calling to the man.

He rose taut inside her. Calan lifted her up, drove himself as far as she could take him and felt her shatter with a husky moan.

His own furious release came heartbeats later, hot and swift, jetting up to fill her.

Her hands tightened, never leaving his cheek.

Kiera had wanted to be free, to trust herself, and he'd taken her the last step of the way. Already she wanted him again, with a fascination that left her giddy.

But when she tried to move her legs, she

collapsed. Her arms were shaking. Her body simply gave way, poured across him in delicious abandon. "You just may have killed me, Calan."

His finger traced her wrist. "You've still got a pulse." He turned slightly. "Which is more than I can say for me." His hands eased her forward, drawing her into the curve of his arm, while her thighs were cradled against his.

He gently traced the flushed skin above her breast. "Very sexy."

She opened one eye and blew a tiny strand of hair out of her face. "You're a dangerous man. I have no strength left. Not anywhere."

He traced the little peak of her nipple slowly. "Not anywhere?"

She smiled. Worked her thighs closer to his. "Nothing that I can feel." Her eyes closed. "Check back in ten minutes."

Then her head nestled into the hollow of his shoulder and she slept.

It was her favorite dream.

The one where a man's powerful arms closed around her. She couldn't see his face but he felt familiar.

A stranger yet not a stranger.

And then the heat . . .

A man's rough cheek scraped Kiera's

breast. Warm breath touched her neck. With a little gasp, she twisted to her side.

Rain tapped at the windows as the man's thigh moved, pinning her body against a soft rug.

No dream held this much detail.

When she tried to ease her arm free so she could look up, Calan slid her back into the crook of his arm and pulled a heavy throw over their entwined bodies.

She blinked, a little dazed.

His finger traced her lips. "Someday you'll tell me why you're smiling."

She watched the rain trail down the window. "And someday you'll tell me what you really do with that explosive gear."

"It's possible."

She leaned back with a sigh and kissed his shoulder. "I'll tell you now. It's from being here with you. All this is the way it's supposed to feel. I keep wondering if it's a dream."

"There is one way to find out." Calan rose on his elbow, kissing her slowly. He traced the curve of her hip and cupped her breast. "It feels very real to me."

The throw fell. Their legs met.

Sleep was forgotten.

Kiera sighed when Calan's hands teased her sensitive nipples. She should have been exhausted, but any contact with his body left her restless to have him again. How could he understand her so well? Why did a near-stranger feel like someone she had known all her life?

The questions faded as he slid his leg slowly between hers. She didn't want him to be slow. She didn't want care and logic. Determined, Kiera rolled away and settled on his chest, wrapping her hands around him.

He turned, bringing her back beneath him, his hands tracing her shivering stomach. He found her heat. While she struggled, he tongued the warm skin beneath his hands.

She made a breathless sound and pulled him closer.

A small chiming sound came from his pants, draped over a nearby chair.

"Hell." His jaw clenched. Calan rolled away and pulled the soft blanket over her shoulders, kissing her hard. "I'll be back as soon as I can."

He didn't bother to dress. Cradling his phone, he strode out into the hall.

Was it his friend Nicholas Draycott calling?

Kiera felt a cold weight on her chest. Old plans and old bitterness goaded her. Was it a mistake to be here with a man she didn't really know? She had finally started trusting her instinct, and she was tired of making every decision based on cold logic. For one single night Kiera didn't want to be cool and practical. Right now her instincts assured her that she could trust Calan with her body and her life.

She caught the comforter against her fingers, wincing a little as she sat up. Her body felt languid and beautiful, molded by their fierce lovemaking.

But something dug at her memory, making her uneasy.

A moment later she fit the pieces together. He had bumped the cut on his leg when he'd kicked the table aside only an hour earlier. She had seen blood and the dark outline of the wound.

But now, as he'd walked away, only a pale welt remained. No blood, no cut.

Maybe she was wrong. Maybe the cut had been in a different spot.

Kiera closed her eyes. No, that was impossible. Everything about the past hour was burned into her memory. She'd seen the trail of blood, and now it was gone. Only a faint scar remained.

Suddenly she had the feeling that Calan MacKay was not who she thought he was.

Not *what* she thought he was . . .

The thought chilled her.

Questions continued to dig at her as she clutched the blanket and slowly gathered her clothes. When he'd kissed her, she'd forgotten all her careful plans. In the hot flare of desire, everything outside this room had been forgotten.

Kiera stood very still, watching the pattern of the rain shadowed on the window. She had been seduced by the power of her own dreams. Now it was time she had answers about who Calan MacKay really was.

"Kiera?"

She turned slowly. He was standing in the door, his cell phone in his hand.

"We need to talk." She took a breath. "You're not bleeding, Calan. It's been barely an hour." She had to force out the words. "Now your leg has healed. I see it but I don't understand how it's possible."

A muscle moved at his jaw. "I don't want to waste the time we have in questions or talk, Kiera. I have to leave very soon. Will you trust me and give me a little more time?"

"I want to," she said slowly. "I'm not sure why, but when I'm with you I feel completely alive. Colors are different. *I'm* different. I feel as if I'm part of something much bigger."

"And you never expected to feel like that."

Kiera nodded.

"It's the same way for me."

"What's happening to me, Calan? I've always known exactly where I was going and how I was going to get there. Then I meet you and I forget everything important."

Her hands trembled.

Only from the cold, Kiera told herself.

"I know just how you feel."

"So what are we supposed to do about it?"

"Follow where it takes us. Trust in what we feel. One hour, one day at a time."

"You make it sound so easy."

"Trust is never easy." He said the words harshly. Yet again Kiera wondered about his past and what had left so much pain in his eyes.

"Part of me says you're right. The other part says that I'm being dangerously stupid."

"You'll have to choose. We all have to choose." He smoothed the wool throw around her body. "You have to decide what you want most, comfort and safety or the truth." He saw her expression of protest. "You can't walk away, Kiera. Nicholas is entitled to the truth, and you're entitled to a family you never knew existed."

"There's something else," she said slowly. "I should have told you sooner, but I didn't know how to deal with the questions. I went to Draycott Abbey last night."

He didn't move. "You went inside?"

"I walked through the grounds, trying to sort out my emotions. I had the strangest feeling that I was being watched. Then as I was leaving . . . I was attacked."

His face was impossible to read. "Attacked by whom?"

"Two men. Others came in a car. I managed to get away."

"And you didn't call the police?"

"How could I? There would have been a thousand questions to answer. It was wrong, I know that. So I'm telling you now. These men spoke a language that sounded Slavic, Calan, and they were no ordinary burglars. Nicholas Draycott and his family — I think they could be in serious danger." She pressed a hand against his chest. "You need to warn him."

"I will."

"Right now, Calan."

"Fine. I'll call him in a moment."

"If something happens, I — I couldn't forgive myself. And what happened with

291

those men in uniform at the abbey could be connected." She frowned. "I haven't changed my mind about the viscount, but he has to know."

Calan nodded.

"As for the rest, I need time to think. Nothing makes sense right now."

"How do I figure into this time you need? Are you going to deny what just happened between us?" His hand cradled her jaw. "Because I won't let you pass it off as simple sex. It was damned well more than that, and you know it."

She trembled at that simple touch. She wanted him again, even while her mind whirled in a dozen directions. "No, it wasn't just sex, and it certainly wasn't simple."

"So?"

"Someone very wise once told me to take things one day, even one hour at a time." She traced the hard line of his jaw. "Remember?"

"Maybe I should keep my mouth shut," he muttered.

"That same person also told me that the important things knock you off your feet and leave your world in turmoil." She leaned her head against his chest, letting the heat of his body warm her fears. "So I'm moving as fast as I can. I'm trying to keep up while the ground is shifting under my feet. Give me time," she whispered.

"I'll try. But when I touch you — I want everything. And I want it forever."

So did she, Kiera thought. She smiled, feeling his fingers smooth her hair. "I feel like a ruined piece of knitting. There are a dozen threads unraveling in my head right now."

"You're smart and you're honest. You'll do the right thing." His lips moved over her cheek. "Just don't take too long." He glanced down at his watch and frowned. "I have to leave. Damn it."

"I don't suppose you can tell me why."

"I'm afraid not."

"Is it something to do with *him?*"

Calan nodded.

Kiera took a sharp breath. "Is he in danger?"

"Yes. You could be, too."

"Me?" She laughed, shaking her head. "That's crazy."

"Is it?" Calan smoothed her cheek and tilted her face up to his. "It took me a few hours, but I saw the resemblance. Other people might have seen it, too."

"But I don't know anyone here."

"Think about it, Kiera. There are dozens of guests and workers at the hotel where you stayed. Think of all the people you traveled with. You've been around hundreds of people in the last few days."

The possibility struck her hard. "Are you saying that I need protection?"

"Hopefully, no. But I don't want you to go back to the hotel. You can stay here, or you can go to the abbey with me."

Her throat turned dry. "I'm not going there, not to meet him." She pulled away, pacing the room. "Not today. Not tomorrow. I — I won't be rushed or manipulated, Calan."

"This is no trick to make you change your mind. You could be in danger. I need you to understand that."

"But you won't tell me why? I think I'm entitled to —" Something moved against her hip. Looking down, Kiera realized it was her sweater draped over the chair. When she reached into the pocket, she saw the light flashing on her cell phone. The unit was in silent mode, vibrating to indicate a call coming in.

She looked at the number and frowned.

"What is it?"

"My cell phone. It must be a mistake. I don't recognize the number." She shoved the phone back into her coat pocket. "So this has something to do with those men at the abbey last night?"

"Probably."

"Then tell me —"

Her phone vibrated again. Impatiently, she pulled it out. It was the same unfamiliar number.

"Maybe you should answer it." Calan leaned over her shoulder, glancing at the number. "It's a London exchange."

Kiera tapped a button. "Yes?"

Static rippled. "Is this Ms. Morissey? Kiera Morissey?"

"Who is this?"

"A friend. Someone who has something very important to you."

"I don't understand."

"Then listen." Rustling filled the line. Kiera heard the sound of sharp, panting breath.

"Hello?"

"Kee, is that you?"

Panic kicked at Kiera's chest. She knew that breathless voice almost as well as her own. But what was her youngest sister doing in London? She sounded terrified. "Maddy? What are you doing in —"

"*Enough.* Now you see that we are most serious. So you will listen, Ms. Morissey. And then do just as I tell you. Is this understood?"

"But why —"

The phone jerked. She heard her sister cry out.

"No. Stop."

"Now you will listen to me. Understood?"

"Y-yes."

"You will drive to the car park near the old church in Winchelsea, overlooking the marsh. You will wait there. Is it understood?"

"Yes." Kiera gripped the phone. "I'll come. Just — don't hurt her. *Please* just —"

The line went dead in her hands.

CHAPTER NINETEEN

She couldn't move.

Horror squeezed down like a fist. Maddy was the youngest of Kiera's sisters. Innocent and eternally optimistic, she had a special skill for music and could remember any sound, tone for tone. For the past six months she had been working in Paris. When Kiera had told her she was coming to Draycott Abbey, she had been totally opposed.

How had she gotten to London? Those men —

Kiera stared blindly at the phone. The caller had an accent just like the men who had attacked her at the abbey.

"Kiera, what's wrong? You're ghost-white." Calan took the phone just as it would have fallen from her hand. "And who is Maddy?"

"M-my sister. Someone has taken her, Calan. I've got to go. They're going to hurt her." She grabbed her clothes and frantically began to dress. "I have to —"

He took her shoulders gently and turned her around to face him. "Tell me what has happened. I can help you."

"There's n-no time. They said —" Her voice broke.

He held out her blouse, his eyes very hard. "While you dress, tell me exactly what they said."

"Maybe I should call the police. But they'll hurt her, Calan."

"Dress," he said firmly. "There are people who can help, but I have to know everything."

Kiera took a shaken breath as she gripped her blouse. With stiff fingers, she began to force the buttons closed. "They knew my name. They said they were very serious." She stared out at the gray light, reciting from memory. " 'You will drive to the car park near the old church in Winchelsea, overlooking the marsh. You will wait there. Is it understood?' " She yanked on her shoes. "Why would they want Maddy?"

"We're going to find out," he said coldly.

"Wait." Kiera spun around, staring at him. "She looks a lot like me," Kiera whispered. "But even more like the picture in the library than I do. Do you think . . ."

"I think we will have to be very careful."

He slipped her coat around her shoulders, then reached down to the table. After fumbling a moment, he pressed her bag into her hands. "We will get your sister, Kiera. I know this part of Winchelsea. The church stands in a very deserted area overlooking the marsh. It is a good place for people who do not want to be seen."

"But surely the pastor or the church members —"

"The church has been closed for at least ten years. The windows are boarded up and there is scaffolding over the outside walls."

"She needs her medicine, Calan. My sister had rheumatic heart disease. She has a bad valve, hypertension. Without her medicine —"

He pulled her to his chest and cradled her face gently. "We'll get her back, Kiera. Believe this." The absolute authority in his voice made her nod.

She believed him. She didn't know how he would do it, but he would. "I'm ready." She pulled her bag over her shoulder. "And — thank you. This isn't really your problem."

"Like hell it isn't." He kissed her hard, then released her. "I'll tell you what I have in mind as we drive."

■ ■ ■ ■

"I don't like the look of it." They were parked above the beach. The rain had stopped, but the sky was dull with racing clouds.

"Why? What's wrong?"

Gunmetal clouds veiled the distant marsh.

"No sign of a car or any tracks. That small gravel drive is the main road to the church. They must have taken another route."

"I can't see any gravel road."

"I can," he said flatly.

Below them sheep moved slowly, lighter gray against the predawn silence of water and sky.

"Are you sure that's the right church?" She stared at the skeleton of stone with its single spire vanishing in the swift clouds.

"It's the only one in ten kilometers," he said grimly. "They chose an excellent location." He took off his jacket, frowning. "I'm going down for a look."

She started to open her door, her face determined.

"No. Stay here, Kiera." He gripped her shoulder. "It's absolutely crucial. Don't follow me. Don't leave the car. Don't make any noise." He dropped his sweater on the floor. "I need to know what we're up against, and I'll find out faster if I go alone. You have to trust me."

"What if they call again?"

"Tell them you should be here in fifteen minutes. Tell them you've just passed Ashford."

She didn't answer, working through her choices. But she didn't know the terrain. Even if she did, how could she fight a group of armed and desperate men?

"I need your promise, Kiera. Don't leave the car."

After long moments, she nodded. "Fine. Just hurry. But be careful, Calan. These men — they sounded very dangerous."

"I can be very dangerous, too."

He left his jacket beside him on the seat and then opened the door.

Wind gusted through a solitary row of willow trees. The tall grass shook.

And then the gray marsh swallowed him.

Five minutes passed.

Ten minutes.

Kiera's gaze was locked on the distant church, watching for the slightest movement. But no one appeared in the indistinct landscape. Only the sheep ambled on, heads down, oblivious to the drama around them.

A movement caught her eye, down near one of the ditches on the far side of the marsh. A bird cried shrilly, exploding into the air.

A shadow — or maybe an animal — was reflected in the still water for a second. Then it vanished into the mist.

Another wolf?

"Impossible. Wolves aren't ever seen in England now." She closed her eyes and rubbed the bridge of her nose. The waiting was a torment, every second consumed with thoughts of Maddy and what could be happening to her.

How had they found her sister and what did they hope to gain with her abduction? If they hoped for an impressive ransom, they were out of luck. No one in their family had that kind of money.

But Nicholas Draycott does, the little voice whispered with icy clarity. And if the kidnappers knew that Kiera and Maddy were relatives . . .

She locked down her frantic thoughts. Imagining the worst was no help. If she caved in to fear, she would be no good for anything.

A sudden movement in her pocket made Kiera gasp. She realized her phone was vibrating. Her fingers were stiff, and she nearly dropped the phone before she found the button to receive the call. "Yes?"

"Where are you?" There was no introduction.

"I — I'm just north of the marsh."

Silence. "What does the street sign say?"

Damn. She ran through Calan's brief directions. "I can't tell in this fog. I know there was a sign for Ashford a few minutes ago."

He muttered something to someone out of range. The two spoke in a rough staccato. Kiera felt sweat on her palms but she bit back her questions.

"Ashford. So you will be here in ten minutes if you are fast. And you *will* be fast, Ms. Morissey?"

"Yes. Of course I will."

"And you come alone. If not, then your sister will pay for your mistake."

"I'm alone," she said firmly.

"Ten minutes," the man repeated.

The connection broke. As Kiera put away her phone, she scanned the bleak gray marsh. *Where was Calan?*

Madison Morissey was shivering. It felt like an eternity since they'd taken her, another eternity since she'd been pushed into this cold van.

She was fighting panic, her knees drawn up tight to her chest. They had taken her coat and sweater when they'd grabbed her outside the hotel. They'd shoved a rag with some kind of chemical over her mouth, and she'd awakened gagged and masked, hands and feet bound, traveling inside a small van.

Her arms and legs ached, stiff with cold beneath heavy strapping tape. But cold was the least of her problems. They'd taken her bag with her medicine.

She should have taken her pills hours ago.

She forced down a wave of panic. At least she'd spoken to Kiera. Kiera would come and together they'd think of something. Kiera always thought fast on her feet.

Wincing, Maddy leaned back, resting her head against the cold metal of the van's interior. She was relieved to be alone. The worst part had been hearing people nearby, knowing that they watched her, talking about her while her own vision was cut off beneath the cotton hood they'd thrown over her head.

She raised her head, cataloging every sound she could pick out, from the cry of passing birds to the low, sucking gulp of water nearby. They had been driving for hours. Sounds were her only clues to her location. She might need them to find her way later, if she and Kiera escaped.

No, *when* she and Kee escaped, she told herself flatly.

She focused on the noises outside the parked vehicle. A seabird sailed past, its keening cry echoing in the silence. Long grasses whispered with dry intensity in a gust of wind.

Sounds were Maddy's job. No one remembered timbre and pitch with the clarity that Maddy did.

They were near a body of water. Someplace isolated, without passing people or the sound of cars. Not far from the sea, judging by the salt smell.

Once she heard a faint bell. A railway crossing?

Then there was only silence.

She shuddered, telling herself again that Kiera would come. Then they would find a way to escape.

She locked her hands and settled down to wait. . . .

Kiera saw the long grass flatten on the other side of a canal. Nothing else moved.

She stared at her watch.

She was expected at the church in two minutes. If she wasn't there, they would hurt her sister. Anger swept over her. How

305

had she gotten swept up in Nicholas Draycott's problems? Again the Draycott family had brought pain to her and those she loved. She *hated* all of them.

She'd tell him that to his face once this was over.

Something struck the back of the car. She spun around, trying to see through the drifting layers of fog. Feathers. Small black feet. Just a bird.

She forced her body to relax. She had to make a choice, anticipating what lay ahead. She couldn't leave her sister's fate to Calan.

Her phone vibrated where she gripped it in her sweating hand. She answered instantly. "Yes."

"Ten minutes," the cold voice said. "You are still not here."

"I'm just over the hill. I see the church," she said quickly. "I'm coming down now."

She heard him cover the phone, heard the rustle of clothing and movement.

"Very well. Two minutes. Not a second more."

Kiera shoved the phone into her jacket. Her hands shook as she turned on the motor, using Calan's keys. She had no more time left. Her caller had been very clear. They would hurt her sister if she didn't do exactly what he said.

Her heart pounded as she turned onto the little gravel road. Behind, somewhere in the fog, she imagined she heard the howl of a dog.

A dark shape ghosts through the tall grass.

Six meters away a man in camouflage crouches, watching the road leading down to the church. He smells like cigarettes and fear.

The animal moves on in silence, his body hidden.

Down the hill he hears furtive movements and circles closer. Two men here. Motionless. Waiting.

He smells gun oil and the tang of old cordite carried toward him on the wind. They are close to the road, weapons braced at their shoulders. Between them a third man lies unmoving. His body holds the smell of drying blood.

He passes on.

Minutes before, five men approached the church. Now only three are left, along with two more he has seen going in and out of the big building. He's found a way through the marsh that will bring him unseen to the back of the church.

The Hunt stirs, filling his blood.

When a man emerges from the biggest truck, weapon over his back, the animal changes direction. The man opens the back of the truck, pulls out two canvas bags, and then moves around to the passenger door.

The animal follows, a black nightmare leaping from the fog. The rifle drops into the mud. Blood strikes the big tires.

The man falls, eyes open. He does not move.

The door to the church stands open. The animal raises his head, checking the smells carried on the wind, searching each one for signs of danger. Slowly he circles, stopping at the edge of the clearing.

Inside the ruined church he sees the front of a white vehicle. A man leans on the door, talking fast.

Dim memories hammer in the animal's mind. His friends will be coming. He must do anything necessary to keep the woman safe until they arrive. But he can feel precious minutes passing.

Suddenly a car motor whines up the hill he had just crossed.

The hairs stir on the back of his neck. He knows the sound of that engine. He knows who is inside.

The animal pivots hard. Digging for traction, he leaps the nearby fence and races along the marsh, trying to cut off the car.

He is too late.

■ ■ ■ ■

White fog drifted past the car windows.

Two minutes drew out, feeling like an agonizing eternity.

Kiera heard the cry of seabirds as she gripped the wheel. Every turn was dangerous with the fog hiding deep ditches beside the narrow gravel road.

Finally she came to a small gate that was standing open. She drove past, turned a sharp corner and stopped. The old stone church rose up before her, windows boarded. Scaffolding spidered up the walls and white tape crisscrossed the broken steps.

The grass near the marsh shook.

Wind, Kiera thought. She took a deep breath and parked in the deserted circle of mud that had once been a parking area, craning her head. Nothing moved around her.

Where were they?

She gasped as her door was flung open and she was yanked from the car by two men wearing black hoods. The bigger one tore away her bag and shoved her against the wall of the church. Another man appeared, spitting sharp questions.

She recognized his voice from the phone calls.

Behind her the car engine roared to life and sped away.

She was shoved hard against the church. Heavy cloth was pulled down, covering her face while they patted down her clothes and took off her jacket. Wincing at another rough shove, she was pushed blindly through the mud toward the side of the church. She remembered that this wall had been hidden by a tall hedgerow overgrown into a wild green barrier.

How would Calan know she was here?

Would he see her footprints? Could he find the car?

She shut away the chaos of questions. Instead she forced every bit of will into planning for what was to come.

CHAPTER TWENTY

Kiera's heart was pounding.

She couldn't see a thing, thanks to the heavy canvas mask they had thrown over her head after pulling her from the car. All she could think about was her sister — where she was and whether she was hurt. She was about to demand answers when the bottom of her mask was jerked up and heavy strapping tape wrapped around her mouth. She was spun around roughly and shoved forward, first over muddy soil and then across uneven bricks. When she stumbled, someone yanked her upright and forced her blindly through what felt like a doorway.

Ten steps.

Another doorway. The threshold catching her foot.

Seven more steps.

She heard the bang of metal and then the sound of a car or truck door opening. A big hand gripped her waist, lifted her, tossed her sideways. With her hands bound, she couldn't break her fall, sliding until her head struck a wall of cold metal.

She was inside a truck or van, Kiera thought. She had no clue whether she was alone or not. She stretched out her legs slowly, feeling corrugated metal beneath her calves. Almost certainly a van.

Was it empty?

She waited, listening for any sound, but the van was silent. Was it some kind of test?

She didn't move for long minutes, the only sound the hammer of her heart. Clothing rustled. Kiera could have sworn she heard a low wheezing sound. She leaned closer. This time she was certain about the noise.

It sounded like the little wheeze that Maddy made when she was having trouble breathing. Warily, Kiera wiggled sideways and stopped.

She heard another wheeze. She repeated her movement, then stopped once more.

The wheeze came again.

Stiffly, she moved her bound hands closer to the source of the sound. Her fingers met something warm. Another hand.

Kiera felt trembling fingers open, grip hers and close down hard.

She had found her sister.

■ ■ ■ ■

A man in dusty khaki pants crouched behind a ruined stone fence, watching the road to the church. His rifle rested in place in front of him. No one would come down the road without being seen.

He looked smug and a little bored. He was used to harder jobs in more dangerous places. So he didn't turn when the wind rustled through the grass behind him. He didn't notice the shadow that fell briefly.

Claws slashed. Blood spattered. He fell before his hand could reach the rifle.

Something pulled his body away over the muddy ground, until it was hidden in the tall grass.

Zarof glared at his assistant. "Where are Konstantin and Anto? They should have reported in twenty minutes ago."

"At least four men have lost contact."

"Then send someone out to check."

"I did. We haven't heard back from Konstantin yet."

Something crossed Zarof's face and he turned slowly, his angry gaze searching the fog-swept marsh. "Give him five more minutes to answer. And then I want you to go. Complete this thing. We're close now. Do not fail me."

The man nodded stiffly. "As you will."

Zarof turned, his face grim as he picked up a large canvas bag and strode into the ruined church.

They had been lucky during their surveillance. They had managed to take one of the soldiers in Viscount Draycott's protection team. He lay on a makeshift table now, arms and legs strapped down. So far he had refused to talk, but that was about to change. Zarof gestured to one of his men, who put a water tube down the man's throat.

Seconds later he screamed, the sound muffled but desperate with pain. It would not be long now until Zarof had what he needed to know. Water was excrutiating and efficient. He nodded to his assistant who slapped their captive hard, rousing him.

"Now I ask you again. What is the code word recognition for Viscount Draycott's security team?"

"Told you —" The man groaned the words. "No codes. Face recognition only. No . . . chances taken."

Zarof scowled, jerking a hand to his assistant. The tube was reinserted. The screams resumed shortly after that.

■ ■ ■ ■

Their hands locked. It was the only warmth and hope in a world suddenly turned to a nightmare. Kiera's thoughts raced wildly, but every practical choice was closed to her. They were gagged, bound, their faces covered by masks.

Think.

She felt Maddy's body turn, so their hands were at right angles. And then she felt her sister's fingers tap on her wrist, just above the strapping tape.

Memory swirled back. Two little girls with healthy imaginations and too much time on their hands, playing spy games.

Her sister tapped again, four times.

Four meant start. The silent code had given them hours of amusement, their own secret communication evolved over a dozen years.

Kiera frowned, trying to remember the rules. Four taps meant a number. Numbers for every letter in the alphabet. She squeezed her sister's hand in affirmation. Waited.

Eighteen taps. *R.*

Twenty-one taps. *U.*

Fifteen taps. *O.*

315

Eleven taps. *K.*

R U OK?

Kiera squeezed her sister's fist hard, twice. Their old answer for *yes.*

R U?

There was a moment of hesitation. And then her sister's squeeze once, followed by a weaker second squeeze. It had to be bad if Maddy was qualifying her answer. Somehow Kiera had to get them out of this place, away from these madmen.

She frowned, realizing Maddy was tapping on her hand again.

F-o-u-n-d. A pause. *S-c-r-e-w-s.* Another pause. It didn't make sense, Kiera thought.

Maddy continued. *W-e c-a-n u-s-e.*

Something small and sharp touched Kiera's palm. A metal screw with a pointed tip. Maddy must have found them on the floor of the old van. Finally they had a tool.

Small as it was, it could cut their taped hands. She coded back an answer.

Y-e-s.

She thought she heard Maddy's muffled wheeze as she carefully took the screws into her hands and went to work on the tape. As they worked, Kiera heard a sound that made her heart lurch.

A man screamed half a dozen times, caught in torment. And then suddenly the screams ended.

Zarof scowled at the body of the dead English soldier. He had not talked, only babbled nonsense at the end. Always the same thing, that there was no team code for surveillance members. Face recognition only.

This would make Zarof's mission far more difficult.

"Do you believe him, Zarof?" the other man said quietly. "Could a man lie under such pain?"

Privately, Zarof doubted it. The SAS soldiers he had worked with were superbly trained, but every man had his limits. No man could hold out forever.

"It makes no matter what I believe. We found no code. So we turn to the original plan." He glanced at his watch and jerked a finger toward the nearby doorway. "Get them ready." He pulled out his walkie-talkie. "Then go find the men who have not reported in. It is time," he said.

Fog swirled over the quiet canals and whispered through the long grass. Only the ruined spire of the church was visible briefly, and then the clouds swallowed it again.

Near the top of the hill, where the drive curved sharply, another man toppled silently to the grass and was dragged away, hidden in the fog.

Nicholas Draycott tapped his fingers on the steering wheel and then checked his watch. "How much longer before we're out of this traffic?"

Izzy Teague muttered under his breath. "According to my GPS, we're less than fifteen kilometers from the interchange. But at this rate it still might be an hour until we reach the church. We'll have to find an alternate route."

Nicholas reined in his impatience. Calan had sounded worried when he had called, and it took a great deal to worry his friend. Now Calan wasn't returning any of his mobile calls, and Nicholas feared that the situation was unraveling.

Their destination was a ruined church overlooking the marshy coast. Calan had warned him to remain in cellular contact at a park service parking lot north of the marsh. Izzy was to approach the church on foot and rendezvous with Calan in five minutes.

But with the traffic snarled, there was no hope that they would be on time.

"What about your friend? What is one man going to do against a dozen armed extremists?"

Nicholas smiled a little grimly. "Never underestimate a Scotsman. Especially when he is a MacKay of Na h-Eileanan Flannach."

"Beg your pardon?"

"The Grey Isles, sometimes known as the Flannan Isles. One of the farthest specks of land in Great Britain, shrouded year-round by mist, and no place for the weak." Nicholas stared into the shifting light. "Calan can care for himself well enough. If any man at all can save the kidnapped woman he mentioned, Calan can."

"I hope you're right. Seems a tall order for one man, just the same."

Nicholas called his friend's mobile phone again. Like all the other times, he got Calan's voice mail. "This could get nasty, since we'll be driving on back roads, but we aren't likely to have much traffic."

"Because no one else knows the way?"

"No. Because no one else is crazy enough to drive through the marsh in a fog like this."

"If anyone can get us there, you can, Nicholas. Let 'er rip." Izzy's smile faded as he saw patches of gray canals and narrow ditches nearly obscured by fog. In the uncertain visibility every turn held a potential for disaster.

Izzy glanced at Nicholas and shrugged. "Nasty. But it beats the hell out of a desk job."

CHAPTER
TWENTY-ONE

Fog brushed the marsh.

Near the top of the hill, where the drive curved sharply, another man toppled silently to the grass and then was dragged away, hidden in the mist.

Gray walls.
Gray ceiling.
Dirty gray windows.

Kiera forced her mind to be calm and focused as she stared around her. The men had come for her and for Maddy with no warning, yanking them to their feet and shoving them into this dark room. One man paced, muttering on a cell phone. Two others stood guard at the door. All the men were tall, dressed in dusty fatigues. Their faces were covered by black canvas hoods.

So far her captors had not noticed the dusty screws rolled up in the cuffs of her sweater. Nor had they stopped to check the tape around her wrists with more than a cursory glance.

Someone shoved her into a rickety chair and removed the tape on her mouth. Her sister was pulled to a table nearby. "My sister is sick. I'll do whatever you ask. Just please get her medicine."

A hand struck Kiera's neck, whipping her sideways. Pain exploded through her head and the room flashed white. Then she was shoved back onto the chair, a cup of cold water thrown in her face.

"No words from you. No talk at all unless it is to answer the questions I will make. You understand me?"

She nodded stiffly. Across the room she caught Maddy's terrified gaze. Now that Kiera's eyes had adapted to the half-light, she saw her sister clearly for the first time. The pallor and the dark circles under Maddy's eyes were unmistakable.

The taller man paced the room, his brisk, decisive movements marking him as the leader. From his voice Kiera recognized him as the one who had called her cell phone.

He gestured to someone outside the room and a motionless figure was dragged in, dropped at Kiera's feet. "You see? This is what will happen to your sister if you give me one word less than the truth."

The man was dead. Blood dotted his torn sweater as his eyes stared blankly at the ceiling.

Kiera forced down a reflex to gag and nodded.

"So now we begin. You are a relative of Nicholas Draycott."

What was she suppose to say? How much did these people know? She realized that her sister's life — and her own — depended on the answer she gave next. "We are distant relatives. Our families were — estranged."

The man stopped pacing and swung around to face her. "Estranged? Then you are enemies?" Clearly he did not like this news.

"Not enemies. Just — out of touch."

"But you know where his family is staying? You know how many guards protect him?"

Kiera hesitated. There was no choice but to lie, and she would have to do it perfectly. She hesitated, then nodded, trying to keep all expression from her face. "I know those things."

She heard the excited rush of his breath beneath his mask. "You will tell me his schedule, every detail. You will tell me when he is expected at the abbey next."

She gave the only answer she could. "I . . .

will tell you." She looked down at her locked hands, trying to appear undecided. If she looked too comfortable, they would be suspicious. She looked worried, biting her lip. "And if I do, you won't hurt my sister?"

The man behind her raised a fist, but the leader cut him off with a sharp phrase. "Your sister will be safe as long as you answer these questions."

"Then I will tell you everything I know."

Her captor called out sharply. Another man trotted in with paper and pen. He shoved her toward the table and then pushed a chair in behind her.

"You will write me a picture of this place. The address, the police who guard him and the code words they give you. Write it now."

Kiera's hands trembled.

She leaned over the table, hiding every emotion. She would give them a map of the narrow streets near the British Museum, an exclusive area where they might expect to find a wealthy family living.

She offered up a silent prayer and then began to sketch out a map.

Footsteps hammered in a nearby room. The big man turned and called out an angry question, arguing with someone in the doorway.

She forced them from her mind, trying to

remember the names of the streets from her visit there three days before.

Suddenly she heard the cry of something that could have been a wolf. She almost dropped the pen, but managed to tighten her grip and force herself to continue. All that mattered was writing down the words that would save her sister. Meanwhile, Maddy's breathing had become more strained. Kiera tried to write faster, sketching in street names and drawing up memories from tours she had organized to London.

When she looked up, only the leader was left in the room. He paced, speaking sharply into a walkie-talkie and snapping out orders.

Clearly, something was worrying him.

He crossed the floor and yanked the paper out of her hands. "If you lie, I will kill her while you watch." He reached behind Kiera and retaped her hands and mouth roughly. The hood was dropped back over her head.

Then there was only silence. Long moments passed, and no one moved. Over the pounding of her heart, Kiera heard a low rustling. Someone was moving near her. Her sister's cold fingers gripped her hands, tapping in a quick rhythm.

L-e-a-v-e.

She understood and tapped back. Maddy

moved closer, sawing with her screw to free the tape from Kiera's wrist. Her dusty hood slid free.

Emotions rushed through her at the sight of her sister's pale, anxious face. Quickly, she pointed up at the rickety ladder left behind by some construction team that had abandoned repair work on the building.

Maddy nodded. Tape still covered her mouth, and there was no time to remove it. Kiera put her foot on the ladder, feeling the dilapidated wooden rungs sway dangerously. Slowly she climbed, passing a grimy, cracked window. Looking down, she saw muddy ditches half covered by drifting fog. Something dark moved along one of the ditches, then vanished.

Kiera heard an angry shout.

Silence and then a snarl. Or had she only imagined that low, wild sound?

Breathless, she helped Maddy up the last rung and into a small space that looked like an unfinished storage area. Crumbling walls rose to low, exposed roof beams where the renovation had stopped abruptly. Directly ahead of them an unpainted door stood closed against one wall.

Maddy wheezed as they scrambled forward. Kiera grabbed a torn military parka draped over a nearby chair, tossing the padded nylon around her sister's shoulders. Shivering, she took a hat and muffler for herself, relieved to have anything that would take the edge off the penetrating cold here at the coast.

Outside, feet pounded past, followed by shouts and the whine of a car engine starting. She ran to the heavy door. Together, she and Maddy rammed the wooden frame with all their might.

Nothing moved.

They tried again, putting all their weight into the movement again and the rustic lock shook. With their next push the edge of the door splintered and gave way.

Caught off guard, Kiera grabbed at thin air as she lurched out into the fog thirty feet above the ground. Even in her terror she was dimly aware of blurred figures racing through the mist.

She threw one arm sideways as her foot slipped. She clawed desperately, trying to grab the splintered edge of a derelict balcony half hidden by exterior scaffolding.

Then she felt Maddy behind her, gripping her waist, pulling her slowly back into the doorway. Strain left her sister's face white and beaded with sweat despite the cold.

Kiera tumbled onto the floor. Her whole body felt bruised as she rolled to her side and sat up. Somewhere below them a man barked angry orders in a way that made her think their disappearance had been noted. She pushed to her feet, glad to have Maddy's hands to steady her. Her sister's firm, determined grip spoke louder than words, warming her amid the chaos and panic of their escape.

Together they would find a way out of this nightmare. Calan was somewhere nearby in the fog. All they had to do was find him.

Warily, Kiera pushed open the half-splinted door and looked out. Below the collapsing balcony more scaffolding zigzagged along the side of the building. Most of the wood had rotted through, leaving big gaps.

Below them a door slammed. Kiera looked at Maddy, pointing outside.

She sat down on the splintered wood, her legs hanging over empty space. There was no going back. They would have to jump and pray that the rotting wood held their weight. Kiera wished she had time to free her sister's mouth but at least Maddy had worked the tape loose enough to breathe clearly already.

Fog swirled up.

No way to jump now. Not without a better view of the scaffolding.

She felt Maddy's fingers grip her shoulders. She motioned for her sister to sit down next to her, in position for the first moment that the fog gave way.

But Kiera realized that her sister's eyes were wide with panic. She was staring down, wheezing, her body rigid with fear.

A huge dark shape climbed slowly up the scaffolding. All fur and muscle, it growled fiercely. Through the fog Kiera saw white teeth open. The animal shoved her on her back, its teeth only inches from her neck.

Memory swirled.

The night at Draycott Abbey there had been a huge dog near the stone fence. Was this —

There was no time to think.

The dark eyes glittered with an arresting mix of intelligence and cunning as one huge paw struck Kiera's chest, pinning her against the splintered wood.

CHAPTER
TWENTY-TWO

Kiera had an impression of brute strength held in check by keen intelligence. She felt the quiver of powerful muscles as the dark body locked over hers.

Slowly the great animal sniffed her borrowed hat and scarf.

When Kiera tried to move, white teeth bared inches above her throat.

She went completely still. Dark fur brushed her face as the wolf leaned down, sniffing her neck, her hair, her cheek, then rose to its full height. Powerful jaws closed down on her hand. Kiera closed her eyes, braced for the searing agony of her wrist being torn in two.

Nothing happened.

She opened her eyes, disoriented as the big jaws moved, exerting only enough pressure to urge her to her feet. There was no mistaking the intelligence of those gray eyes. Part of her mind, stunned and disoriented, tried to process what was happening. He was smelling her, reading her expression somehow.

Almost as if he was trying to communicate. . . .

"Maddy?" she whispered.

"Right here, Kee."

Kiera looked back and saw that her sister had managed to remove the strapping tape from her mouth. "Good job. Now follow me."

"Are you sure? I mean — is this safe?"

"Not much choice," Kiera whispered. "He wants us to go back inside, and I never argue with teeth locked around my hand." She rose awkwardly. Immediately she was tugged over the floor. At the far corner of the room, fog swirled beyond a broken window.

The animal pulled Kiera to the wall, then released her and rose to its hind feet, resting its paws on the splintered sill. After a quick glance back, it leaped up to the window and vanished.

Kiera's breath caught. Then she heard the thud of the animal dropping down onto some kind of wooden scaffolding out of sight.

She squared her shoulders. "I'm going up, Maddy. Help me push that box over here.

Once I'm out, I'll help you up."

Together the two women turned a dusty packing crate on end, and Kiera scrambled up. She looked down at a gray world of sullen fog. The roof stretched away from the window. The wolf had vanished from the scaffolding. Ten feet away a towering oak tree bordered the far edge of the church's facade.

The tree would give them a way down.

There was no time to wonder how or why the animal had found this place or where he had gone. It was nearly impossible to see down. Kiera's hands bled as she crossed the splintered windowsill. A shout echoed from the corridor below as Maddy jumped up, wheezing. Footsteps hammered closer. Through restless tendrils of cloud Kiera saw a straight path across the roof. She moved out onto the sagging roof and prayed it was more stable than it looked. Neither Kiera nor her sister looked down. There was no time to think, no time even to be afraid. They stepped out onto the roof.

As the fog broke in a sudden gust of wind, Kiera looked back, stunned to see a dark shape stalk over the scaffolding below the broken window. It was almost as if the creature was staying behind for a reason.

Protecting them.

The dark eyes rose, staring at her with a look of such intense intelligence that the hair prickled along Kiera's neck. She couldn't move, caught by some bond of awareness between them. That contact brought her a sense of safety in the nightmare around her.

"Kee, we have to go."

Maddy tugged at her arm. Even then Kiera couldn't move, caught by some strange, trancelike contact with the dark figure in the mist.

A muffled shout broke the stillness. A man emerged in the window.

Kiera shoved Maddy forward.

As the fog closed around them, Kiera heard a growl. A man cried out in shock and fury.

And then silence.

"There it is."

Nicholas Draycott pointed north to the dilapidated church rising from the fog-swept marsh.

"Bingo." Izzy pulled on a Kevlar vest, buckled it in place and nodded to the viscount. "Stay here. It's you they're looking for, but they can't have you."

Nicholas began an angry protest. The last place he wanted to be was crouched in a car like a frightened rabbit. But Izzy was right. If he was caught, he would become a precious bargaining chip. So he would stay in the car, waiting just as Calan had told him to wait. "Call my satellite mobile as soon as it's clear to leave. If you need backup, I can have a chopper here from Hastings in ten minutes."

"Good to know. Watch your six." Izzy opened his door silently, gave a little two-finger wave and vanished into the fog.

Panic drove Kiera and Maddy forward, gripping the high tree branch. Now the fog became their friend. Every swirling tendril hid their escape. As the cold began to set in, her teeth chattered uncontrollably. Hand over hand they crossed the rough bough, moving forward by feel alone. And then the branch ended. They had reached the tree's dead center.

The only way was straight down.

"I'll go f-first," Kiera chattered. "Give me ten s-seconds. Then you follow."

Maddy squeezed her sister's hand. "Thank you for coming, Kee. If you hadn't . . ."

But there was no time for thanks or anything else. Maddy's hand fell from Kiera's shoulder. "Be careful, Kee."

"Count on it." Carefully, Kiera wrapped

her legs around the main branch and started shimmying downward.

The descent was slow and agonizing. Every ridge and shoot dug at her thighs. Halfway down, her palms began to burn, a layer of skin torn away by the rough bark.

Leaves rained down on her, and she realized that Maddy had begun her own descent.

Kiera listened intently. The shouting had stopped, and now she was caught in a white blanket of silence, trapped between banks of swirling fog. But the silence was deceptive. Kiera knew her captors could appear at any moment. Every second was precious.

Her hands slipped, sticky with her own blood and she locked her arms around the trunk to break her fall. Small branches tore at her face and leaves slapped at her eyes. Dizzy with pain, she scanned the ground, little pools of water shining somewhere below her. So far there was no sign that they had been followed.

She leaned forward, gauging the distance to the ground. Ten feet?

Fifteen?

There was no time to worry about how she would break her fall.

She murmured a prayer and simply let go.

The jolt of impact hit her shoulder like a

truck and she almost blacked out with the pain. Then she rolled sideways, struggled to her knees and cradled her throbbing shoulder. She'd landed at the very edge of a ditch. A few inches more and she would have been fighting her way out of the mud.

A man with bleached-blond hair and a broken nose suddenly lunged for her arm. Kiera pulled back just in time, but slipped in the mud, falling backward. The man lunged again, cursing in vicious bursts that didn't require a linguist's skill to understand. She crawled backward, struggling to stay out of reach.

Then her sister appeared on the bank behind him — angry, silent and determined. Maddy was holding a thick piece of wood that appeared to have fallen from the old scaffolding. As the man lunged for Kiera, Maddy's angry blow hit him in the shoulder, knocking him sideways. Her second blow hit him in the neck. But the blow only slowed him down. He spun toward Maddy.

Her next blow hit him squarely between the eyes.

He staggered, clutched at his head and then collapsed with a groan.

"That was for stealing my medicine, groping me in the van, and thinking that you could hurt my sister."

Kiera smiled crookedly, shivering with cold. "I'd high-five you, Maddy, but I haven't got the energy." She clambered onto the bank, sighing in relief as she felt a heavy jacket pulled around her shoulders.

"I found this on the other side of the tree. There was a whole box of ammunition stacked underneath it," Maddy said between wheezes. "These men are planning something very bad, Kee. Someone has to do *something*."

"Right now you and I have to find a way out of here. But I remember where they drove the car." Kiera zipped up the oversize jacket and started along the edge of the ditch, moving cautiously through the restless banks of gray. A small road curved around the old church. She remembered that a man had driven Calan's car into the trees there just after she was taken captive.

She turned, scanning the curve in the road. Her teeth were chattering. Her shoulder was on fire, but joy overwhelmed any sense of discomfort.

Calan's car was just down the hill parked on an angle, half-hidden behind a yew hedge. They were going to get out of this place before they were discovered. Kiera ran down the hill and yanked open the car door. No keys.

"Maddy?"

"Already on it." Kiera didn't hesitate, sliding into the driver's seat. In the family her sister was known for her nimble skills at hot-wiring a car, courtesy of their father, who had always joked that if things got truly bad, they could survive on his and Maddy's ability as car thieves.

The car hood rose. A moment later her sister tapped. Kiera smiled crookedly at the wonderful sound of the engine growling to life. As she gunned the motor, Maddy slid into the passenger's side, and they backed out onto the road.

There was no sign of movement as they passed the deserted canals and slowly climbed above the marsh. Maddy leaned down, fiddling with the heater, and the two women luxuriated in a blast of hot air.

"Your wrist is bleeding." Maddy leaned forward, pulling up Kiera's cuff.

"I'll be fine. We have to get you to a hospital. You need your medication."

Maddy wheezed a little as she sat back, resting her head against the seat. Her face was very pale. For once she didn't argue.

"Just rest." Kiera peered out at the fog. "I remember there was a police station about five miles back. We'll head there first. You're going to be fine."

There was a blur of motion behind Kiera. She swung around sharply. Her captor from the church loomed up from the rear seat, gripping Kiera's neck.

"No police," he said viciously. "You were warned."

He raised a pistol, and Kiera swung the wheel, sending the car into a sharp skid while the man cursed and slammed her forward against the steering wheel.

CHAPTER
TWENTY-THREE

Stars exploded white-hot in front of Kiera's eyes.

Blinded, she tried to control her skid while she struggled to recover. She heard Maddy shout and then the hammer of fists.

"Maddy — no. Be careful."

The man yanked open the passenger-side door. In one powerful movement he forced Maddy sideways out of the moving car. Then his pistol leveled on Kiera.

She tried to look back, but cold metal dug under her chin.

"If you slow down or turn around again, I will shoot you. Then I will throw *you* out, just as I did to her. You understand this?"

Kiera's fingers were white, clutched on the steering wheel. "Why do you hate Nicholas Draycott so much?"

The gun twitched against her neck. "Because he interferes in our country's future. Because he's arrogant and cold, and he thinks he can help shape the destiny of my country — he who is no one and nothing to us. But he will certainly fail. We will see to that."

Kiera heard the madness and the implacable hatred in that voice. But Maddy was all that mattered at the moment. She leaned over the wheel, squinting into the fog.

"Where am I supposed to be going?"

"No more talk. I will tell you exactly where to go when it is time. We will start with your map."

His cell phone rang, the sound muffled somewhere in his jacket. Kiera heard his hand fumble with the flap of his pocket.

She jammed hard on the brakes, throwing the car into a dangerous fishtail turn. They had barely ended the turn when she accelerated again, snapping the man backward. He cursed as she twisted the wheel, skidding in the other direction.

Kiera wrenched open her door and lunged out, away from the car, landing facedown in the gravel.

Pain clawed at her face and shoulders.

Something hissed by her head and burned through her arm. She screamed with shock, her body rolling along the bank above the marsh.

Another shot. Her chest seemed to tear

open in a searing burst of agony.

Everything blurred.

She looked up to see an orange fireball shoot through the air. The burning car skidded sideways and turned, headed back toward her, flames shooting from under the engine.

A black outline soared through the restless orange curtain, silhouetted sharply against the flames. There was painful beauty in the strength of that body and the fierce determination of the high, flying leap. Powerful paws struck the back of the car. The violent movement sent the car down at an angle, plunging over the bank away from Kiera.

She heard the roar of another explosion.

Dirt and gravel rained down on her face.

She was too exhausted to move.

Pain brought her back to consciousness. The car's black metal frame stood outlined like a twisted skeleton against the flames.

Her eyes burned from acrid smoke as she struggled to stand up. She couldn't seem to breathe. Her legs shook and then gave way.

Fighting a terrible weight, she clutched at her chest and then slowly toppled sideways.

Strong hands touched her face. Dimly, she felt warmth as if a blanket had been wrapped around her.

More words. Someone leaning over her. The sounds held no meaning.

As the crushing weight on her chest grew, Kiera stared up at the pale sky and knew that she was dying.

CHAPTER
TWENTY-FOUR

"Kiera, *talk* to me." Oblivious to the cold mud, Calan crouched beside Kiera's motionless body.

Her pulse was shallow and her eyelids fluttered slightly. Blood oozed from a wound at the center of her chest. Another bullet had grazed the corner of her shoulder.

He spoke to her again, but she didn't seem to hear him. Down the hill footsteps splashed through the ditch, and Izzy Teague loomed out of the fog, a canvas backpack over his shoulder. He frowned as he tossed a blanket over Calan's muddy shoulders and handed him his jacket. "Someday you'll tell me why your feet are bare and you're not wearing a scrap of clothing. Are you hit?"

Calan shook his head. The blood on his hands was all from Kiera. More blood welled up with every heartbeat. "She took at least two bullets. Can you do something for her, Teague?"

"It will have to be in a hospital. I can't treat a chest wound out here. I've already called Nicholas, and there's a helicopter on its way from Hastings. But . . ."

Calan didn't release her. There was a look of desperate resolve on his face. His fingers opened gently over the wound above her heart. "But what?"

"It's bad, Calan. I'm not sure they'll make it in time."

Fury and despair churned up and Calan gripped Izzy's arm. "Do something for her *now*."

"I'm not a magician. If one of those bullets grazed her heart, the odds are about as bad as they come." Izzy shook his head slowly. "I would only make things worse."

"I don't give a damn about the odds." Calan growled the words, bent over Kiera, his fingers gently stroking her hair. "There has to be something you can do, Teague."

"She needs surgery and X-rays and fluids." Izzy's voice was taut with frustration. "How am I supposed to do that in the middle of a muddy field, with no equipment and no blood?"

Calan's eyes narrowed. "How long until the chopper arrives?"

Izzy rubbed his neck. "Ten, maybe fifteen minutes."

"And that much more time back. She won't make it, will she?"

"I don't know, Calan. Damn it, I just don't *know.*"

In Calan's arms, Kiera's body shook. She took a short, gasping breath.

"Your guess is she's got a bullet at or near her heart. That's where the angle of the wound appears to be."

"Impossible to know for sure without an X-ray, but it's a solid probability."

"And if the bullet could be removed?"

"Out here in the field, without sterile equipment? Impossible."

Calan was already sliding a blanket under Kiera's body. "Tell me. What if it were *out?*"

"Hypothetically — if it was lodged at or near her heart, and if it was removed cleanly and fast, with blood volume adequately controlled — but that would take a machine, Calan. If *all* that happened, I'd say her chances for surviving were slight, yet better than hopeless. But it can't be done."

It could.

It would be dangerous, Calan knew. Maybe right at the edge of insanity. But he was making the choice blind, by heart and instinct alone and praying he'd taken the right turn because there was no going back.

She was white, motionless in his arms.

346

Blood oozed through his half-open fingers. He couldn't let her die without trying to help her.

What good were his skills if they couldn't save the woman he knew, in this instant, that he was joined with by destiny?

He shoved Izzy's jacket off his shoulders, glancing up as Nicholas jumped over a narrow ditch in the fog.

Izzy glared at him. "I told you to —"

"The brigadier's men are down on the coast road. Things are just about mopped up there. The whole place looks like a war zone." Nicholas only then saw the woman who was cradled protectively in Calan's arms. "What happened up here?"

"She's dying, Nicholas. I have to remove that bullet so she can have a chance."

"Out here? But how —" Nicholas frowned as Calan touched Kiera's face very gently. "She's — she looks like . . ." Nicholas sank down to the mud, swaying as if he'd been kicked. "Elena?" he whispered. "How can that be?"

"She's your sister's daughter. A mother betrayed and a daughter who learned bitterness and mistrust. A long story, Nicholas, and there's no time for any of it now." Calan shot a look squarely at Izzy. "Get me your best antiseptic."

Izzy growled a protest, but the look on Calan's face stopped him cold. "You're serious about this? Nicholas, how can he —"

"Do what he says, Izzy."

Muttering, Izzy pulled a brown plastic bottle from his gear bag. "Here's the antiseptic," he said reluctantly. "But how —"

"Scrub my hands. Then paint them up to the wrists. Be sure you get the nails."

"You're a crazy man, MacKay. I know field hygiene, but *this* can't work. If that bullet doesn't kill her, then you will."

"How far out is the helicopter, Nicholas?"

"Another eight minutes now. They're having trouble finding us in this pea soup."

Calan's jaw set in a hard line. "That's what I thought. Get the sterile equipment and dressings ready, Izzy. Open that blanket, Nicholas. You'll have to keep her still, no matter what. No movement of any sort will be safe once I start."

"Once you start *what?*" Izzy peered down, angry and suspicious.

"We're wasting time. Leave the things I need and wait over by the car, Teague." The order snapped off Calan's tongue. "Don't come back until Nicholas calls you."

"I don't see —"

"Go, Izzy." Nicholas's eyes darkened with impatience. "It's her only chance. Let Calan do this."

Shaking his head, Izzy stood up. After a last glance at Kiera, he stalked away into the fog.

Calan rolled his shoulders. His eyes followed the distant line of the ruined church as he took deep, focusing breaths. He didn't look at Nicholas as he held his hands carefully level, just above Kiera's chest.

"Let me see the bullet hole, Nicholas. And whatever happens — take care of her and her family. Help her. Together you can put all the ghosts to rest."

"I will. Be careful, Calan." The Englishman flinched as Kiera's eyes fluttered open and she gasped twice, flailing against Nicholas's arms.

"*Hold* her, damn it. No matter what you see or what happens."

Then Calan brought all his focus to his hands. With savage control, he dropped in one hard instant from sanity into the cruel, dark place where his Other waited, cunning and hungry. Muscles rippled along his back. Tendons shifted and fine black hair rose across his neck and chest. Calan drew back from the physical form at the last minute, shuddering against the violence of his shift, fighting to control who he was and everything that he intended to do, despite the fury of his Other and the fearsome price it would cost them both.

His fingers twisted, misshapen bones cracking, then shaped to short, powerful paws covered by dark fur. He closed his eyes, drawing back, caught in the moment before he returned to human form.

He snarled in pain, focused on his hands.

His fingers seemed to lose physical form.

Sweating, Calan held his hands at the thin boundary between animal and human form, when atoms spun and energy played out in a vast network that held only probability. He eased his shimmering fingers against the hole in Kiera's chest and followed the trail of battered skin in search of the bullet fragment. Without form, his fingers traced the bullet's path.

Calan took a harsh breath, battered by unthinkable pain as he fought his change and the rebellion of all his muscles. He was a hunter not a healer. His body quivered, desperate to change. But he swore to use every second of life to save the woman in his arms.

Sweat dotted his chiseled features. His heart fought in angry, unpredictable beats as he gently found the outline of a bullet lodged inches above Kiera's heart. "Be ready." His voice was hoarse.

Almost like a growl.

He struggled against the restless hunger of his Other beating beneath his skin. Calan pulled his hands free, memorizing the bullet's path.

"Give me the surgical tweezers, Nicholas. Quick —"

His hands took solid form. He grabbed the fine titanium handle from Nicholas and followed the jagged path downward by touch and memory. Kiera gasped restlessly as he found the bullet and closed the tweezers over the metal edge.

Sweating, he pulled the metal up, away from her heart, inch by careful inch.

His hands were rock solid, without a tremor despite the Change that howled through his blood. In Nicholas's arms Kiera took a raw, sighing breath. Color rushed in to fill her face.

Calan leaned forward and his eyes closed.

"Calan — can you hear me?" Nicholas's voice was very dim. "Let it go. You've done all you can. You're barely breathing."

Calan let the Change free, let his body's energy flare into the shift. Tendons and muscles twisted wildly, power shooting through him. But it was too late. He felt his heart squeeze in his chest. The sharp, irregular hammer turned to crushing pain as his heart stopped.

He collapsed backward on the ground.

When Nicholas Draycott looked down, a bullet lay cradled on Calan's still and bloody palm.

CHAPTER
TWENTY-FIVE

"Izzy, you need to look after Calan *now.*"
Nicholas Draycott shifted to one side as Izzy
Teague crouched in the mud beside Calan's
rigid body.

"What in the hell did he just do?" Izzy's
voice was tense as he pulled a stethoscope
and syringes out of his field kit bag. "At
least Kiera's got a strong pulse now, though
I can't figure out how. I also don't know
how Calan got that bullet out of her without
any more blood loss. Just keep an eye on
her, Nicholas. If her pulse goes thready, I
want to know immediately."

Nicholas nodded, shooting a worried look
at his old friend, whose face was now
bluish-gray and beaded with sweat. "Her
pulse seems light but steady. What about
Calan?"

"Faint breathing. Airway is open." Izzy
dug in his bag and pulled out a syringe.
"He's going into shock. I'm giving him

fluids." When he inserted an IV line, the Scotsman's eyes fluttered briefly, but he showed no other response.

Izzy pulled out an aluminum thermal blanket and spread it loosely over Calan. "Someday you'll tell me what went on out here. For now let's pray he can hang on until that chopper finds us in the fog. There's not much more I can do."

Over their heads came the drone of motors and the dull *thump-thump* of a chopper banking over the marsh.

"About time," Nicholas muttered. "But Calan is still losing color." He frowned as his friend fought for breath.

Kiera's eyes opened. She gasped and tried to sit up. "Maddy —"

Nicholas held her still. "Your sister is safe. You're out of danger, Ms. Morissey."

"Calan?" She was looking over Nicholas's shoulder, her eyes dark with worry. "I saw some kind of animal. The car exploded, but Calan never came back." She gave a sharp gasp when she saw Calan, ashen-faced. "No . . ." She glanced at Izzy and then at Nicholas Draycott, flinching a little when she saw his face clearly. "You — he said you were his friend. Help him. Do *something*. I — I can't lose him. I *won't*."

The motors droned loudly and a helicop-

354

ter appeared through the fog. The big skids had barely touched down when two men in dark uniforms jumped out and ran toward them.

"Nicholas Draycott," the Englishman called out. "This is Ishmael Teague. We've got three casualties here for immediate evacuation."

"Yes, sir." Two more men appeared, carrying a stretcher.

"Where is my sister?" Kiera asked hoarsely.

"She's waiting near the car." Izzy Teague removed his stethoscope and gestured for the team to lift Calan onto the stretcher as the casualty with top priority for treatment.

"But her medicine —"

"She'll be fine until we reach the E.R. But you need to relax now. You've been through a major ordeal."

Kiera put one hand lightly on the bloody, torn shirt that Nicholas had rebuttoned at her chest. "I remember gunfire. Then I hit the ground and everything hurt at once. My heart seemed to tear." She ran a hand over her face. "I'm so tired." She shook her head, trying to see Calan as he was carefully settled on the stretcher. "What's wrong with him? Please — I need to know."

"You'll have answers soon," Nicholas said.

"We all will." He stood back as Kiera was lifted onto the next stretcher. Her eyes closed.

Nicholas stood back next to Izzy. "How bad is Calan?" he asked quietly.

Izzy closed his bag, his expression grim. "I won't speculate. His heart appears to be in serious arrhythmia. That could lead to cardiac arrest." He shouldered his gear bag. "Praying is never a bad idea."

Kiera was caught in restless dreams of gray cement rooms with roofs that collapsed all around her.

Cold bit into her skin. All her energy seemed to be draining away from a deep red hole at the center of her chest. No matter how hard she pressed, the energy kept pouring out over her hands.

She tried to sit up, desperate to ask about her sister and the man she loved, but the fog was everywhere. No one heard her.

She whispered Calan's name, her hands searching blindly. Then the fog swallowed her.

The small hospital was not prepared for a sudden influx of patients, but the capable staff went into overdrive. The wounded attackers had all been transported into military custody. Maddy and Kiera had adjoining rooms and were receiving around-the-clock care. Calan was downstairs in a separate wing, in intensive care.

Maddy's energy had come back first. After checking on her sister and Calan, she called her family back in France, and then tracked down Nicholas Draycott. Their confrontation quickly turned into an emotional interrogation. The Englishman's answers did not completely satisfy her, but they painted a far different picture from the one her mother had presented in the weeks before her death.

It became clear to Maddy that Nicholas Draycott was not quite the villain she had believed. Doggedly Maddy demanded answers about the estate manager who had handled the viscount's affairs during his absence. This was the man who had truest blame. Once Nicholas heard the whole story, in Maddy's version, he placed a phone call to the man he had not seen for over ten years.

There was no answer at the man's house in London. His telephone number in Kent was out of service. Nicholas assured Maddy that he would get to the bottom of the ugly business. What he did not tell her was that if the story proved true — and he was quickly coming to believe that it was — his retribution would be swift and fierce.

Meanwhile, he saw to it that all three of the patients had constant attention. It was his greatest wish to see them all back at Draycott Abbey, recovering in the quiet beauty that had helped him back to sanity so many years before. It would be a safe haven now that the brigadier's team had everyone from the church in custody. An additional group of terrorists had been tracked down in London.

In every sense, the threat against Nicholas and his family appeared to be over. But he had arranged for private protection officers for his wife and daughter in case any of the splinter-group Croatians and their British collaborators had managed to escape the brigadier's net.

Kacey Draycott had arrived at the hospital within a day of hearing about their recent danger. Equipped with an armful of magazines, fresh flowers from the abbey's garden and a basket filled with Marston's best pumpkin walnut scones, she set about charming Nicholas's newfound relatives.

Nicholas was still reeling from the discovery that his sister had died only several months earlier. To that was added the shock of learning that he had three nieces with every reason to hate him. Since duty and family bonds were the most important things in Nicholas's life, the discovery had taken him to the edge of despair.

Kiera still slept, drained after her ordeal. She did not know that Calan was in critical condition. The exact nature of his heart arrhythmia remained a mystery to the cardiac staff. It was Kacey Draycott and not her husband who was at Kiera's bedside when she came awake.

Kacey rang the call button as Kiera blinked and looked around her. "Where —" She sat up with a gasp, yanked back the sheets and tried to stand up. "Where is Maddy? My sister —"

"She's fine. I'll get her for you."

Kiera released a long breath and nodded. "Calan — I have to find him, too."

"Take it easy. He's right downstairs, Kiera." Kacey spoke calmly. "You can see him in a few minutes. The doctor's with him now."

Kiera stared at her. "You're a nurse?"

"A friend. Tell me anything you need, and I'll get it. Coffee, tea. Magazines. A computer to write e-mails or a cell phone."

Kiera closed her eyes. "Calan. I need to see him now."

When she tried to stand up, Kacey Draycott crossed her arms, a look of determination on her face. "I'll check to be sure he can have visitors. Then I'll go find a wheelchair to take you there. It's that or nothing. You won't last five minutes if you try to walk."

"Says who?" Impatient and angry, Kiera swung her legs over the side of the bed — and swayed dangerously. She closed her eyes and sat down. "Tomorrow I'll walk," she muttered.

"I'm glad that much is clear. I'll be back in a few minutes. I've left you a Thermos with tea beside the bed, along with Marston's homemade scones."

But Kiera didn't hear. Her eyes closed in exhaustion. She sank onto the bed, dropping back down into restless dreams.

Nicholas Draycott and Izzy Teague were pacing impatiently in the hall when Kacey went outside.

"How is she?" Nicholas demanded. "We heard the call button. A doctor is on the way now."

"She woke up and seemed completely lucid. Exhausted, of course. Stubborn, too. Not surprising, given her Draycott blood." Kacey stepped back and watched a doctor and a nurse stride into Kiera's room. "She was demanding to see Calan."

"He's still unconscious," Izzy said quietly. "He's not allowed to have any visitors yet."

"I wasn't going to tell her that. She was agitated enough without more bad news." Kacey glanced at her husband. "He's still the same?"

"I'm afraid so."

Izzy rubbed his neck. "His heart arrhythmia hasn't responded to any treatment so far. Nicholas was right to send for a specialist from London. To get him to come all the way out here must have meant pulling a whole lot of strings."

"It was a small thing to do," Nicholas said flatly. "Calan was hurt because of me. I put him in this dangerous situation. I never should have gotten him involved."

Izzy's eyes narrowed. "Hold on just a minute. If you're trying to take the blame for what happened to your friend, you're making a big mistake. It was his choice to help you, just as it was his choice to do whatever it was he did to save Kiera's life."

"I keep telling myself that. It doesn't make me feel the slightest bit better," Nicholas said bitterly.

Two hours later Nicholas was outside Calan's room waiting for an update when

361

the elevator doors opened.

Calan's great-aunt appeared, scanning room numbers carefully. When she saw Nicholas, relief filled her face. "I just had a phone call from the hospital. They told me that Calan had been hurt, but they wouldn't give me any details."

"He's downstairs in intensive care." Nicholas took her arm. "Why don't we sit down. Calan can't have any visitors yet."

Agatha MacKay's face went pale. "What happened, Nicholas?"

"There was an . . . incident. Calan missed the gunfire, but something has affected his heart. The diagnosis is still unclear, I'm afraid. He may need a temporary pacemaker. Do you know if he has any history of cardiac arrhythmia?"

Calan's great-aunt ran a hand across her eyes. "I'm not sure. His side of the family has always been very closed. My husband, when he was alive, never spoke much about family matters. I'm afraid I can't help you very much." She frowned, watching an orderly push an empty gurney into the elevator. "But aren't there tests that can be done? Things like X-rays or ultrasound exams?"

"For some reason Calan's condition doesn't fit any existing model. If we knew his medical history, it would help the staff to decide on treatment."

"I can search my letters and old records when I get home. But I would like to see him before I go, even if it's only a brief visit."

"His doctor will have to decide that. They're with him now."

She nodded, looking tired and a little dazed. "Have you spoken with Miss Morissey, Nicholas? You know . . . her story?"

"I do," Nicholas said flatly. "But we've had no chance to speak about it."

"It sounds tragic. I do hope you can get to the bottom of what happened."

"Not for a while, I'm afraid. Kiera was hurt, too." Nicholas motioned down the hall. "She's in the room next to her sister, who is a patient, too."

"All three of them are here?" Agatha MacKay sank down in the chair that Nicholas had drawn up. "I suspected that something was going on. Calan never tells me much of anything, not that I expect him to discuss his work. But where did this all happen? Was it at the abbey? Were you or any of your family . . ."

Nicholas had already planned a sanitized account without any sensitive details. "No, the incident did not take place at the abbey. All my family is fine, thank heaven. But that is in a large part due to your great nephew's bravery, Agatha," Nicholas said. "And I'm going to do everything in my power to see that Calan recovers."

The woman looked more worried than before.

"Agatha, maybe we should find someplace more comfortable for you to sit."

"Not yet. I need to see Kiera first. But this . . . incident you mentioned. It involved you, Nicholas? They didn't come after Calan, did they?"

Nicholas frowned. "I don't know what you mean, Agatha. Who would come after Calan? He never mentioned any problems to me."

The old woman cleared her throat. "Of course not. I was — mistaken. There has been no contact with his brother or his uncle, I take it?" Her voice was cold. "Not that I would know how to contact Magnus, even if I wanted to."

"I don't know how to reach them and Calan hasn't been conscious long enough to pass on any information to me or the hospital."

"So they haven't been told." His answer seemed to make Agatha MacKay strangely relieved. "I will see Calan as soon as his doctors permit it. Now I would like to see

Miss Morissey." The old woman's determined tone made it very clear that neither hospital protocol nor nursing regulations would stand in her way.

"She may be asleep. She has been through a great deal."

"Then I'll wait. While I do, perhaps you will tell me exactly what has happened to her, Nicholas. And I only hope . . ." Agatha's voice trailed away. Whatever else she would have said was forgotten as the door to Kiera's room opened. A bandaged hand closed around the door frame.

The fingers locked, white with tension.

Kiera's eyes were clouded with anxiety as she walked slowly through the door. "Where are my sister and Calan?" she said hoarsely. "I'm not taking any more medicine until I've seen them both." She swayed a little, and Nicholas lunged to grip her arm.

He didn't scold her for being out of bed. The look of anguish on her face was too deep for anger or reproach.

CHAPTER
TWENTY-SIX

Kiera stood through raw force of will, ignoring the pain at her chest and the effort it took to stand up. Questions about Maddy and Calan haunted her, their condition burning through her mind. She had to know they were safe.

"Your sister is downstairs in X-ray right now. She should be finished in about fifteen minutes." Nicholas Draycott spoke slowly, as if he was considering every word. "If there's anything I can do for you — anything at all — I hope you will let me know."

Kiera looked at him squarely for the first time. Emotions warred in her face. There was none of the hatred she expected to feel. "Just take me to Calan. I can't think about anything else now. As long as Maddy is safe, nothing else matters, don't you see?" She took a slow breath. "Calan wanted me to ask you what happened. He told me to listen — really listen to what you told me. So I will," Kiera said quietly. "But I have to see him first. He looked so pale in the helicopter. If I lose him —" Kiera looked away, and her voice broke off sharply.

Izzy emerged from a nearby room, pushing a wheelchair. He cleared his throat as he made a neat turn and angled the chair behind Kiera with a flourish. "Nobody is going to lose anybody," he said briskly. "Now we've got that straight, let's go for a ride." He helped Kiera sit down. "And if the nurse says you can't see Calan, we'll go find someone else who says you can." He glanced at Nicholas Draycott. "He won't tell you this, I see. But since your uncle there happens to have endowed almost every room in this facility and he is spending a hell of a lot of money on your care right now, I don't think breaking a few rules will be that hard."

But Kiera's hopes of seeing Calan failed.

He had gone straight from one set of tests into another room for more tests. The closed looks of the staff made it clear that his situation was grave.

The afternoon shadows ran into night. The day staff went home and the night staff moved efficiently into their place. The hours ran together for Kiera, exhausted after her own ordeal. Recovery was slow. Every movement made her chest ache. She refused sleeping medication, wanting to be available as soon as Calan was able to have visitors. Maddy and Kacey Draycott became unlikely co-conspirators, bringing Kiera frequent progress reports so that she would make no more rash attempts to walk downstairs to find out his current condition.

On the afternoon of her fourth day in the hospital, Kiera awoke and finally felt clear-headed. She was still in considerable pain, but the pounding throb had settled to a low, continuous ache. And with the return of her energy, she made it clear that she had to see Calan.

Reluctantly, she agreed to use the wheelchair that her sister and Kacey Draycott made certain was on hand. Kiera was relieved to see her sister was entirely recovered. Even the horror of captivity appeared to have receded beneath Maddy's natural optimism and endless curiosity. Meanwhile, there were half-a-dozen military guards posted around the hospital, Kiera noted. Apparently Nicholas Draycott and his government connections were taking no chances on further problems. Izzy had given her a guarded account of what had happened after she had been wounded, and Kiera didn't ask for details. She was only too happy to put the bitter memories behind her.

Finally she had permission to enter Calan's room. She ran a hand through her hair, leaving it in spiky chunks. She probably looked like a walking disaster.

The first sight of his face left her reeling. He was so pale. His breathing was so shallow that it was barely noticeable. Machinery whirred quietly behind the bed, flashing lights and spiking sensors marking his vital signs.

Kiera wanted to hold him tightly. As she leaned over the bed, she was overwhelmed by a need to reach out and somehow make him safe and well again. She hated feeling helpless in the face of his condition. "I don't understand what happened." She frowned at her sister, who didn't answer. "No one will tell me anything, and I can't remember any details. Was he shot or did he fall?"

"I think you'll have to ask my husband," Kacey said quietly. "He was there. He knows. He won't tell me any of the details, either. I'm sorry."

"I want to know," Kiera said flatly. "I *have* to know.

Kacey nodded. "I'll find Nicholas." She glanced at Maddy. "Maybe we should go outside and wait, so you can be alone with Calan."

Kiera nodded, barely aware of Maddy's hand on her shoulder and then the sound of their footsteps behind her. She moved the wheelchair forward toward the bed, and then leaned over, sliding Calan's hand between her fingers. It seemed fiercely important that she make contact with him, no matter how briefly. As she watched the faint rise and fall of his chest, Kiera had the strange sense that he was aware of her presence, and that the words she said next would be infinitely important.

She took a deep breath, staring at his motionless fingers and marshalling her thoughts. "Mainly, I want you to know this. I think I love you, Calan MacKay." Her voice broke for a moment and then she continued. "I never expected it to happen. I'm not even sure that I wanted it to happen," she said with a little anguished laugh. "I came to England to close the door on the past. Instead you opened entirely new doors for me. I fought and argued every step of the way, but you helped me to open my eyes when it was much easier not to look around me. They won't tell me what happened to you or even what to expect. But I want you to know I will be staying right here. I'll be as close to you as they will let me be, right beside you until you wake up." There was no movement to show that he heard her, no flutter of his eyelids or tremor in his fingers. But somewhere in her mind, Kiera sensed that her words had registered. The instinct was as deep and powerful as the sense of wordless contact she had had with the dark wolf on the marsh, but she refused to believe there was any connection.

With her eyes closed, she leaned over his motionless body. Gently, she rested her fingers on top of his. Maybe he didn't hear anything she said. Maybe her efforts were hopeless. But a deep, wordless determination gripped her, and she refused to let him go without her best struggle.

From the corner of her eye, she saw a nurse in the doorway. Clearly, her time was up. But leaving was the last thing Kiera wanted to do.

"It's time, Ms. Morissey. I'm sorry," the nurse said quietly.

Kiera realized her cheeks were damp. She brushed the tears away impatiently. "When can I see him again?"

"In six hours." The nurse's voice fell. "Unless . . . his condition changes."

"He'll be better. He's strong and he's a fighter," Kiera said fiercely. "I know it."

The nurse nodded briskly. "Of course he will be better. But now you need to rest. I'll push you outside. Your sister and Lady Draycott are waiting for you."

Hearing the name and the title so abruptly came as a slap to Kiera. The old instinct for anger and distrust surged to life, only to fade just as quickly. Kiera was not the same woman who had climbed over the abbey's old stone fence only a few nights earlier. Somehow she would have to face those changes, and that included accepting the fact that Nicholas Draycott was a decent man.

So much to accept. So many changes to face.

But none of these things mattered if she didn't have Calan to share the future with.

Maddy squeezed her hand. None of the women spoke on the way back to Kiera's room.

He was a tall man, and there was a sense of distance in his eyes as he watched the three women pass. He recognized Nicholas Draycott's wife, but not the two others.

Which was the woman that his nephew had so rashly risked his life to protect?

Magnus MacKay clenched his fists inside his rain-streaked jacket, cutting off a curse.

372

It had been years since he had seen his nephew. As the laird of the Grey Isle, Magnus had carried the grave responsibilities of protecting the dangerous and ancient secrets of the clan from enemies and outsiders alike.

He would take his nephew home, back to the fog-swept island where he belonged. There Calan would recover in the old way, using the old skills. His powers would finally be complete.

He would be safe there on the Grey Isle, away from these English strangers who could never understand his gift. Soon he would be the new laird.

The rest of his past was irrelevant.

His future was with the clan and he would remember nothing about what had happened here.

A cold gust of air played across Agatha MacKay's neck. She shivered, pushing aside her barely touched scone. All day she had been filled with a sense of dread, as if a trap was about to slam shut.

A shadow fell from the window behind her. She turned — and her formless dread took on full, sharp outlines.

He looked older than when she had last seen him. Older and much harder, Agatha thought. It was hardly surprising. The Grey Isle could turn anyone old before his time.

"You've come," she said flatly.

"With no thanks to you. You might have reached me with the news instead of having it come from a stranger in London whom I had sent to keep discreet tabs on my nephew. You've never liked us," he said coldly. "My great-uncle should never have married someone outside our clan."

"He married for love, not duty," the old woman said, her own voice harsh in turn. "But I suppose that's something you will never understand."

"*Love* is an empty word," he repeated harshly. "It belongs in a weak man's book of tales."

"You're just like your brother, aren't you? How proud he must have been of you. I wonder if you realize how much you lost the day that Calan was put to sea. Yes, I know all about that piece of savagery." Agatha MacKay shook her head, and then she stood up slowly. "There will be no stopping you, will there?"

Magnus's cold, forbidding expression was answer enough.

"He'll hate you for it. He'll hate you *almost* as much as I do."

Magnus MacKay smiled thinly and

shrugged his powerful shoulders. "Will he? But your feelings and your wishes are of no interest to me, old woman. Stop muttering and take me to my nephew."

CHAPTER
TWENTY-SEVEN

Six hours crawled past in a blur.

Six hours of restless uncertainty and growing urgency.

Now Kiera stood up slowly, carefully gaining her balance as she took stock of the quiet hospital corridor and of her life to that moment. A look, a touch, any sign of recovery — that was all she needed. It seemed that she had spent far too much time in her life on travel and furthering her career, and that time should have been spent learning to trust and grow in the company of an amazing man like Calan.

Kiera made a fierce promise to start making up for all that lost time. When Izzy, waiting, ever watchful, made a move as if to follow her into Calan's room, she held up a hand. "Please. Give me just a few minutes alone with him first."

"Of course," Izzy murmured. "But I'll be right outside."

It still hurt to walk and the stitches above her heart ached, but Kiera forced all her pain and stiffness from her mind. Smiling, she opened the door, blinking in the sunlight that spilled from the window. Then she ran a hand over her eyes.

The room was empty. The bed was neatly made and all signs of personal belongings removed. Shock hit her in the chest like a fist.

"Where is he — what's happened?"

"What do you mean?" Izzy peered into the room and cursed softly. "Must be some kind of bureaucratic decision. Maybe his condition has been upgraded. No one told me anything about it."

Kiera's heart lurched. What if it was something else? What if he — ?

No. Her whole being rebelled against the thought that Calan had died. On some level she would have known immediately. The shining thread of contact stretching between them was too strong for her to have missed its sudden snapping.

She spun around, pushed open the door and glared down at the nursing station. "I want to know where he is, Izzy."

"So do I," Izzy growled.

Footsteps raced up the corridor behind them. "I must have just missed you in the elevator." Nicholas Draycott strode toward them. His face was haggard, his mouth set in an angry, flat line.

"What's happened?"

"Not here." He pushed open the door to the room where Calan had been a patient. "You need to sit down, Miss Morissey."

"Kiera. I think we're beyond being formal, don't you? Just tell me what's happened to Calan."

Nicholas waited until Kiera was sitting down on the bed. Then he ran a hand through his hair. "He's gone."

"Gone *where?*"

"North, I suspect. Up to Scotland. His uncle came and signed him out against medical advice."

"Why didn't you stop him?" Kiera lurched to her feet. "He wasn't in any shape to travel."

Cold anger sliced through Nicholas's voice. "Do you think I don't know that? I tried to stop them. I made calls to everyone I knew. But I'm a friend, not a relative the way Magnus and Agatha are."

Kiera ran a shaky hand over her face. "Agatha MacKay was involved in this insanity?"

Nicholas nodded. "She signed the discharge request along with Calan's uncle."

"Aren't you going to do *anything?*" Kiera

blew out an angry breath. "Let's go after them. Let's just —"

"I tried. They have the full weight of the law on their side." Nicholas stared out the window. "Magnus has taken him by ambulance to Hastings, and from there I gather they are traveling north by private plane." Nicholas toyed with something inside his pocket, an then glanced at Izzy, whose eyebrow rose slowly. "At least I'll be able to track him."

"How can you do that?" Kiera stared from one man to another. "You're not making any sense."

"With this." Nicholas Draycott held up a small black chip. "It happens to be a new piece of technology that Calan is developing for his company. We have been testing it over the last few days at the abbey, and I saw to it that Calan had one of these taped to his chest under his bandages." He smiled wryly. "As a precaution all of us have been wearing them. You, too, Ms. — Kiera."

"Well, I'm glad that one of you has done something sensible." She frowned down at the flannel robe pulled over her hospital gown. "I'd better go change. I'll look into flights to Scotland while you begin tracking that chip."

Nicholas Draycott blocked her way, his

face impassive. "I want to see Calan safe just as much as you do, but I won't let you endanger your own health in the process."

"What I do or don't do is none of your business," Kiera said flatly. "Now, if you'll just move aside —"

"I won't. I'm certain that your sister will agree with me about this. And whether you like it or not, I *am* a blood relative. As your uncle, estranged or not, I have a duty to help you in any way I can. So I'll provide a car for you. I'll hire a small plane for the trip to Scotland. But not until your physician has given you clearance to travel."

Kiera started to snarl a protest and then stopped. He was being generous in his offer of help, and she would be no help to Calan if she slowed down their pursuit. "You're certain that chip will work?"

"So far it's performed impeccably."

"Has anybody told you that you're unbelievably stubborn?"

Nicholas smiled faintly. "Every day."

Kiera stared at him. "And you're telling the truth about renting a private plane?"

The Englishman nodded. "But there is something that we need to do first."

Golden sunlight cut through banked clouds. Two hours later Nicholas Draycott passed a

380

broad hedgerow and raced up the long driveway that led to Agatha MacKay's house. He was a good driver and they had made excellent time from the hospital near Hastings. Kiera's doctor had reluctantly cleared her for travel, and Nicholas had put no further obstacles in their way.

His planning had been impeccable, and so far Calan's experimental tracking equipment had worked perfectly. When Nicholas explained its design, Kiera had a new respect for Calan's intricate work. He had built his company from scratch according to Nicholas, linking his satellite mapping technology to carefully designed products in high demand around the world.

Nicholas Draycott's pride in his friend's achievements was obvious. The two had been friends since a miserable summer in camp together. When Calan's relationship with his family had ended abruptly, Nicholas had been Calan's confidant. When he had finally left Scotland, still a teenager, Nicholas and his parents had helped Calan make a new life in England.

As far as Nicholas knew, there had been no further contact between Calan and his family.

Except for Agatha and her husband. And then Magnus MacKay had shown up at the hospital the night before.

As the Englishman spoke, Kiera saw the core of honesty and duty that framed his actions. It was impossible to hate Nicholas Draycott. It was growing harder even to distrust him. But Agatha MacKay was a different story. Kiera was furious that Calan's great-aunt had been involved in his removal from the hospital.

Yet it was hard to stay angry when she faced the tired, worried old woman who opened the door to them.

"I wasn't sure that you would come, Nicholas. Not after what happened at the hospital. You're going after them, I hope?"

"We'll be in Scotland tomorrow," Nicholas said.

Kiera hid her surprise, well aware that Nicholas planned to reach Scotland that same afternoon. She noticed that Nicholas did not tell Agatha about the chip or any details of his plan to track Calan. He was taking no chances on Agatha's loyalties, it seemed.

"I have everything packed for you. I've drawn you a map — at least as far as my memory permits. It's been forty years since I was in that part of Scotland, so you'll forgive me if there are gaps. Use this book as your best resource." The old woman ran her fingers gently across the weathered leather cover of a slim volume. "Read every word. It will tell you all the things I can't. If Magnus knew that I had it . . ." She made an angry sound. "But he doesn't and he never will, because my husband never told him. Guard it well. In those pages lies the key to Calan's life. Now go. You have very little time before —"

"Before what?" Kiera interrupted.

"Magnus will do whatever he can to hold Calan. Things are different there. Time can be misleading. You will have to win him back, and the struggle will be a cold, hard thing. But you can read that on the way. It's all in the book. Go to Portree on Skye. From there follow the map I've made. *Hurry.*"

Kiera cradled the book, frowning. "*Why* did you help Magnus?"

"I had no choice. He would have taken Calan, one way or the other. At least this way I knew his plan. As soon as they left, I knew I could contact you." The old woman looked uncertainly at Kiera. "I hope you will forgive me. I did what I thought best. How could I not, when I love Calan like the grandson I never had?" The old woman pressed the book into Kiera's hands. "Now, go. The rest is written in this. Be careful of

Magnus's wrath, for he will strike from behind and when you least expect it. I can still remember —" Agatha MacKay closed her eyes and shook her head. "It seems like a dream now. That they should still exist at all is a marvel."

Nicholas's eyes narrowed. "They?"

Agatha MacKay shook her head. "You'll find all the answers in the book of the clan. Make haste lest you are too late. And . . . give Calan all my love." She swept open the door and waved them outside, looking agitated.

A cold wind whipped at Kiera's face. As she walked, the cover of the book lifted against her fingers. The old pages seemed to move, ruffled in the wind.

They spoke.

Their low whisper was like a warning in an ancient language she could not understand.

"Do you believe her?" Kiera asked quietly.

"Twenty-four hours ago I would have said yes. Completely and absolutely." Nicholas Draycott frowned as he watched a small private plane being prepped for takeoff. Dark clouds piled up on the horizon. Another unseasonable storm with low visibility was expected by afternoon, adding further urgency to their departure.

Nicholas cleared his throat. "I should tell you that I've finally managed to locate our old estate manager. We lost track of him, but I've learned that he died two years ago in a mental home. I was told that he was paranoid and delusional. At the end he was certain people were coming after him. I'm deeply sorry about this, Kiera. I wish I had known what my sister was enduring while I was in Asia. It's intolerable that all my affairs were left in the hands of such a man. Before this, my family had never had a reason to distrust him."

Kiera let out a breath. "I believe you. I may never know everything about what happened. I'm glad that you told me."

"I will help you in any way that I can." Nicholas studied her face. "Do you love him, Kiera?"

She stiffened at the abrupt question. Then she slowly nodded. "With all my heart. Such a short time I've know him, but somehow he has changed me and everything I thought I wanted."

"Love will do that." Nicholas looked down at the book unopened in Kiera's lap. There had been no time for more than a quick glance as they raced to the small airport. "And will you love him just as much once you know everything about him? There are secrets in that book, details about his clan past and his difficult future. Will you feel the same then?"

"Just as I do now, with all my heart."

"For Calan's sake, I hope so." He stood up as the man on the runway turned, waving to them briskly.

Ten minutes later they were banking over Dover's white cliffs, headed toward Scotland.

Kiera opened the book and began to read.

We come from the same blood.

We come as one from a place of stone and mists. Our name was different then. We wore the past in the cloth our women worked, each color framed of the old knowledge. Every cloud had a meaning, every pebble a lesson. We were as one. No outsiders were given to know the way to our guarded places.

All that changed in the great rebellion. Our secrets stood in danger of being revealed.

Now as a man of clan MacKay, you hold the book and read the secrets. By blood you are bound by them. You will be claimed by this truth forever.

Fear and believe.

And then understand. . . .

Kiera shuddered, feeling a cold slap of warning. The book seemed to move in her fingers. She was not a man, not of Calan's clan.

Yet she had to know the truth.

She gripped the book. Grimly, she continued to read the yellowing pages.

> The gifts are three and set clearly below:
> The Naming.
> The Calling.
> The Binding.
> Without a true clan name, one can neither be called nor bound. Mark this well. Call one by a true name and he must come. Bind one by a true name and he must yield.
> Love one by a true clan word and he must be caught forever.

Kiera felt something brush the skin at her neck, in warning or in promise she did not know.

> The curse and the gift come from the Calling.
> The Change and Hunt are for the clan. Not for personal gain or glory. Not for revenge. Not for love.

You hunt for the need of the blood.

You hunt for the need of your kind.

The animal that you meet in your first dream will be your constant shadow . . . and your truest future.

The words went on, framed almost in poetry. But the pictures between the words were harsher, with fierce animals and grotesque shapes, formed of man and wolf. Kiera closed her eyes to other shapes as the knowledge roared in her ears. They could change.

They could *Change*.

It was impossible.

She remembered the great wolf outside the abbey's stone fence. The same great animal had seemed to hold unnatural strength and intelligence as it guarded her flight from the ruined church.

Calan.

She sank back, the book shaking in her hands. Even as her mind rebelled, the cold, infinite truth slid home.

She looked at Nicholas and saw the weight of knowledge in his eyes. "You knew this?"

"Not all. Calan has never said much. But enough."

Kiera still struggled to understand what she had read, how legend and magic wrapped around a bloodline, protected by storm and fog on a small island with a cove found on no maps. As a MacKay of the Grey Isle, Calan was a creature who should not have existed, a human capable of transformation that no science could explain.

The black wolf.

She closed her eyes as the memory of their bond leaped into her mind. She followed the bond, fighting at first and then slowly accepting what she felt.

The burning, restless blue-gray eyes. The intelligence beyond that of any animal.

"I don't believe it," she whispered. "I can't. It's . . . ridiculous. Highland fantasies with strange creatures torn from fog-shrouded legends?" Her voice broke. "Anyone can write a book and fill it full of tall tales and gloomy legends. No man could do what those pages describe."

Will you love him just as much once you know everything about him? Nicholas's question haunted her.

Was she brave enough to accept all that Calan was?

Kiera felt the strange silver mark at her wrist burn suddenly and she wondered if it carried its own kind of magic. Then deep in her heart, even as she fought against the words she had just read, Kiera felt the cold weight of truth. Calan was the thing that the book described. He had come from a line of such shape changers.

She took a deep breath. "It's true, isn't it?"

"So far as I know what truth is. I've seen him change three times now." Nicholas rubbed his neck. "It is a thing to make you question all your established thoughts of physics or humanity. Don't ask me to explain it, because I can't. I know only what my eyes have seen." Nicholas Draycott sat forward suddenly, pointing out the small window. A broad rocky cove curved against whitecapped water. "There's Jura below us. We should be in Portree within the hour."

Kiera nodded. But she was thinking about a man with too much pain in his eyes, a man whose hands had taught her trust and pleasure beyond imagining. Those same hands and limbs could change to fearsome form, from all she had just read. As a relentless hunter, he would always be fighting to control his own strength and dark instincts. How could she ever feel safe around such a man?

Man.

The understanding came to her slowly as she watched the sea run in high swells beneath the airplane. She had felt Calan's

390

humanity. It had wrapped around her, comforted her, touched her on too many levels to count.

Calan the man was real. His laughter and touch were real. Whatever else he was, he would never lose the part of him that Kiera could trust. Even as her mind flinched against images drawn from myth and superstition, Kiera felt the certainty of trust bloom.

She would bring him home. To *her* home. To her family, not the cold gray island.

And Kiera accepted that Nicholas had to be part of that future.

As if he sensed her turmoil, Nicholas hesitated and then rested one hand on hers. "Give it time. You don't have to accept or understand everything at once. But he's a man worth fighting for, and I've never seen him in love before. He told me that it could only happen to him once — if at all. He seemed to think it very unlikely. I'm glad that he was wrong." He gestured at the book, half-open on her lap. "And if you're done reading about the history of the clan MacKay, I'd like to have a look myself before we land."

CHAPTER
TWENTY-EIGHT

It was just another bleak, windswept cove wrapped in gray water. They had passed dozens already.

But somehow Kiera *knew* this one was different.

She stared at the finger of land jutting up into angry waters. The pilot shook his head, sweeping a glance over the brooding horizon. "Naught down there but water and stones. You're certain this is the place, Lord Draycott?"

Kiera scanned Agatha MacKay's hand-drawn map one more time. They had left the Isle of Skye with bad weather close on their flank. The light was going fast. If they made a mistake, they would lose another day before they could orientate against the map.

"We went in the wrong direction," Kiera said slowly. "After that last mountain, we crossed three little islands. According to

Agatha's map, there should only have been two. We need to go back."

Nicholas Draycott looked undecided. "Kiera, the light is going. We don't have much time . . ."

The certainty.

The bond so strong she felt it hammer at her chest.

"*No.* He's back there. Take us back to the mountain. Then head west." The roar of the plane engine was a constant thunder against the microphone that all three of them wore.

Nicholas Draycott started to ask a question. But he looked at her eyes and nodded. "Just like she said. Back to the mountain."

And now a thread of contact, gossamer fine, seemed to tug her, showing the way. Kiera closed her mind to uncertainty and followed.

"There."

Her hand pressed against the plane's cold window. Two islands rose beneath them, half-swallowed by racing clouds. The pilot banked and headed west. Now the landmarks were just as Agatha had drawn them.

A high peak to the north. Then a stretch of deserted sea. Calan was down there. He needed her.

The island was tiny, a speck against restless water. Without Agatha's map, they never would have found it. Staring at the jagged rocks, Kiera felt the hairs tighten on the back of her neck.

A warning — too clear to miss.

Her eyes hardened. Let them try to keep her away from Calan. She had negotiated with bandits in Outer Mongolia and traded chickens for safe passage among headhunters in Borneo. Calan's family didn't know what they were up against.

Kiera smiled coldly. She was glad to have Draycott blood if it made her stubborn and imperious. She welcomed all those strengths now.

The crooked cove lay half-hidden against a sullen headland. She was going to take Calan home.

The pilot found what little protection he could, putting them down right on the beach in the lee of a jagged cliff. There was no sign of any cottage or even a road.

For a moment Kiera's certainty faltered.

Then the thread of contact reemerged, stronger than ever.

He was here. Somewhere close.

The sun faded, caught behind racing clouds. Somehow here in the strange light distances were distorted, just as Agatha had warned.

"I can only give you thirty minutes, Lord Draycott. There's a high-pressure ridge moving in from the west, and we need to be in the air before it reaches us."

Nicholas nodded, turning to survey the grim cove. "I didn't get to finish Agatha's notes. What are we supposed to do next?"

Kiera took a deep breath. "We're supposed to call him."

The Englishman's brow rose. "Not with a cell phone, I presume."

" *'By voice and by will.'* At least that's what the book said. *'By truest name.'* "

She thought of the strange words that might have been Gaelic.

She put her hands on her hips, squinting into the wind. Clouds swirled around her. The wind seemed to rise, howling in sullen fury almost as if the island itself fought her.

"Calan!" She sent a message of love in her thoughts at the same time she called to him. "Calan Duthac MacKay of Na h-Eileanan Flannach — I make my calling to you." Calling out in the wind, she felt almost foolish. She welcomed Nicholas's voice when he joined her.

There was no response. But the island itself seemed to reject them, the sea churning up white and angry only steps from her feet.

Time was running out.

"Calan Duthac MacKay, I call you. I bind you with word and heart." Kiera stumbled over the Gaelic phrases that she had seen in Agatha's old book, but her voice was fierce. For good measure, she repeated the words twice more.

The third time the effect was electrifying. The wind roared to a howl and she was nearly knocked off her feet.

She felt Nicholas move closer, gripping her arm to hold her against a nearly horizontal gust. Something had changed. . . .

"Straight ahead at the top of the cliff," he muttered.

"I see them." Six figures made their way between jagged boulders. Kiera's heart leaped, but then hope faded.

Instinct told her that Calan was not among them.

She frowned into the wind, hunching her shoulders, glad now to have Nicholas Draycott beside her. "Calan Duthac MacKay, I call you now, by the love I bear you."

The wind carried a distant shout across the beach. Gravel raked her face.

The first two figures came into clearer view. Kiera straightened against what felt like a physical blow of hatred.

"Magnus MacKay at their head," Nicholas said harshly. "Somehow that doesn't surprise me."

The tall man who crossed the beach toward them stared from eyes as cold and hard as the stones that ringed the cove. "Leave now. You're neither one wanted here."

"I'll leave when I have Calan." Kiera lifted her voice, loud against the wind. "Calan Duthac MacKay — I call you." More men ringed the beach, scowling behind Magnus. The island itself seemed to amplify their hostility.

And still no sign or sound from Calan.

"You're too late," Magnus cried angrily. "Your meddling caused his death. He's gone from here, gone from all of us. He gave his life to save you, woman. He used all his energy to bring you back, thinking naught of himself." His voice was hoarse with pain. "So get yourself gone from my island. Or haven't you done enough harm to me and mine?"

Kiera closed her eyes.

Dead.

Lost to her forever.

Then the bond shimmered, pulled like a thread over the beach and up the rocky cliff.

She touched warmth — and belonging.

"He is alive. You are lying to me."

A tall figure separated from the rocks across the cove. Now Kiera saw a small stone cottage built right up against the cliff face.

Calan stood motionless, a bright tartan caught around his waist and no other clothing. The folds of wool stirred in the sharp wind as he turned toward the beach.

Kiera called his name, using the old phrases from the book of MacKay.

The bond between them snapped hard, hot and white as desire, almost knocking her off her feet.

"I bind you. I am bound in turn. The calling and my bond will last forever." She raised one hand.

And then she began to run, with Magnus MacKay's curses ringing in her ears. . . .

Calan covered the sand, moving stiffly. His jaw was set. Then his arms were hard and strong, opening. Tightening around her, safe haven for them both as their bodies met.

"I am called, *mo cridhe.* I am bound. I and my Other hold to you."

They heard Magnus's scream of fury behind them.

Too late.

The wind rose as Nicholas Draycott

gestured to the pilot. Scuffling feet crossed the sand.

"He'll destroy you," Magnus screamed. "You'll destroy *each other!*"

The wind roared, gravel pelting the beach. The other men wrestled Magnus, still fighting, to the ground.

The wind abruptly died.

Sunlight shot through a ragged hole in the sullen clouds.

Kiera slid Calan's arm over her shoulder, while Nicholas braced him from the other side.

"Let's go home," she said firmly. "I think that there are a few things we really should discuss."

"The wolf," he said, his eyes wary.

"The marriage date." Her chin rose. "And then how many children. I'm thinking four." She touched his bruised shoulder gently. "At least for a start."

Against the hammer of the wind buffeting the plane, Kiera looked down at the waves battering the tiny island. It still seemed impossible that a community could live in such isolation, their secrets protected by storm and fog.

But the evidence was right beside her.

When Calan moved, she saw the spiraling

mark on his wrist. The same silver lines covered her own. Even now the skin throbbed, and the bond between them sang with power.

In time she would understand all of it, but now was not the moment for questions. She gripped Calan's hand, driven to feel the heat of his skin to reassure herself that he was safe.

Across from them Nicholas pulled out a small box from beneath his seat. The Englishman straightened his headphones and then opened the box. "Izzy gave me strict orders to give you this medicine. Two pills, and then I'm supposed to contact him with your temperature and vital signs as soon as I can."

"Not absolutely necessary, but I doubt it will hurt." Calan glanced from Nicholas to Kiera. "Something's different between you. No more cold or distance." He nodded slowly. "About time."

Then he took Kiera's hand between his strong palms, with the folds of the thick wool tartan beneath them, bright in the sudden sunlight as the clouds passed. "Let's go home."

Epilogue

Call one by a true name and he must
  come.
Bind one by a true name and he must
  yield.
Love one by a true clan word and he
  must be caught forever.
      — The True Book of Clan MacKay

Draycott Abbey
Midnight
The night is alive.

Mystery shimmers at the corner of his glance. He walks the soft grass, touches the worn stones of Draycott Abbey. Near his hand a mound of lavender and the scent of a woman.

A woman he can never forget.

For so many years he has feared discovery and the power of his own fierce hunger. Only one woman has met his dark need. Now only she can test that fear — and make him whole again.

The wind draws him through the roses and down toward the moat. His clothes drop, forgotten as the thousand scents of night flow around him. Muscles flex and blood sings, power surging through him like long-forgotten hopes.

Across the valley he feels the weight of moonlight on his bare hands.

Alive.

Alive — with such power as no mortal man can know.

Will she accept this thing he can become? Will she flinch and will he lose her forever, the one true and beautiful thing that life has given him?

No more lies. No more shadows between them. He must give her the truth tonight.

A bird cries. Moon rising.

The dark, racing shape is gone, swallowed by the darkness.

She walked through the night, following the slope down from the great oak above the moat. In the sudden silence of the forest Kiera knew she was not alone. Old fear struggled with new shocks, and with every step she beat down her uncertainty. Her bitterness was done. She had no more hatred for the abbey or its owner. Her mother's pain was put to rest, and the healing could begin.

Kiera had gathered the things her mother had sent her to find, and in doing so the abbey had worked its magic. Elena Draycott's daughter had found her future shimmering in the eyes of a man who had seen too much pain and far too many shadows.

Moonlight touched her shoulders. A bird cried from the darkness. The little hairs stirred at her neck as she felt the weight of a presence.

The roses whispered. She heard the rough breath of an animal hidden in the tall reeds.

The leaves shook, and then the glimpse of sleek fur. Powerful muscles bunched as she faced her stark nightmare, cast in fully physical form, blocking the path before her.

So big, she thought, her heart frozen in her chest.

So . . . intelligent.

She had guessed this would be his shape. But to be face-to-face, close enough to see the wind flatten the dark fur . . .

She summoned her courage and her will, turning away from the safe and familiar past to find the hope of the future in those keen, unblinking eyes.

If she flinched, she would lose him.

That much Kiera knew.

She must accept him as he was, with no fear for the powerful thing he became. If not, he would vanish into the darkness and she would never see him again.

And all her hopes of happiness would be lost with him.

She stood tall, facing him without fear. "I'm here. Whatever you are — whatever it is you do — I'm not afraid."

The low growl made her muscles tighten, but she held her ground, determined even when the long fur brushed her leg, skimmed her knee, and she felt the hot breath of the animal against her hand.

Such power could tear her apart in seconds.

She accepted the truth of it, but that made her love stronger, slowly reaching out until her fingers met the warm pelt. Muscles tensed at her touch. The great animal turned, its gaze locked with hers.

Power. Longing. Hunger. Unknown worlds in those burning, blue-gray eyes.

Kiera reached out for the future, never looking away.

The bond between them snapped hard, hot and white as desire. The force of his love almost knocked her off her feet.

Her fingers tightened, locked in that long fur. "Calan," she whispered. Then her voice rose in fierce command. "Calan Duthac MacKay of Na h-Eileanan Flannach — I make my calling to you. I bind you with word and heart, your body to mine. Your shape to mine." The old Gaelic phrases were still rough on her tongue, but there was no uncertainty in the voice she raised.

"I bind you, Calan MacKay, and I am bound in turn."

The strong muscles clenched. She felt the stir of the wind as the animal passed, lost in one leap into the tall grass.

Her hands opened in the air where he had been. She yearned to feel the fur against her palm, to touch so much power. Strangeness fell before a desire so swift that her whole body shook. In a sigh she licked lips that felt hot and achingly sensitive. She had never known such need to touch and bond.

Wind brushed her shoulders.

"I bind you, Kiera, heart of my heart." Callused fingers touched her cheek, turning her to meet the sweet shock of his naked body, where he gripped her close.

"I bind you with word and heart, your body to mine." His lips grazed hers, then clung to her mouth. He dragged in a harsh breath. "Your shape to mine."

She met his kiss, her hands tangling in his hair until there was no space between their aching bodies. "I bind you and am bound in turn," Calan said in a voice thick with desire. "I and my Other hold to you. It is done," he said gravely.

Kiera knew it was done for all his human life. No papers or lawyers could change this bonding, done in the old way. Her knowledge of Calan's uniqueness was still limited, but each day he told her more.

He tilted her face up to his, frowning. "You're done with bitterness, and the Draycott past is truly healed?"

For answer, she kissed him one more time, her mouth hungry and searching. Her sister would find her own answers at the abbey. For Kiera the shadows were put to rest.

Then Calan's hands were on her face, her hair. Wind touched her shoulders as they fought to see who could tug away her clothes first, blouse and sweater flying onto the dark grass.

Skin met yearning skin. Calan's fingers moved slowly over her body. He claimed her . . . and was claimed in turn.

Moonlight spilled over the quiet glade and a bird called from the old oak at the top of the hill. But tonight the Other hunted no longer.

Draycott Abbey was at peace.

AUTHOR'S NOTE

Moonlight on weathered stone.

The rich scent of roses in a spring wind.

I hope you've enjoyed this new journey to Draycott Abbey. Calan carries dark memories, and I have the sense that he has more secrets to reveal. My next book, *Bound by Night,* brings Calan face-to-face with his oldest Scottish friend, now his harshest enemy. When their conflict threatens Draycott Abbey and the life of Kiera's sister, the abbey ghost must intervene.

With disastrous results.

Watch for *Bound by Night* next year.

Meanwhile, if you're interested in my earlier Draycott Abbey stories, visit my new Web site, www.draycottabbey.com, for a complete list of the books and novellas in this magical series. Stop by for new videos, excerpts and sketches of new stories to come.

If you'd like a signed bookplate to go with

your book, please drop me a note at: bound bydreams@christinaskye.com. If you have a reading group, let me know so I can send you a kit of special materials for your group.

Researching a new book is always a joy for me. I'm always delighted to pass along information about my favorite research books when I'm done. If you are interested in Scotland's grand past, you'll enjoy *At Home in Scotland,* by Lesley Astaire and Roddy Martine (New York: Abbeville Press, 1987). Their book offers an engaging look into the glorious private estates of Scotland, far less seen than their counterparts to the south. Sometimes quirky, often dramatic and always unforgettable, these homes are captured in inspiring detail.

For photos of the scenic north coasts, see Charlie Waite, *Scottish Islands* (London: Constable, 1989). The drama and brooding power of Scotland's mountains and shores are captured in these remarkable photographs.

For a book filled with anecdotes and historic photographs, savor *The National Trust: Country House Album* (Boston: Little Brown, 1989). A skillful writer, Christopher Simon Sykes shows what really happened on busy, socially connected country house weekends in the last century.

Of course only *one* estate has a guardian ghost and his loyal cat companion. Only one estate hides banks of rare heirloom roses and dark secrets.

And if Izzy Teague has worked his way under your skin, you can find more details about his difficult, shadowy past at my Web site. Visit www.christinaskye.com/izzyfiles for details from his secret cases and personal history.

During the first month of sale of *Bound by Dreams* in the winter of 2009, Izzy will be offering special prizes to randomly selected members who sign in. Be sure to drop by and ask him a question. You might be lucky and win the shirt off his back.

The T-shirt, that is.

Meanwhile, I've savored all your messages. Thank you for telling me again and again how much you've enjoyed your visits to magical Draycott Abbey. Already a new story of haunting shadows and dark betrayal is unfolding. Adrian and Gideon will soon be charged with more dangerous duties. The safety of the abbey has been betrayed.

The testing has begun.

Until your next visit, happy reading.

Christina Skye